24 Hours in Hell

With Best Wishes

ALAN E LONGWORTH

Order this book online at www.trafford.com/07-2704
or email orders@trafford.com

Most Trafford titles are also available at major online book retailers.

Edited by Lois Weightman.
Cover Design: Alan E. Longworth.

Note for Librarians: A cataloguing record for this book is available from Library and Archives Canada at www.collectionscanada.ca/amicus/index-e.html

Printed in Victoria, BC, Canada.

ISBN: 978-1-4251-5971-9

www.trafford.com

North America & international
toll-free: 1 888 232 4444 (USA & Canada)
phone: 250 383 6864 • fax: 250 383 6804
email: info@trafford.com

The United Kingdom & Europe
phone: +44 (0)1865 722 113 • local rate: 0845 230 9601
facsimile: +44 (0)1865 722 868 • email: info.uk@trafford.com

10 9 8 7 6 5 4 3 2

TABLE OF CONTENTS

24 HOURS IN HELL

I SAW A flash in the night sky. I heard the whine of the missile. The sound of our jeep exploding rent my ears. Brilliant light blinded me, yet through the light I saw the bodies of my fellow soldiers torn apart and flying through the air. I have no recollection of what happened next.

Deep in the recesses of my mind, my thoughts and feelings began to collect themselves. I felt a burning sensation where I knew my face should be. My fingers twitched. I willed my arm to move. To my great relief I felt movement. I lifted it to have my hand feel if the skin had been burned from my face. I ran my fingers across my closed eyes. I felt for the orbs under the eyelids, in fear I might have been blinded I forced my eyelids apart. The blackness faded, I saw light. The unmistakable smell of burned skin and flesh mixed with the smell of burning oil and rubber filled my nostrils. My arm reached over my chest to see if the other arm was still attached to me. It was. I forced my brain to draw my legs up into the fetal position. Both legs obeyed, I knew I was alive but I could not summon the strength to sit up and take stock of my situation. I rotated my head to the left. The remains of the jeep burned furiously about fifty feet away. I tried to focus my eyes upon it. After a few moments I could discern that the front of the vehicle had disintegrated while the rear half lay upon its side self immolating in its own fuel supply. Thick black smoke poured skywards from sputtering tires.

As my thoughts began to coalesce, I realized that the blast had hurled me away from the vehicle. Had I not been standing upright behind the deck-mounted machine gun, the outcome might have been quite different. I had lived through a rocket attack. While, at this stage, I had no idea if my comrades had survived, I had a feeling deep in my gut that they had not. Suddenly the vivid memory of an instant in time when human body parts flew into the air right before my eyes shook me to my core. My body shivered and trembled, further proof to my confused brain that I was indeed alive.

I lay prostrate on the dusty ground. The blast had forced all the air from my lungs. I struggled to breathe. There was an urgency to get up to check on my fellow soldiers and to assess my own situation. Sucking in air to give me strength to rise, my thoughts began to bring me to the reality of what had happened in that split second, God only knows how many minutes ago.

Thoughts of my mother flooded into my head. She had expressed a mother's fear for her son when I had told her I was being sent to Iraq. I remember how, with boyish bravado, I told her nothing would happen to me. Frankly I shared her anxiety, but did not want her to worry unnecessarily. I recall my own fears diminished in the company of the guys in my platoon, but having said that, there always remained a sense of doubt in the back of my mind. Now those doubts had become reality. Our reconnaissance mission had gone terribly wrong. I found myself lying in the dust of a foreign land, behind enemy lines winded and with facial burns.

On my back looking up, the night sky appeared to be just as spectacular as it always had been at home on the family farm in Wisconsin. My eyes searched for familiar constellations but found none. A sudden unexplainable panic struck me. How would I ever find my way home when I couldn't read the stars? I tried to sit up but the strength had been sapped from within me. The shock of the blast had begun to subside and pain appeared where before there had been none. A burning sensation crept across my face; reminding me of the rising spring flood waters slowly inundating the low lying levels of the Wisconsin hay meadows. I felt an odd sensation in my shoulders and buttocks. Slowly it turned to the pain of severe bruising. I realized that it would be the result of being hurled to the ground by the great force of the blast.

My next sensation was the fear of not being able to move from where I lay and dying alone in this wasteland of dust and death. I had been in Iraq long enough to know that human life had little value here. I knew that my death would be celebrated by whatever faction had fired upon our jeep. At home in the state of Wisconsin my death would be recorded as a sacrifice to our great nation. At the family farm it would be considered a tragic loss of an only son, tearing the heart out of both mother and father. It would mean that four successive generations of the Wyman family, on the family farm, would come to an end.

For some inexplicable reason, I had a vision of my now aged parents, driving away from the farm for the final time, the long string of heritage having been torn apart in the desert lands of a place so different than the green fields of Wisconsin. I still could not rise from the ground having no idea if I have lain here ten seconds or ten minutes. I do not know whether I slipped into unconsciousness or if my mind, in some obscure way, attempted to relieve me of the stresses of the moment.

I saw myself at three years old playing in the farm kitchen while mother made a meal for the family and Jake the hired hand. So far as I was concerned at that age, Jake was one of the family. He always sat at the table with the rest of us. He worked alongside my father in the fields and dairy barn. Mother busied herself frying home cured fatback bacon for the breakfast. I could swear now that the smell of the bacon crossed the ether and came to my nostrils in my dream or altered state of mind.

My mother was fair haired, slender in build. She had deep piercing green eyes able to express tender love and disapproval with equal ease. It was her decision to call me Rodney at my birth, but as long as I can remember I was just plain Rod. Mother never wore makeup while on the farm, but on the days she and dad drove into town, I remember she wore a soft shade of lip rouge spending little extra time creating a pleasing hairstyle. She always wore a different dress for shopping but in the farm kitchen she wore an old cotton dress with a print of faded roses. Over it she wore a pinafore of plain white sturdy cotton. I always thought my mother looked beautiful when she dressed to go shopping in town. I remember I once told her; she smiled, picked me up and kissed me over and over. Mother offered me great comfort and security; as a result I was a happy child.

On the long lazy summer days, I played out in the farmyard always able to find something to amuse myself. At times I would chase the chickens just to hear their protesting squawks. Father had rigged up a swing for me it hung from the branches of a big shade tree. He erected it in exactly the same place his father had hung one for him many years earlier. On hot days the long cattle water trough became my exclusive swimming pool. I never had swimwear, out on our lonely farm there was no need for propriety; the only witnesses to my skinny dipping were the baleful stares of a few Holstein milk cows. Sometimes father would take me with him on the tractor. I would sit on his knee and pretend I was the driver of this snorting monstrous machine.

At other times I would swing by the hour under the shade tree. There, I was a trapeze artist in the circus. Occasionally I would play in the red sand dug up by a long since gone number of rabbits. I spent hours building speedboats, fast cars and airplanes and even more hours piloting my creations through land and seascapes created in my own mind. My creations were often demolished by the cows during their grazing wanderings; it never concerned me, for the next creation would always be better than the last.

My mind transported me to my upstairs bedroom in the back of the farmhouse. It had a six pane window dressed with dark green curtains reaching to just below the sill. The bottom part of the window slid upwards, on warm summer nights when it was propped open, the night breezes would shake the curtains making me think of angels watching over me like mother said they did. From my window I had a view of a pond out beyond the farmyard. Sometimes after I had been sent to bed I would look out and see the reflection of the moon on the water. The small trees around the pond framed it in black similar to an ornate picture frame. In the daytime the pond was a haven for a family of wild ducks with brightly coloured feathers. Within the ponds waters lived frogs, minnows and all manner of little water insects for me to catch in jam jars.

Opposite the window sat my bed, which had an iron head and footboard. Mother always brought me to my bed at that time in my life. She would read a story and have me recite a prayer before tucking me in. I had a large toy box at the foot of my bed. It contained both damaged and undamaged toys, books, odd socks and my winter hat. The room held a chest of drawers along one wall where mother stored my clean pressed clothing, some extra sheets and blankets for the winter. Against the other was a couple of old kitchen chairs relegated to my room after my parents bought a better kitchen set at the local auction barn. I rarely sat on the chairs but mother would sit on one when she read to me at bedtime. The walls of my room were wallpapered in stripes with all manner of animals. It had obviously not been done professionally for some of the animals in the corners did not match the ones on the main walls. I can remember mentally trying to put them back in the right place while lying in bed waiting for sleep. There was a picture of Jesus on the wall above my bed. It used to scare me when I was very small, for Jesus was holding his heart in his hands and I knew even then that our inside parts should stay inside.

The memory of inside body parts stirred me from my dream, or state of unconsciousness. I sat up quickly. It surprised me, for a while ago I did not have the strength to rise from the dust. I wondered how long I had been in a state of oblivion. Was it minutes, seconds, hours? I staggered to my feet. The jeep still burned brightly, suggesting I had only been unconscious for a minute or so. I limped toward the burning wreck. I tripped but did not fall. I looked down and saw a severed arm with a corporal's stripe on the sleeve. It was Matt Jackson's arm. My stomach discharged the meal we had consumed before leaving the base. I retched until my torso hurt like the rest of me. The only sound was the flames licking up through the wreckage. I found a body alongside the jeep. One arm was missing and the face completely blown off the skull. I knew it had to be Matt. I also knew there was nothing I could do for him; his life's blood had soaked into the sand. I began to look for Smokey Watts, our driver. I found what was left of him. He had caught the worst of the blast, which had disintegrated his body. Parts of him were cooking in the burning wreckage. The smell of it hit my brain and I wanted to puke again, but there was nothing left inside me but fear.

Now I had a dilemma. Should I try to bury the remains of my comrades or should I hurry away in an attempt to get back to our base to report the incident. The military had never briefed me about what to do in this situation. It seemed very un-Christian to just leave my buddies to rot soon to be covered with the ever present bluebottle flies then to eventually have their bones bleached by the desert sun. The wooden handled shovels in their holders on the jeep burned along with the vehicle. The option to bury their remains no longer existed unless I dug a shallow grave with my bare hands. But the hard packed sand of the desert made this an impossibility. Even if it were not so, I would have to wait until daylight to gather the body parts together.

Soldiers don't cry. What a line of bull those words are. I began to weep. Not for myself, but for Smokey and Matt. They, like me, had hopes and dreams of a life after our time in Iraq. I believe Smokey had a wife and child waiting for him stateside. I didn't know Smokey well; he was just one of the guys in the platoon. I began to think of his child growing up without a father never knowing as I did, the love and security of a caring father. I thought too of his young wife who perhaps loved him with an intensity that would prevent her from moving on with her life coming to love another man. Smokey probably had a mother and a father somewhere back in the land of the free, who would perhaps mourn his death until they too passed away. Thinking about the terrible loss of Smokey to four other people far away disturbed me; my tears fell scalding my burned cheeks.

I resolved then and there that if I got out of the Goddamn mess I found myself in, made it back to the base, then home to the states, I would attempt to locate his family just to tell them that Smokey didn't suffer at his death, sparing them the awful details.

I knew Matt much better. He had been in the military longer than I and he had risen through the ranks to corporal. We were not close friends, his rank was of course an obstacle to closeness in a personal sense, but we were close as fellow soldiers. We were on the same team. This war was a tie that bound us all together regardless of rank. We all knew we had to fight as a cohesive entity. None of us were entirely sure what we were fighting for. There were a great number of theories. The main one was the ownership of Iraqi oil. Another was to free a people held in bondage by its leaders, the list went on. To us on the ground, packing rifles, it really didn't matter what the reason was, we were in an inhospitable place where any number of groups of armed men sought to kill us. In order to ensure our own survival we had taken on the task of killing others. Matt took this task seriously.

I looked down again at the remains of his body. I don't know why the thought came to me, I wondered if his family, wherever they were, had photographs of him, for his face would never be seen again by anyone. The thought, although somewhat illogical, brought forth a new flood of tears. It also conjured up a vision of my own father were he never to see my face again.

I hold great memories of my father. The only times he ever chastised me were when I might unknowingly place myself in danger. Such as the time I ventured into the stall of our big Holstein bull, in my innocence thinking it was just another gentle milk cow. Dad grabbed me pulling me clear of the lowered head and flared nostrils. There were other instances, where dad just quietly explained the danger I had placed myself in. I suppose I considered my father to be Godlike. I certainly looked up to him and paid attention to his lessons on life and the art of dairy farming. He dressed in the fashion of most other farmers in our area. Brace and bib overalls, a checked wool shirt and stout work boots. In the summer months he wore a straw hat, in the winter a knitted toque. Dad had a serious looking face with bushy eyebrows; he shaved every morning after the milking was done. Dad's look of seriousness hid his true nature that of a gentle and loving man. In all my life at home on the farm I never heard him once yell at mother.

We Wyman's were not wealthy farmers, but we wanted for nothing. We had food a plenty as I recall. Mom had her own car, an older Chevrolet and dad had a fairly new pickup truck which I learned to drive out in the big pasture. The millisecond memory of the sound of Dads pickup when I drove it brought me back to the here and now. I heard the sound of an engine off in the distance. This was no dream. The sound was real.

I turned my head toward the direction of the sound I saw headlights approaching fast, bobbing up and down in the rough terrain. Then I heard whooping and yelling. Instantly I realized that it was most likely the ones who had fired the rocket now were on their way to gloat over the kill guided by the burning jeep. No longer could I consider not leaving my dead comrades. I was fully aware that should I be found here still alive I would be captured, probably tortured at worst at best sent to my maker immediately via a shot to the head or knife at my throat. Momentarily I forgot all about my own injuries and finding strength I never knew I possessed. I ran into the desert at the far side of the road from which the vehicle approached. I had no weapon; all had been consumed in the jeep. I suppose I must have run about a hundred yards from the wreck when I ran into a scrubby bush similar to sagebrush. In fear I dove behind it and lay on my belly to observe what would happen. I prayed that the men were not experienced trackers who could find my footprints and discover my place of refuge.

No sooner had I flopped to the ground when the vehicle, a pickup truck with five or six men carrying rifles, leapt to the sandy earth circling the burning jeep. I heard excited voices as they discovered the remains of my comrades. I saw one man kick Matt's body probably to be sure he was dead. Then they began looking for souvenirs.

My heart skipped a beat as one of the men approached the bush I was hiding behind. Had he spotted my footprints in the sand? My heart stopped! Since he carried a rifle while I had nothing, getting up to run would be suicide. I made the decision to lay face down accepting whatever my fate might be, a bullet in the back of my head or…? My ears searched for every sound. I heard footsteps come right up to the bush. I heard the sound of a rifle in a pair of hands. Then I heard the rustle of cloth. The next sound was of urine splashing at the other side of the bush three feet away from my head. I dared not even breathe in or even breathe out. I lay utterly motionless and soundless for what seemed an eternity. Finally the splashing stopped. The silence was deafening. I thought my lungs might explode holding my breath so long, yet I did not hear the sound of retreating feet. A voice in an unknown language called from near the jeep. The man beyond the bush answered him as he walked away.

I exhaled as softly as I could. So far they did not know I existed. I wondered how long they would stay near the jeep. I knew I could not just stand up and head back to our original point of departure. Even though it was still dark any noise by me could alert them, I might become just one more trophy, or worse, become a prisoner and face almost certain torture and humiliation. Pictures of my captivity might be sent out via television to the western world. The thought of the possibility of my parents seeing their son in that predicament tore at my guts.

My breathing returned to what I would consider normal under the circumstances, but my heart rate was high, pumped with adrenaline from my fear. The spilled gasoline from the jeep had begun to burn itself out, but the tires still burned sending up plumes of stinking acrid black smoke visible against the night sky. I saw the flash of a match and then the pencil thin glow of a lit cigarette. Several other cigarettes were lit from the first one. It was obvious the men were in no hurry to leave. I began to worry if the men stayed until daylight I would be a sitting duck. I had to make a life or death decision. Stay here to risk capture or death, or try to move under the cover of darkness. I chose the latter. As quietly as I could, I began to crawl backwards always keeping my eye on the flickering flames. I was fully aware of the fact that I would be making an easily follow-able trail but it was my only option to get away from the men around the jeep without possibly being noticed.

I had traveled backwards about fifty feet when I bumped into a bush. It probably wasn't so, but to me it sounded incredibly loud. I stopped moving and remained motionless for a while. The men were still hanging around the jeep apparently not having heard anything to alert them to my presence. I felt it safe enough now for me to crawl forwards away from the danger of being seen. Now I could cover more distance quicker, but I still did not dare stand up to walk or run in case I could be seen in silhouette against the night horizon. I thought it best to stay clear of the road we had traveled down, but I would skirt it a half mile or so away making my way back across the enemy territory line. As a matter of fact in reality there was no such line. Here in Iraq, the enemy was everywhere. The people we were fighting were indistinguishable from the general population. This was not a conventional war we were involved in; the enemy by and large had no uniforms to denote who they were.

Dressed in my military fatigues I would stand out like a sore thumb alone in the desert. If I were to encounter civilians not involved in the conflict they would know I was an American and not a threat to them; however I would not know if they were a threat to me. I knew I had to avoid contact with any other people until I reached my platoon's base. There was a further problem. Our intelligence had informed us the enemy took the uniforms of our dead and wounded personnel, using them to get close to our installations. I was aware that even if I reached the base, walking alone, I could be suspected as a suicide bomber and shot by my own platoon members.

I felt I had crawled far enough from the accident scene that I could stand up and walk. Warily I rose to my feet and looked around. I had traveled over a small rise and so the fire was no longer visible, but I could still see the smoke black against the sky. Now I was out of immediate danger, my fear subsided. However now that the adrenalin rush was over I felt the scalding burns on my face. My mouth was dry and my throat was parched. I cursed myself for taking off my water canteen as I manned the machinegun. I had no idea how far we had traveled before the missile hit us, so I had no idea how far I had to travel in the desert before I could quench my thirst. I started to walk. The massive bruising on my buttocks agonized every stride I took. The fear of possible capture and the fear of never getting back to my family in Wisconsin gave me the impetus to ignore my pain striding out in the direction which I hoped was the correct one. I fixed a point of land far off in the distance in order to keep myself on track to avoid walk in circles. Skirting around the unidentified scrubby bushes would make it all too easy to change direction without being aware of it.

I remembered my father telling me how he kept his plowing furrows so straight. He said 'See that third fencepost from the corner son, aim the tractor straight for it and do not deviate from course for anything your first furrow will be dead straight. We farmers have not much in which we can display our pride in what we do to the city dweller, but a straight furrow is one of them. It is open to the sky, visible to all, but only another farm person can appreciate the workmanship and the pride that went into it.'

Father told me many things as I grew up; at the time I thought it was just conversation. I realized later that father was educating me in a way that didn't seem like I was being taught anything. Young as I was before I joined the army, I knew a great deal about dairy farming. Father in his quiet way had imparted a great agricultural education to me. I realize now that it was his way of ensuring the Wyman farm dynasty would carry on uninterrupted. Yet here I was in a foreign far off land with the dynasty in extreme danger of being torn asunder. The thought brought back the memory of a vision I had earlier. In which I saw my parents leaving the Wyman farm for the last time. Behind them was a big sign, Dairy farm for sale 250 acres of good land. Across the top of the sign was a smaller one carrying the word, SOLD. Father drove his pickup with mother at his side. Both had grown older, I saw they were both crying. I knew that I hadn't made it home. It was a mixture of memory, present thought, and a waking dream. I wondered how I would die. Would it be thirst, torture, or a bullet from afar? A sob came from deep in my chest a few more tears scalded my burned cheeks as I walked steadfastly toward the landmark on the night horizon. I knew I cried not for myself. I cried for my parents broken dreams.

I can only think now that it was the tears in my eyes that prevented me from seeing the object in front of me. Granted it was dark and I was concentrating on my focal point in the distance. Suddenly I found myself very close to it, a big black object sticking out of the desert. I stopped dead in my tracks. Could it be a military vehicle? My eyes searched the dark hulk then I realized it was a farm type tractor with a front mounted bucket. My heart began to race. Who owned it? Were they close at hand? What was it doing out here in what I assumed to be the wilderness desert? I listened intently for any sounds of human activity. There were none. I walked around it. I felt at the radiator it was cold. I tapped at the fuel tank and by the hollow sound, discerned it was empty. I assumed it must have been abandoned after running out of fuel, but why was it here far from the road to the right? My mind suggested a number of scenarios. Perhaps a family drove it here in an attempt to escape the senseless violence. Perhaps there had been a futile attempt to rid the ground of the scrubby bushes to plant a crop. Could it had been driven here as a prank by some misguided youth. I discarded the last scenario I knew that such an act in this crazy country could bring a death sentence without the benefit of a summary trial, even upon a thoughtless youth.

A vaguely familiar smell registered upon my sensory brain. What was it? I sniffed the air in attempt to identify it. The smell was from somewhere in my past. Suddenly I recognized it! It was the smell of rotting flesh. Occasionally on the farm we would have a cow abort her calf that had died within the womb sometimes it was necessary for the vet to dismember the calf in order to remove it, for failure to do so would result in the death of the mother due to blood poisoning. This explained to me why the tractor stood out here. It was obvious a cow had been brought out to be buried but the tractor had run out of fuel before accomplishing it. My idea of starting the tractor and driving it towards the base was of course dashed. I would have to continue walking.

In the darkness I had walked no more than twenty feet beyond the tractor when I found myself falling. I must have dropped about eight feet before hitting the soft bottom. Now the smell was overpowering. Had I landed on the damn cow? I put out my hands but it was not a cow's hide that I felt. In the blackness of the pit, I felt cloth then smooth human skin. My hands explored further, I felt a bearded human face, and I knew it belonged to a man. I felt another body beside it. It was that of a child. I began to panic. I had to get out of this pit. I looked up at the sky seeing that the pit was dug ramp like at the far end, away from me. I attempted to stand up but my feet started sinking into the rotting bodies. In my panic, I crawled over God only knows how many dead and decomposing men, women and children. I crawled up the ramp and when I reached the top my body forced me to try to puke, but there was nothing inside me yet I retched and retched till felt my intestines were about to be ejected. I felt an odd sensation of movement upon my hands. The urge to scream tore at my throat when I discovered my hands and clothing were crawling with maggots. Now my body and uniform stunk with the vile smell from the decomposing bodies. I shuddered at the sensation of the maggots crawling across my flesh.

I hurled myself down to the ground and began rubbing my clothing and skin with dry dusty sand. It only worked partially the maggots had squirmed inside my clothing. I stripped off my uniform feeling utter disgust. When I was naked I rolled around in the sand to cleanse my skin of the offending larva. I shook my clothing violently to rid them of the maggots, then I felt one wiggling on my burned forehead. It was far too sore to rub with sand so I threw handfuls at my face and knocking it away. Holding my clothes I ran from the pit.

Nothing in my life, either on the farm or in the military, had prepared me for such an experience. I felt sure it would haunt me for the rest of my life no matter how long or short it might be. We had been told, of course, that mass murder and graves were not uncommon in war zones. They had been found in Bosnia not too long ago and it had occurred in many countries in Africa. We were also made aware that Saddam Hussein's troops had carried out mass killings for years in the North of Iraq in Kurdish territory. Now that things in the south had deteriorated, different factions were committing the same crimes. To the populations in the Western World such crimes were abhorrent. Yet we tended to read about these things in our newspapers, shake our heads in disbelief then turn the page. To us it was not real; they were just newspaper and magazine stories. But to experience it as I just had the crimes became a horrific act.

A couple of hundred yards from the massacre site I stopped to put my clothes back on. Now I had time to think. As I struggled to pull my pants over my boots I wondered who those people were. What had been their crime? Why the children? Surely they were innocent of any crime; what of the murdered women what could they have done to warrant such treatment? I remembered again an officer telling us that in this land human life had no value. Ten, twenty, a thousand, it made no difference, if someone in command, be it a military or religious faction, decided that he wanted rid of certain people then it was done without remorse or conscience . My thoughts returned to the tractor. Had it run out of fuel before the bodies could be covered? Or did it sit there ready to bury the next batch of innocents after a gallon of gasoline had been added?

Now dressed, I began walking again, the appalling stink staying with me as it had inundated my uniform. My face, which I had pelted with sand, began to burn even more. I desperately wanted to rub it, but touching the seared skin just made it worse. I had become terribly thirsty from vomiting. My shoulders and buttocks hurt. I thought seriously about lying down to rest for a while, but deep inside I knew that would be a mistake. I would be only a matter of hours before the sun came making the desert baking hot. I had to get some miles in before daybreak. I fixed my gaze on the prominent feature I was aiming for striding as best I could, each step causing pain and discomfort.

I thought it might help if I took my mind off my situation by thinking about my young life in Wisconsin. I believe I was five when my mother took me to school for the first time. Having been an only child on the farm, I was unaccustomed to being surrounded by a group of excited children, but Mrs. Southworth, our teacher eased me into playing and working together with the others. I came to love school after the first couple of days, of course missing the attentions of my mother. Soon I was eager to ride the big yellow school bus with the other children. I became friends with a boy my own age called Ron Ramsey, we were inseparable. We shared our stories and packed lunches, played together in the schoolyard and shared a seat on the bus. Ron also came from a farm family but he had a bunch of siblings. He was the youngest, the oldest boy was seventeen working full time alongside his father. Ron, like his dad and brothers, had bright red hair. Folks used to say you could tell the Ramsey's walking in the dark with that red hair. They said their heads looked like the reflectors on the back of trucks, but I never thought so.

I maintained my close friendship with Ron until we reached the age of about fourteen. For reasons that are not clear to me, we kind of drifted apart. I suppose it was we had reached puberty we had differing views on life. We did see each other from time to time, but there was no common thread left between us. At fifteen Ron left home to become a live-in farm worker in the next county. I suppose he had put himself in the same position as Jake, the man who worked alongside my father.

I have no recollection of a time when Jake did not live in our home. He had his own bedroom upstairs next to mine. He was a quiet fellow, basically he spoke only when spoken to. It was never made clear to me nor did I ever ask, but I think Jake had come to us from an orphanage not as an adoptee but rather as farm labour. To all intents and purposes he became a family member. He was a hard worker and did father's bidding without question, although Dad would never have asked Jake to do anything he would not do himself.

I always had the feeling that Jake had a serious lack of self confidence, probably as a result of living his young life without the love and guidance of parents. There might be some who would think of Jake as being mentally slow, but such was not the case. His quiet attitude, in my opinion was as a result of being warehoused through his formative years. I never knew exactly how old Jake was but I figured him to be about thirty five. Under my father's hand, Jake had become an expert dairyman, there being nothing on the farm he was not capable of doing well. I don't remember him having any kind of a social life, he seemed content to listen to the radio or watch television in the evenings. I can only assume he saved the better part of his wages, apart from his work clothes he never seemed to spend any money. He neither smoked nor went out drinking;

he didn't even own a car. Instead he had an ancient Shwinn bicycle that someone had given him when he first came to live with us. Above all, Jake was dependable. I wished he were here with me in this God-awful place. His quiet determination would be a great comfort in the nightmare in which I found myself.

The terrain before me began to slope downwards making it a little easier to walk, but placing my feet lower with each step I took; pulled on the bruised muscles in my buttocks. I guessed it had been about an hour since the rocket attack on the jeep. I kept all my senses as sharp as I could. I constantly looked all around me listening as hard as possible. The only sounds apart from a light wind teasing my ears were my own feet on the hard desert ground and the rustle of my uniform pants as they brushed the taller scrubby foliage. Trying to use my sense of smell was an exercise in futility. My clothing smelled so bad one might think any other aroma would be cut down before it got to me. But it was not so. The acrid smell of wood smoke drifted to me on the night air, my olfactory senses sent a warning shot to my brain.

I stopped walking. I sniffed the air in an attempt to locate the source of the smoke. My father always used to say 'where there's smoke there's fire' but in this case where there was fire, there was extreme unknown danger. On the other hand it may be completely innocent; perhaps it came from the chimney of a mud brick cottage housing a family of ordinary non violent Iraqis struggling with day to day existence. My life and liberty depended on being absolutely sure which. The smoke had spread so thin in the night breeze that I could not read the source with certainty. I resumed walking but now more cautiously. I walked like a blind man. The sun still dwelled far beyond the rim of the earth so not even a flicker of light helped me to find my way.

I stumbled upon the edge of a draw probably formed eons ago by rushing waters. It was then I saw the source of the smoke. In the light of a flickering campfire I was able to make out a circle of humans lying down, likely sleeping. Were they soldiers, Religious warriors, or refugees in hiding? Realizing that I was standing in silhouette at the rim of the draw, I dropped to my belly until I could make a proper assessment of the situation. I lay still. Breathing softly, listening with such intent that I swear it hurt my eardrums. I could hear the crackle of firewood sparks and I think I could hear snores, but the sound was unclear. Then a different sound came to me. With unhurried steps human feet approached from my left. A sentry? I wondered. I lay stock still, face down in the sand. My heart began to pound. Would the sentry see me or worse trip over me? I tried to quiet my quickened breathing as much as I could. The sound of the footsteps grew closer. Now the sound was behind me. I wondered would this be the place where I die. My heart raced. Would it be a clean fast bullet? The sound of the moving feet passed me then stopped. I guessed it was about fifteen feet beyond where I lay. I heard the rustle of cloth. I wondered could he be drawing a large knife from his belt. A burst of light struck my anxious eyes. The smell of sulfur from a lit match reached my nose. It was followed by the unmistakable smell of burning tobacco.

With excruciating pain I moved my head to look. In silhouette I saw a turbaned man in long clothing with a cigarette burning in his hand. He sat down on a rock so close to me I could hear his exhalation of the smoke. I lay immobile not knowing how long he would stay there. If he stayed until daylight the game would be over. Time was running out for me to travel a fair distance before the sun began to bake the landscape. I had no choice but to lie here as immobile as the rock the sentry sat upon, unable to move a muscle. I watched him smoke his cigarette then grind the butt into the sand. I prayed that he would get up and leave but he stayed put, surveying the low horizon.

I began to think about the grave danger in which I found myself. It was my fault that I was here in Iraq at all. I remember the look of horror on my parents faces when I told them what I had done.

'I have joined the Army' I said. My mother burst into tears and my father told me.

'Son.' He said 'You have jeopardized not only your future, but indirectly ours. Your grandfather and great grandfather would turn over in their graves were they to hear what you have just told us. You say you have done this over a slip of a girl who was obviously not worthy of you.'

My father's words hit me hard. To be chastised by him who had always trusted, respected and loved me unconditionally, added to the hurt I already felt. I realize now that my father was right as usual. I had walked into the recruiting centre suffering from a deep sense of loss after being jilted. In a way I suppose I felt like the men who had joined the French Foreign Legion where I would choose extreme danger for myself and make Maryanne feel terrible about driving me to such an act.

But real life is not the movies! She had found another beau before she even told me she didn't want to see me anymore. She could not have cared less what I did after that. For me it was too late to change my mind. I had signed all the documents and now I was a bona fide member of the United States Army. I reported to boot camp in a matter of weeks and shortly after training I boarded a plane for this God forsaken place. Sergeant Barlow had picked me randomly with Smokey Watts and Matt Jackson to come out on this ill fated reconnaissance mission.

The man sitting on the rock stood up. I watched as he took out another cigarette, struck a match lit the end then he sat down again. Under my breath I cursed the day of his birth. I felt like a rat in a trap. I could not move without jeopardizing my safety. Time was passing I had no idea how fast; it felt like I had lain here for hours. I feared the sunrise greatly. If the sentry had not left his seat by then it would reveal my position. I ached to move my body but had to endure perfect stillness.

I met Maryanne in high school. Since she lived close by the school she didn't travel on the yellow bus so our meetings, for the longest times, were limited to the school hallways. We shared our first pre-pubescent kiss by the lockers. It was a fumbling affair, but it became the first building block of a long relationship. I realize now that to have had only one female friend was a gross mistake. There was no way I learned how to make intelligent comparisons of character. With the benefit of hindsight, I realize now that Maryanne had no interest in farm life and as such had no intention of sharing my life in that endeavour. It should have been a red flag, but I ignored its waving because of the high school culture of boys having a girl friend and vice versa. It is clear to me now that Maryanne used me for her own ends having no intention of making our friendship a lifelong one.

As we continued on into puberty she would hold my interest by using her sexuality. When we found ourselves completely alone Maryanne would allow me to fondle her breasts and very occasionally we might engage in heavy petting but she drew the line at total intimacy. Despite the discomfort the abstinence caused me, I respected her wishes, but the thoughts of a future full sexual encounter with her held me in a vise like grip.

I suppose some would call it puppy love, now in the light of reality, that is exactly what it was. It was not a relationship based upon trust, respect, and a real desire to totally share our lives together, but rather a childish notion of love on my part. Looking back I think I was merely a stepping stone to someone more exciting than I. By the same token I had used my entry into the military as a stepping stone to relieve me of my emotional pain of the moment. The foolishness of youth had landed me in a place where my life had no more meaning in the greater scheme of things than a weed in a meadow.

The sentry man stood up slowly walking back the way he had approached. At last I felt safe enough to breathe normally. I raised my head watching him until he disappeared from my view. To my intense relief I did not encounter him again. I deviated from my direct path to the point of reference. I walked as carefully as possible higher up the draw away from the encampment below, intending to cross it when I was out of earshot. I had no idea how much time I had lost lying prostrate on the ground. It may have been an hour, or possibly a duration of only ten minutes. In any event dawn had still not begun to break. It concerned me that there might be other sentries about so I proceeded with great caution. I suppose I had covered about a quarter mile before I decided to cross the draw. It was not nearly so deep here I crested the other side pausing at the top to search for signs of human activity. Finding none, I found my point of reference and headed unerringly towards it.

I kept all my senses sharply tuned for any sound, smell or light that could put me in more danger than I already was. I walked briskly, dodging the taller bushes for what I estimated to be an hour. The smallest amount of light began to appear behind the Eastern horizon. Within less than another hour, light would flood the land. In spite of my suffering I quickened my step to maximize the safety the dark offered me. It was almost dawn when I stumbled into it. I found myself on the edge of a small village. It had been hidden behind a stand of large trees I wondered did it contain any humans.

I stopped dead in my tracks. I worried that an alert dog might waken the inhabitants. But there came not a sound, nor did I see any smoke coming from the cluster of mud brick houses. I stepped up to a large tree. I hid behind it to look for signs of life; I recognized that something was amiss. The doors to the houses were all open, several of them swinging back and forth squawking on dry hinges pushed by the dawn breeze. Then I noticed the house windows were all knocked out of their frames. The village had every appearance of having been ransacked. A stray cat had sensed my presence coming to me no doubt looking to be fed. Its guts were drawn in as though it had not seen food for a number of days. It smelled at my stinking pants, then rubbed itself against my legs. An odd sensation came over me. It was a sense of reality within an unreal situation. Memories of our farm cats flooded back into my mind. They didn't want for much just a dish of daily milk and an occasional gentle stroking of their fur. Why had no one fed this animal? Was the village deserted?

I left my hiding place behind the tree and crept softly to the nearest house. I looked through the broken window, even in the dawn gloom I could see that the interior had been trashed. I stepped through the open door. I wondered if perhaps I could find some food, or more urgently a drink. There was nothing, even the cupboards had been torn from the walls. I left the house and went carefully to the next one. Again I found nothing edible or drinkable. It was then I realized that the houses had no plumbing. I was beginning to believe I would not find any drinkable liquid. Then I realized the missing inhabitants had probably carried their water from a well somewhere in the village. I stepped into the third house only to be met with a stench I was more than familiar with.

In the largest room, to my absolute horror, I discovered a woman's body hanging from a beam by the wrists completely naked. The body covered in the most appalling welts, cuts and bruises. Her hair had been shorn completely off and the ever-present flies had laid their eggs. Maggots writhed all over her head and face while those who had lost their grip squirmed in a heap directly under her. On the floor lay a pair of blood stained rough wooden clubs which I assumed had been used to beat the unfortunate woman to death.

I stepped back in intense horror. Had I anything left in my stomach I would most certainly have heaved it out. I staggered outside into the clean morning air. My experience in the pit had shocked me beyond belief, but this sight, this mark of human depravity toward a fellow being left me stunned and sick. I wondered what in God's name this person had done to deserve such a savage end, being left to rot with absolutely no dignity. I began to dry retch. I desperately needed a drink of water. I went to the next house and found that it too had been ransacked. It dawned on me that the dead people in the pit were probably the ones from this village. Had they been massacred for their food supplies I wondered? Or were they killed because of their religious beliefs? I would never know and if I did, I knew I would never understand.

The sun had risen beyond the horizon flooding the village with pale light. At the far end of the flat stone clad street I spotted the village well. I had guessed correctly. The water pail lay askew on the ground its rope still attached. I hurried towards it in anticipating a drink then washing off my body and disgusting clothing. I picked up the pail and dropped it into the well. Instead of a splash I heard the clunk of the pail hitting something solid. I leaned over the edge and looked down. About fifteen feet below the rim, the bodies of a number of quite young children floated on the surface. Once again the smell of rotting flesh rose to meet my nostrils revolting my senses.

It was obvious that the water would be fouled by all manner of bacteria; to drink it would mean certain death, probably within a short time of ingesting it. I wondered if the children had been dropped into the well because they were too young to walk to the killing ground at the pit. Had it been done while the parents were forced to watch? My mind reeled at witnessing the aftermath of these barbaric acts. I had come to this country with a fairly open mind, naively believing the country would be peopled by good folks, like I was used to back home but living under a repressive regime. Many of us G.Is believed that if we were to get rid the country of the corrupt leaders, it would become peaceful and the population would not have to live in fear. It was painfully clear to me that the atrocities I had witnessed this day were not military atrocities. There was no evidence of shelling or heavy arms fire in the village; it had been done by a small group of murderous men with no mercy or respect for human life or dignity.

I continued my search for drinkable water going through three more houses with no results. In the seventh house I searched for any canned foods that might contain liquid. I heard a sound and I stood stock still. Was it human or animal? I did not move a muscle as I strained to hear. I heard it again. It came from somewhere within this house. But where? There was a scratching sound, and then what I thought was a whimper, a child's whimper. But how could it be, it was obvious to me the village had been deserted for a number of days. I fought with my instinct to say, 'is someone here?' But I held my tongue then I heard it again.

The sound seemed to be coming from around my feet. Looking down I found myself standing amid a pile of rags and pieces of broken furniture. The sound came again, this time I was convinced it was a child's weak voice.

The thought struck me like a thunderbolt. Perhaps a parent had hidden a child to escape the massacre. I scuffed the debris away with my feet revealing a crude trapdoor. I tapped on the boards with my boot resulting in the tired wail of a child. My first thought was that I had to get the child out of there. My second thought, could this some kind of booby trap? I was very much aware from my training that often human bodies were used to conceal a land mine. I discounted the thought. If it were such a trap surely the child would have triggered it and why would even the most demented murderer mine an empty house in an equally empty village? I moved the rest of the debris then lifted the trapdoor. I placed my head into the hole seeing a wide eyed terrified child staring up at me. In the gloom of the underground hideaway it looked like a girl of possibly three or four years of age.

I smiled to re-assure her that I would do her no harm, but one look at my face and she began to scream. It was then that I remembered that my burn blackened must look like a monster's face to so small a child. I held out my arms for her to come and be lifted out, but fear had gripped her. She reeled back away from my hands. Her little lungs screamed so loudly it worried me that if there were someone, perhaps one of the perpetrators of the massacre, still within the village she would give us both away.

I leaned further into the hole, grabbed her holding her small body to my chest until she calmed down. There was evidence that her parents had left her food and water but she had consumed it all. I climbed back into the room still holding her tightly. The child had been forced to do her bodily functions where she had lain. She smelled bad, but not nearly so bad as I. Between the two of us there must have been an awful stench.

Now I faced the biggest dilemma of my entire life; any decision I had ever had to make prior to today paled in comparison to the one I had to make now. My upbringing and teachings in Wisconsin told me clearly that I should not abandon this child to wander the desert alone. But, I had my own life and safety to deal with. The child might be lucky and find someone take her in. On the other hand she could become target practice for the rebels who had raped her village, or she might become a victim of the wild dogs that ran free in the desert. To take the child along with me would be difficult possibly jeopardizing my own safety resulting in both our deaths. I wondered if I ever made it back home to the family farm how I could ever tell my mother I had abandoned a tiny girl to her fate in the scorching desert. What would my mother think of her son then? What of father who had always taught me that life was precious even in the animal world? In the end there was no choice. I had to try to get the child to safety. I took one last look around the room. Hanging on a nail in the wall was a long robe, the kind that the rural people wore. It occurred to me that if I were to get rid of my uniform and wear the robe, I would be less conspicuous should I be spotted walking along with a child in my arms. I put the child down to rid myself of my appalling uniform just keeping my shorts. I put on the robe not knowing what it might be called. Clothing hurled from a smashed chest of drawers was strewn around the room. It occurred to me that if I intended to look like an Iraqi country man I should wear some kind of headgear. Not only that, the sun's heat was increasing, making it necessary to keep my head covered. I found a piece of brown cloth and wrapped it round my head like a turban.

I found a shard of broken mirror on the floor. For the first time I saw my burned face, I was shocked at my appearance no wonder the child was frightened of me. Despite the extreme discomfort of the burns I saw an upside to them. I no longer looked like a white American boy, I smiled inwardly. From a distance I could pass as an Iraqi farming person. The child seemed to be more comfortable seeing me dressed as one of her own people. I looked for some clothing that I could change her into; I could not stand to carry her covered in her own feces. If only I could locate some water I might be able to clean her up properly. Even though we could not communicate with each other she seemed to understand that I would not harm her. I pointed at her feces covered dress and made a gesture of holding my nose. She understood immediately and offering no protest when I lifted it from her trying not to have it touch her face. With some rags I found on the floor, I wiped her as clean as I could without benefit of water. She must have had older siblings, for I found a crumpled and torn dress that was much too large for her. Dressing her in it, I then found another piece of rag in which to fashion a makeshift hat to protect her from the sun.

I made a sign to her that I needed a drink but she did not understand. She just looked at me confused. I motioned her to follow me as I left her home and went into the next house. In my continued search for a drink I found a teapot on the floor beside the smashed stove. It was upright and contained a small amount of stale tea. I poured a mouthful from the spout and my tongue hurled it at my parched throat. I saved some for the child who grabbed the pot and drained it. That appalling tasting stale tea was the most gratifying drink of my entire life; even my mother's homemade lemonade could not hold a candle to it. The cat that had greeted me on my arrival at this village of death had followed me, no doubt expecting I would feed it.

As the child bent down to stroke it I heard a noise that sent terror racing through my veins, my heart shooting to my mouth. It was the sound of an engine. A motorized vehicle approached. I felt a terrible fear that

I had been seen going in and out of the houses. If the occupants of the vehicle had come to search the houses, I hadn't a chance in Hell of escaping. Even if the opportunity arose, how in God's name, could I leave the child to be shot or hurled alive into the well?

I put my finger to my lips to indicate she should be absolutely silent. She nodded. It was obvious she had been trained in the signage, likely by her parents. In all probability it had saved her life. We hunkered down by the back wall of the room far away from the window. The sound grew louder, so loud it sounded like a tank but without the rattle of tracklayers. The noise was deafening in this place of silence. Then it passed by our view, the vehicle was an aging Toyota pickup running without the benefit of a muffler. In the pickup box, four bearded men wearing turbans were holding rifles in one hand and hanging on to metal bars with the other.

The cat, realizing I was not about to feed it, ran out after the truck. A shot rang out then we heard laughter as the noisy truck left the village in the direction of the camp in the draw. When all was quiet we ventured from the house and saw that the cat had been blown into two pieces, lying in the road. I indicated to the child, with sign language, I would take her with me and leave the village but I don't believe she understood. I picked her up. She must have weighed about thirty pounds. I knew I was in for a Hell of a struggle carrying her in my arms beneath the blazing sun all the way back to my base, that was if I was fortunate enough to make it back alive.

At first she struggled. How I wished I could communicate with her, for if she only understood what I was trying to do for her she would be much more relaxed and cooperative. In her struggles she accidentally struck my burned face several times. The pain was excruciating, I wanted to yell out but I dared not. I had never spent much time around little children, now I began to realize how patient mothers have to be carrying misbehaved offspring who have no wish to be carried. The sun had climbed higher and the heat rays bombarded the earth, exacerbating the burn pain on my nose and cheeks. With the child slung low in my arms I passed the fouled water well and walked out of the village. Once clear of the houses I left the road again, there was no telling if the truck would return. I had no intention of being spotted. It goes without saying that the road followed the path of least resistance while I traversed the rough ground on the hillside above it.

With the child in my arms I found it hard to see where exactly my feet were being placed upon the ground. At one point I stumbled on a rock, which moved then began rolling down the hill. I looked back and forth to see if anyone approached either way on the road. Suddenly a huge explosion rent the air. I knew immediately that the rock had triggered a land mine. We were well above the damage zone and the fragments went harmlessly into the hillside. The child screamed at the shock and I held her tight to re-assure her she was safe. But a new fear entered my brain. I realized we were standing in a minefield. I also realized that the explosion would alert the men at the camp in the draw. They had a vehicle and could conceivably be here in just a few minutes.

I knew I had to leave the area quickly. I knew if there was one mine there was almost a hundred percent chance there would be at least several more. Which ever way I moved I would be taking a chance on triggering one. I fought the urge to panic. I stood still. I had to figure out my next move. I reasoned that the likeliest place for the mines to be concealed would be relatively close to the road. Perhaps I was above them already. With my heart in my mouth, a terrified child in my arms, I began to climb higher away from the road. Each small sound that reached my ears made me cringe, would this be my last moment of life? Out of breath and with my muscles protesting the extra exertion I reached a place where I could lie down without danger of being spotted from the road and where I could ease my arms of the weight they carried.

Finding some momentary relief, the child and I lay behind a rock waiting. I had been right; the explosion had alerted the persons at the camp. I heard the roar of the un-muffled pickup as it raced to the village and beyond. I carefully looked around the rock. The truck came to a dusty halt and I saw the men pointing at the newly disturbed earth and the stone in the road that had precipitated the blast.

I heard much heated conversation in a tongue I did not understand but I did get the feeling that they were not about to enter the minefield to investigate further. I could see them scanning the hillside for signs of movement while the child and I remained motionless. She was so good at being quiet and still when I signed her to. I had the feeling that she had been well instructed by her parents in the art of survival despite her young age. I wondered what her name was and if I knew, would I be able to pronounce it. The dress I had found for her was evidence that she was not an only child; I wondered how many of her siblings had been murdered. What really troubled me was how her parents had decided she should be the one to live, then hiding her in the ground inside the house rather than the other children or child. I could not conceive of how a parent would make such a decision. I thought possibly a relative had been informed of the child's presence and she was supposed to have been rescued and that relative had also succumbed to the butchery. I wondered who had given the order to have the village residents annihilated. Was it based upon religious differences? It was common knowledge that different religious factions did commit atrocities upon those, whose beliefs differed. These things happened in any number of countries. Here in Iraq it had been going on for years. But even armed with that information I still could not get my head around the notion that some factions believed it was right in the eyes of God to kill other God fearing fellow countrymen.

The men down on the road began to climb back into the pickup truck, apparently satisfied that the blast had been caused by a loose rolling rock. The vehicle turned around in the road heading back toward the village a cloud of dust followed its progress. It was now safe to get to my feet to continue walking towards the army base.

I was headed in basically a southern direction so the morning sun struck my left cheek and forehead. The pain on my already burned skin felt as though a blow torch was being applied, there would be no relief. In fact as the day wore on I would have to endure much more of the sun's torture. The heavy weight of the child pulled on my shoulder muscles. I wished in vane that I had a haversack I could put the child in; I realize now that I could have made a sling for her from the clothing back at the house. It would be so much easier had I been able to carry her on my back. I tried my ultimate best to ignore the mass of pain that my body had become, mechanically putting one foot in front of the other. It was however a blessing that the child had succumbed to exhausted sleep despite our mutual hunger and thirst.

I suppose I had been walking for about an hour. The sun had climbed higher and had begun its merciless scorching of the landscape. With the child in my arms I could not adjust my makeshift headwear to shade my face. By now I was fatigued. I knew that soon I would have to find some shade under which to lie down to rest. I scanned the horizon in the general direction of where I thought the base might be. I saw a group of trees about a mile away however I would have to deviate from my course in order to reach them. For my sake and that of the child I felt if I did not get out of the sun to rest we would likely both de-hydrate and succumb to exhaustion.

With incredible effort such as I had never experienced before, I placed one foot in front of the other step by step, until I reached the first tree. I put the still sleeping child down in the shade of the trunk then I made my way to the second tree flopping to the shaded ground like a rag doll. How it was possible given my thirst and hurting muscles I do not know, but I fell quickly into sleep. I felt a renewed burning sensation on my face. I awoke to find that the sun's journey across the sky had moved the shadow of the tree trunk beyond where I lay. I lifted my head then horror of horrors, a scorpion stood upon my chest facing me with its tail arched over its back.

Coming from Wisconsin, obviously I had no experience of these overgrown insects. I had of course heard about scorpions and a couple of the guys back at the base had close calls with them. I lay still, terrified. I knew that with one quick dash it could be on my face or neck. I was not sure if its sting was lethal or if it caused paralysis. With Herculean effort I fought the urge not to panic. My hands were on the ground beside me. I wondered if I were to raise my right hand and quickly try to knock it away, would it have a lightning response like a housefly and be on my exposed face before I could get to even touch it. I watched as one front leg rose up from my chest and stepped closer to my face. I had no choice now but to act. I had to make my move carefully and be sure I knocked the ghastly thing away from my head. Slowly and deliberately I raised my right arm from the ground in preparation to knock it away with the back of my hand. The insect began a slow move closer to my face. It was now or never. I lashed out in an act of desperation hitting the scorpion on the side of its body. Before it had any time to react it flew through the air and landed several feet away. I jumped to my feet with all the speed I could muster, even though I feared this thing I stomped on it with my boot. I ground it into the dust to be absolutely sure it offered me no more danger.

When my heart rate returned to something like normal, I turned to see if the little girl was alright. Once again my heart sprang into high gear. The child was not where I had left her. In concerned panic I looked all around me between the trees. She was nowhere in sight. It was the oddest thing. The child was not mine nor even of the same nation, but I had developed a strong bond toward her. I had this need to see that she survived just as I needed to survive. I had a millisecond memory of the farm cattle back home, how a mother cow, instantly her calf was born, considered its safety and well being her life's concern fighting anything to protect it. Within that flash of a memory was born my instinct to offer the same to the child with no name. Within the same millisecond, I realized that were it not for me hearing her and lifting her from the dark pit she had been hidden in, she would have died there and so in a curious sense I had given her life.

It would have been all too easy to just leave in an attempt to save my own skin, but to abandon the child no longer was an option; I had to find her and complete my mission. I scanned the desert where we had crossed earlier but she was nowhere in sight. I presumed she must be among the trees somewhere, unless she had wandered off within minutes of me laying her down. I did not want to shout for her, not only would she not understand, but the shouts might attract unwanted attention. As I hurried through the trees I saw a flash of colour. It was the girl in the dress I had put on her. I hurried to her side and found her bent over something. She picked up a walnut and pointed to her mouth. I cracked it open with my two hands and she devoured the contents. Together we began to look around and we found a number of nuts between the exposed tree roots. I realized we were in a nut orchard. By using two flat stones to break the shells we had a rudimentary meal. Being bone dry they were hard to swallow past our parched throats.

We were busy devouring the walnut meat when I heard the crack of a twig underfoot. It sounded close by. Much too close for me to grab the girl and run and hide so I indicated to her to be quiet. We sat still on the ground hoping we would not be spotted. I fully expected a bullet to end the nightmare of the last few hours. At best I might be taken prisoner. I had heard stories of prisoners being dragged to death behind a speeding car and I wondered what might become of the little girl?

A man stepped into the group of trees under which we had been gathering nuts. He held no rifle nor wore a gun-belt. He wore clothing similar to what I had on, except for his headgear. In his hand he held a pruning saw. The man looked at my burned face which now had developed water blisters. He spoke words in a soft non threatening voice. I pointed to my mouth and ears to suggest I did not understand him. Then he spoke to the child who answered him. She pointed at me; I thought I heard her say the words papa. I knew this would be highly unlikely; perhaps it was an Arabic word that sounded similar. The child spoke again and the man nodded. He indicated a drinking motion to me, to which I gratefully nodded. He motioned me that we should follow him.

I moved to pick up the child but he beat me to it, picked her up in his arms and began walking through the trees. We soon arrived at a small flat roofed cottage. The man called out to the house and a woman in a long dress wearing a scarf kind of thing over her head emerged carrying a pitcher of water and a glass. She poured the glass full; the child gulped it down passing it back for more. Refilling the glass for the child she then handed the pitcher to me. I raised it carefully to my lips and drank as I have never drank before. I saved enough to fill the child's glass a third time then nodded my gratitude.

There was no way these kind people could not notice how badly the child and I smelled. The woman put her fingers to her nose. In impromptu sign language indicated she would bathe the child. I of course nodded my agreement. The man went to a well at the side of the cottage, drew up a pail of water handing it to me along with a crusty piece of hard soap. I cannot describe the feeling of relief the splashing water upon my raw face gave me. I washed my body as best I could with the one pail of water. After I had finished my ablutions, the man beckoned me to enter the house where the lady handed me a plate containing cooked rice and chopped vegetables.

My mind immediately cast back to the family farm. This unknown woman had done exactly as my mother would have done had two bedraggled and dirty strangers knocked upon her door. The actions of this couple reinforced my belief that there were good people everywhere in the world despite the human tendency to paint everyone with the same brush. The little girl was wrapped in a towel, now nice and clean with her hair washed, while the lady of the house laundered her clothing in a pail using an old fashioned scrub board.

I thought I would try to find out the child's name so I pointed to my chest and said,

"Rod." Then I pointed at the lady, silently urging her to tell me her name. She looked at me blankly so I repeated it, then she understood,

"Hayfa" she replied smiling. Then I pointed at the child and the lady looked at me utterly confused, I assumed from her reaction that she must have thought I was her father or grandfather. With my face in such a mess it would have been hard for her to tell my age. After staring at me for a while she spoke to the child, I figured it would be to ask her name. The child responded with something that sounded like "Hanna." Then Hayfa looked at me and said as she pointed at the child, "Shanna." Now I knew the name of my young charge. I nodded my thanks to Hayfa and glanced out of the open door. The sun, now well past noon, had begun to lose its fire. Now that Shanna and I had been refreshed I felt we should continue our journey to the base.

Suddenly I realized that the man who had brought us here was no longer around, it seems he had just quietly disappeared. For me that was a red flag. Perhaps he had recognized that I was American because of my army issue boots and my inability to communicate with him. It was also possible that he had brought us here to recuperate while he went off to report he had found us, perhaps to receive a reward for my capture. I sincerely hoped it was not so and that my earlier thought that I had run into kind and gentle people was the correct one. Either way I felt a great urgency to leave. It occurred to me that the child might be safe with the kindly woman but there was no way I could be sure. She would come with me despite the difficulties. I indicated to Hayfa that I would be leaving immediately. She nodded at the child as if to say, her too. I nodded in return, so the woman put the still wet dress and head cover on Shanna. I picked her up in my arms, gave Hayfa a thank-you bow and strode out of the cottage.

Looking up at the sun I deduced by its location in the sky the approximate time of day and the southerly direction I needed to take. Shanna's weight once again pulled down on my shoulders but I was rid of the appalling thirst of earlier in the day. I moved as quickly as my aching muscles would allow, trying to put distance between us and the cottage just in case my suspicions were fact. I tried from time to time to have Shanna walk along with me but she was painfully slow, so I would pick her up again and carry her piggyback while trying to make sure her little hands did not touch my raw face. We struggled on as the sun slowly lost its fire and sank lower into the horizon. The mere fact that I was no longer getting my face fried made our journey a little more tolerable. Soon darkness enveloped us and I knew we were nearing the base for I could make out its outline about two miles away.

My right foot stepped into nothingness and I lurched forward, hurling Shanna off my back. My foot landed in the bottom of a hole of some kind twisting my ankle and knee as my body weight forced the joints and ligaments into an unnatural position. I fell forward onto Shanna, she began to cry loudly. I don't really think she had been hurt, the shock and surprise had no doubt frightened her. I held her close to my chest and attempted to comfort her. The child was tired and did not wish to be consoled, but I persevered speaking softly into her ear. When her sobbing ceased I tried to stand up in order to continue. It felt as though I had broken both leg and ankle. The pain was excruciating but I still had two miles to go. Once again I hoisted Shanna onto my back and limped on dragging my right leg. It must have taken me an hour to get within shouting distance of the base perimeter.

I heard the whine of a bullet whizzing past my head. My God my own people are shooting at me. Then I heard the report of the rifle then another bullet whizzed by. I knew our guys had night vision equipment and there was no doubt that they could see me. Then the thought hit me like a flash, I probably looked like a suicide bomber dressed in this outfit and carrying a load on my back. A searchlight's beam momentarily blinded me. Slowly I took Shanna from my shoulders placing her on the ground beside me. Fully aware that guns were trained upon me. One wrong move and I would be a dead man at the hands of my own countrymen. I put my hands in the air and held them there for a minute then I slipped the robe garment over my head and dropped it to the ground. I stood in my shorts and boots to show I carried no explosive or weapons.

A loudspeaker boomed out. "Identify yourself!" I yelled at the top of my lungs, "Private Rod Wyman U. S. Army."

THE HANDYMAN

THE LAST thing my wife said before going to work was,

"Harold you have the day off, so I want you to fix that dripping faucet in the kitchen. I have been asking you for months and you always have an excuse for why you could not do it."

To say the least I was angry at her ultimatum. It's not often I get a day off work. Some of the guys had arranged to go to the bar and watch sports on the big screen there. I figured that having the day to myself, I would join them and have a few beers and unwind from the pressures of the job. I have come to know Wendy pretty well after being married to her for the best part of twenty years and I knew if the faucet weren't fixed when she got home the proverbial crap would hit the fan, with ninety percent landing on me.

"I'll get to it as soon as I have finished my coffee." I yelled as she went out the door. I drank my coffee and finished reading the morning paper. I reached for the television remote control box. Suddenly, I realized if I got onto the job right away I could still meet the guys at the bar. So I went out to my tool shed to look for a wrench and a screwdriver. It was a real mess in there. I have a bad habit of putting things down anywhere. The way I saw it, if I had to be neat and accurate at work, I'll be damned if I had to do it at home. Any way I finally found a screwdriver and a large crescent wrench. It was much too big really, but I had no idea where to begin looking for the others.

I went back to the kitchen and looked inside the cabinet under the sink. It was full of junk; at least that's what I call it. I knew I would have to empty the cabinet to get at the shut off valve. I began to remove the bottles of cleaning fluids and dishwashing soap standing them on the floor. Then I lay down on my belly to turn off the shutoff valve. It hadn't been moved in years and I couldn't turn it. It was good that I had brought the oversize wrench with me so I put it on the valve and began to slowly turn it. After about a half turn the whole thing broke off and water shot up to the underside of the sink. It immediately began to fall back into my face.

I thrashed around trying to get away from the torrent of water attempting to drown me. As I thrashed, my feet knocked over the bottles on the floor, and liquid and powdered soap mixed with the water now running all over the linoleum. I knew I had to get the water stopped and quickly. I had to get to the main shutoff in the basement. I ran down the steps and began searching for it. I had never needed it before so I had no idea where it was located. I checked everywhere I thought it might be without finding it. I noticed that a stream of water had begun leaping from step to step into the basement. Then it occurred to me that I may have sealed the shutoff valve behind the big cupboards I had built to store paint cans and garden chemicals.

I rushed back upstairs to get the screwdriver and as I ran into the kitchen I slipped on the soap and water covered floor. I hurt my hip a bit as I went down quite hard. I got back on my feet with suds dripping off my clothing. I raced for the basement door and noticed the living room carpet had changed colour with the absorption of sudsy water. Down stairs I opened the cupboard door to get at the screws finding the shelves were full of cans and bottles. Damn! I had to put all of the stuff on the floor to get at the screws. As quickly as I could I scooped everything off the shelves and threw it to the floor. I found the screw heads.

"I don't believe this." I yelled aloud. My screwdriver was slotted, but the screws were the Robertson square headed kind. I rushed upstairs and went out to my tool shed to find the Robertson driver. As I said before, neatness is not my forte. I finally found it five minutes later in the sawdust box of my table saw. When I got back to the basement the floor had a half-inch of water covering it. Feverishly I tried to undo the screws. Unfortunately I had filled the heads with paint when I painted the inside of the cupboard. There was no way I could get the screws out so I thought the best thing to do would be to pull the cupboard off the wall. I tried lifting pushing and pulling, but it would not budge.

I decided that under the circumstances I would get the axe out of the tool shed and smash the thing off the wall. Desperate things call for desperate measures I thought. I ran back out to the shed and began to search for the axe. I couldn't find it anywhere. I just about tore the shed apart in my urgent search. But the axe was not there. Then I remembered that it might be out at the woodpile, even though I had not chopped any firewood for some time. Running to the woodpile I found the axe there all right, jammed tightly into a knotted log. I remembered now when it got stuck, I left it to deal with later. I realized that I would have to get my sledgehammer to break the axe free of the log. Then I thought, why bother with the axe just use the hammer on the cupboards. I ran back to the shed and started looking for it suddenly realizing that I hadn't seen it when I was looking for the axe. Where the Hell did I leave it?

There came a distant memory of seeing it in my car trunk with all the other stuff it was jammed-full of. I ran round to the carport realizing my keys were still in the house. I ran back inside splashing water from the soaking carpet onto the furniture. The keys were not on the hall table. Remembering I had left them in my other pants pocket I ran to the bedroom, the carpet in there was wet also. My pants and shirt were soaked as I found out when I retrieved my car keys. I ran back out to the car and opened the trunk. The sledgehammer was there underneath the tire chains and the old battery I hadn't disposed of yet.

Clutching the hammer, I ran back to the basement and attacked the cupboard. It took a minute or two but I managed to break it to pieces.

"I don't believe this!" I yelled when I found that the shutoff valve was not behind it. The water level had now risen to two inches. Then I figured the shutoff might be near the front wall of the basement since the water main was out front on the street. The base of the front wall was hidden behind a pile of old suitcases, cartons and a bunch of stuff I couldn't identify and was supposed to have disposed of during last year's big garbage collection day. I began hurling them out of the way. Some of the stuff floated away across the basement. Finally I found the shutoff valve sticking up out of the concrete floor and was able to turn the water off.

By now I was soaking wet and angry. If Wendy had not been so unreasonable none of this would have happened, there would have been no mess to clean up and I could have been sipping a beer with the guys. I went back upstairs to see what supplies I would need to buy at the plumbing shop. I made a list, then changed into dry clothes and went out to the car. The slow leak in the right front tire that I had been meaning to get fixed had finally gone completely flat. I opened the trunk to get the spare when I remembered that I hadn't had it fixed since changing it out on the highway last August. I went back into the house to phone the auto club to send someone out to fix it for me.

"I'm sorry sir your subscription expired last November. We did contact you, but as of this date we have not received your renewal documents."

If I could have reached down the phone I would have choked the woman. It seems that at the times you need them the most you can't depend on anybody. I figured I might as well take a taxi down to the hardware store and back again. I would deal with the car later when the plumbing was fixed. It was a ten-minute wait for the taxi. Meanwhile the main floor carpets were releasing the water they were holding and it found its way down the basement steps.

"Triple H Hardware!" I yelled at the cabby. A glance at his face told me he didn't appreciate my tone. "The one on main Street, and then I want you to wait for me and bring me back here."

He didn't answer. I guess I spoke too sharply, but lets face it I had good reason and there was no need for his surly attitude. The plumbing clerk collected the things on my list.

"Cash or credit card sir?" He asked. I felt in my pocket and groaned. I had left my wallet in the pants I changed out of.

"The store policy Sir is cash or credit card or no merchandise."

"I will come back with the money later I have an emergency situation on my hands."

"Bring the money first Sir; we are not a charitable organization." I could have killed him, the pompous little swine. If he knew that I was a respected citizen working in a credit granting company and had a seat on the town council, he wouldn't dare speak to me that way. I stomped back out to the taxi.

"You are not going to believe this." I hollered at the cabby. "I forgot to bring my wallet so we have to go back to my house and do this all over again." He did not respond but gave me a piteous look. We returned to the house where I went to fetch my wallet. I glanced down the basement as I passed the open door. I see the water level has risen now to three inches. What I do not know is that the water level has put out the pilot lights on the furnace, and gas is bubbling up through the sudsy water into the basement air. I growl at the clerk in the plumbing supply shop. I let him know in no uncertain terms that I am displeased at him and his attitude.

I pay for the goods with my credit card because my money is soaking wet, returning to the taxi. Clutching a new shutoff valve and connecting pipe; we leave for my house. We had just arrived. As I was paying the cabby there was a terrible explosion. I saw my house lift four feet off its foundations and fall sideways against my neighbour's place. It was then that the fire started. I ran to the house of another neighbour, Mrs. Wilson to call the fire department. I knew she didn't work and was more than likely sitting at home. There was a note on her door saying back in ten minutes. By now the flames had engulfed the house, shed and car-port, within minutes the car became an Olympic torch also. Someone else must have called the fire department because the fire truck arrived within a short time. Of course by then the neighbour's house was fully ablaze too. Since my house was a total loss, the firemen concentrated their efforts on dousing the flames next door. By the time all the fuss had died down my place was a steaming pile of wet ashes in the space where the basement had been. My car sat on four rims and the body was a bright red rust colour where the paint had burned off, and a smouldering pile of useless tools sat where my shed had been.

It was then that Wendy drove up. She stared in utter disbelief at the empty space where our house had been and at the firemen battling the blaze in the house next door. She got out of her car and with tears in her eyes; she came and stood next to me. Tearfully she asked.

"What happened to our home Harold?"

"I tried to fix the dripping faucet." I replied.

ROOM FOR RENT S.W.F.

"I BURIED MARIANA Johnston under this group of red roses. I always liked the red ones; in fact I think they are my favourites. They seem to be doing very well this year. I don't know if you already are aware or not, but roses flowering so prolifically need to be well fed. I buried Mariana in a fairly shallow trench so that the roots of the roses could reach down to get nourishment. These large velvet like blooms are proof of my theory. Mind you I did give them some commercial bone meal when I first planted them but their other nutrients and trace elements come from Mariana."

"Are there others like Mariana in your garden, Mrs. Whiteacre?"

"Oh yes. These are my hybrid tea roses in this bed. Let's see, I think it was Nancy Wharton I put under them. Yes it was. I remember now, she created an awful fuss when I told her where I intended to put her. The silly girl seemed quite unwilling to fulfill her destiny. But despite it all she is doing a good job. See the size of the blooms; they are all large with such bright colours, although, I do prefer the reds."

"There are others buried here in your garden then, Mrs. Whiteacre?"

"Oh yes. A good garden requires nutrients in order for plants to reach their full potential. You see this large Wisteria loaded with blossoms, my husband Frank Whiteacre is responsible for it."

"Do you mean he planted it or….?"

"Oh no, I planted it. But it didn't do very well until I put Frank under its roots. Now look at it, it is healthy and it blooms for months. Sometimes people ask me for cuttings but I discourage them, let's face it I wouldn't want Frank's nutrients popping up all over town. Are you a gardener yourself constable?"

"No. I'm afraid not Mrs. Whiteacre. But having said that, I do enjoy seeing the results of the efforts of other gardeners. Tell me, how many bodies are buried in your garden?"

"Now let me see. Frank was the first, and then Mariana Johnston and then there was Hilda Martens. She was a right little madam I can tell you, I put her under the white climbing rose. Hilda was no good in life, and you can tell by the condition of the plant she isn't much better in death. After her was Penny Marshal. She was a very untidy girl and I like things in my house to be just so. I put Penny under the apricot tree. I get some really nice apricots every year now; they are large and very sweet. Then, Wendy Groatman came to live here; she is under the raspberry canes. Let me see, there was Violet Thompson, then it was Joan Carter that's all I think. Oh, I forgot there was Nancy Wharton too; I think I already told you about her, the hybrid tea rose bed?"

"So you have buried at least six bodies in your garden Mrs. Whiteacre?"

"Yes. I think it is six, maybe seven. If I remember any more I will tell you."

"It is Joan Carter that I came to inquire about. Her family back in Detroit gave your home as her last known address. But I am glad you told me about the others, Mrs. Whiteacre. I am sure it will close a lot of unsolved cases. Can you tell me how the situation began and why did you bury these bodies in your garden?"

"I have explained to you already Constable, that I put them in the ground as plant food and the results are self evident just look at these blooms I love flowers Constable, don't you?"

"Yes I love flowers too. But that is not really the point Mrs. Whiteacre, apart from your husband, how come these women came to be in your house and eventually in your garden?"

"Oh that is easy to explain Constable. What did you say your name was?

"It's Wainright, Mrs. Whiteacre. Constable Wainright, Cardston City Police."

"I had a sign in the front window. In fact it's there now. It says. 'Room for rent S.W.F.'

"What does that mean Mrs. Whiteacre, what do the letters stand for?"

"It stands for single/ working/ female you silly man. I thought everyone knew that."

"I do, Mrs. Whiteacre. I ask to see if you had a meaning other than the usual. Let's face it. You are a most unusual person."

"Oh, you are referring to my gardening. Thank you, constable, you are very kind. Yes, I do pride myself on my achievements. Come and look at my vegetable patch? I am very proud of my root vegetables, that's where Violet and Joan are. I have much too many for my own use, I can give you some carrots and a turnip when you leave."

"Thank you, Mrs Whiteacre, that will not be necessary as my wife buys all the vegetables we need."

"Yes. But my vegetables are fed with all natural nutrients making them much better for you than the store bought ones."

"I am sure they are, Mrs. Whiteacre, but I will decline thank you. I am on duty and my superiors might frown upon me bringing vegetables into the station. Now can we begin at the beginning with the death of your husband, the one under the wisteria? How did your husband die, and was the death reported to the authorities?"

"Frank was a miserable man Constable. We could never see eye to eye. We married later in life, and after the first few weeks our marriage soured. He would come home from work in a morose mood. He always claimed he was too tired to help with the heavy work in the garden. Of course I nagged him until he did and refused to make his dinner until the work I wanted done was finished. Even in the winter when the garden was at rest he had the same attitude. In my opinion this was time to do repairs and alterations to the house. I had to nag him every night and weekend to get the jobs done. It went on for years, right until he retired. Then the real trouble started. He said he had things of his own that he wanted to do.

Well! I would have none of it! So one day when he was out in the potting shed I crept up behind him slipping the kitchen carving knife between his ribs from behind. The real heavy work in the garden was complete so I didn't really need him any more. He had no job, so that no one would wonder where he was and come looking for him. I dug a trench under the wisteria then I cut him into smaller pieces putting him in it. The next spring the wisteria blossomed like never before, so I knew I was on to something."

"So you never reported his death, Mrs. Whiteacre?"

"Oh, no, there was no need. I had dealt with the matter by myself."

"Did you not know it was an offence to not only kill your husband, but to conceal it from the authorities?"

"I did what I thought was right constable. Just look at the wisteria blossoms. Have you ever seen better? You have to admit that you wouldn't get blooms like that with your commercial 2-8-12 fertilizers."

"Be that as it may, Mrs. Whiteacre. It is hardly the point. It is against the law to use people as fertilizer, surely you see that? Now how about the Mariana Johnston woman? How does she fit in to the scheme of things? How did you first meet her?"

"Mariana! I didn't like her right from the start. She came to my door saying she had seen the sign 'Room for rent.' I still had Frank's pension coming in because I never told the government he was no longer with us. However with the cost of things I thought I would make a little extra by renting out his old bedroom. Well, since she was the first to call after I put the sign in the window, I let her have the room. She turned out to be a sloppy and careless tenant. It didn't take long before I knew I couldn't live with her like this. Not only that, she refused to do any of the garden work. The little hussy said renters do not have to do manual labour as well as pay rent. Well! No-one talks to me that way Constable. So I coaxed her into the potting shed to do a little pruning on her. Just look at those red roses again constable. Tell me I didn't do the right thing."

"How did you cover up her death, Mrs. Whiteacre?"

"That was easy. I telephoned her employer saying she had asked me to tell them she had a family emergency in New York. She would contact them when she got back; I got rid of her personal things in the weekly trash pickup. See these petals they are like soft velvet. Thank you Marianne."

"How about the others, Mrs Whiteacre? Did you kill them all in the same way?"

"Good heavens no. People are like plants constable. Each one has different requirements. Penny Marshal, I hit with a hammer. Frankly it was rather messy; but thank goodness the garden hose reached right inside the potting shed. The crocuses that are outside where the blood and water ran out were incredibly large this year especially the purple ones. The yellow ones were much better too but not as good as the purple. I have some rhubarb in the same bed but it is too early to say if it is stronger this year."

"And the others, Mrs. Whiteacre?"

"Frankly, I saw no difference in the white crocuses."

"I meant the other victims, Mrs. Whiteacre?"

"I choked Wendy Groatman. She deserved to die slowly. I found out quite by accident that she was stealing my cocoa. Can you believe the nerve of some people constable? Every night for weeks she took a spoonful for herself without so much as a simple please. I went to her room and choked her with my garden twine, the strong green kind. She was only a small girl so I buried her in one piece. The others I stabbed and dismembered as they are much easier to deal with that way."

"Has it never occurred to you, Mrs. Whiteacre, that what you have been doing is reprehensible? You have admitted to the death of a number of human beings. These were victims by your hand for the most unworthy of crimes. To use human bodies as fertilizer stretches the imagination, Mrs. Whiteacre. I have been a Police Constable for a goodly number of years; frankly I have never run into a case like this."

"Constable Wainright. Are you not able to see the benefit of my actions to my garden? Can you not see the quality of the blooms here? The people who lie buried here have made a sacrifice to nature. Humans have always made sacrifices to nature. All the way back through history, many civilizations have sacrificed the human body for the common good. Did not the Inca's spill the blood of children to appease the Gods of nature? It has gone on for centuries. I have done no different than they did.

Perhaps you see me as a person who has done wrong. Perhaps you see me as evil. However I would take umbrage with your findings. Were you a gardener such as I, you would see clearly that I am as much a part of nature as these glorious red rose petals. If you doubt me for even a moment come to my potting shed, I will prove it to you."

"I suppose you realize you will have to come downtown, Mrs. Whiteacre, and the entire property will have to be dug up for evidence."

It was quite obvious to me that the lady was completely unbalanced but for the moment I thought I would try to humour her.

"O.K. Show me." I said. I followed the demure Mrs. Whiteacre into the shed. Before I knew what was happening I found myself fighting a tigress. I felt a knife slip between two ribs and I went down. I could scarcely believe the woman had bested me. The knife ripped across my throat and soon all went black.

"There you go my beauty. Mummy has brought you something to make you big strong and beautiful. Mrs Whiteacre filled in the trench under the lilac tree containing Constable Wainright.

"You will have lovely blossoms next spring," she said, as she went into the house to make a cup of hot tea with milk and sugar.

SNOWBOUND.

AT DAWN I looked out of the cabin's small window in disbelief. During the time we had been in bed oblivious to the world outside, aware only of the sound of ourselves in a frenzy of lovemaking, the night wind had driven snow right up to the window ledge. My car was buried under the lord only knows how many feet of snow The road leading up to the cabin between the tall pines, lay under snowdrifts I estimated to be five or six feet deep.

Yesterday the car radio had said nothing about a possible snowstorm when we drove up here. Had it done so I would have changed my plans to bring Julia to this remote cabin instead taking her to a motel down in the valley?

I turned to look at her, lying under the tan coloured down duvet with her dark hair spread around the white pillow in elegant profusion. Her eyes were closed, and her lips now bereft of lip-gloss had a hint of a deeply satisfied smile. Julia looked particularly beautiful. I had never seen her lying in bed before and the knowledge that she lay warm and naked under the duvet needing only my presence and caresses to rekindle the fire we had lit and quenched in our bodies last night.

Glancing out through the window again, I knew this idyllic scene would quickly change to one of fear and disillusionment for both of us. My immediate assessment of the situation was that we were trapped at the 6000 foot level on Mount Bastion. No one was aware that we were here. We had both been most careful to ensure that. If I could not get Julie back home before her husband Manfred returned from his hunting trip, the gig would be up.

I worked with Manfred, our two families socialized at barbeques and weekend parties around my in-ground pool. Julie had acknowledged my admiring glances at poolside and often displayed her bikini-clad form for my benefit. I don't think Manfred, or my wife Glenda, ever noticed the eye contact Julie and I shared. Over time changing to body contacts. Just small things, like a lingering hand, longer than usual handshakes, or welcoming hugs. For the longest time neither Julie or I ever spoke of these little moments of intimacy, but our eyes indicated to each other that we liked them both desiring the moments to be longer and even more intimate.

I turned again to look at the blowing snow out side the cabin window. Now the flakes were beginning to pile up against the windowpane, and melt with the heat coming from the large pot bellied stove in the centre of the cabin floor. Just for a moment it reminded me of how Julie and I had melted into each other's arms for most of the night, completely oblivious to everything but the music of our writhing bodies.

I was now faced with a huge dilemma. Should I get back into bed and caress Julie into wakefulness losing myself in her arms or perhaps to re-live the splendour that had quickened our pulses for the last number of hours? Or should I dress and try to dig out the car, and the trail between the trees? The cold emanating off the glass begins to chill me, so I go to the stove and place four of the well-dried logs on the embers. Logs that that Manfred and I had cut and split on our October campout and stored in the log box. Thinking about it, a shudder of guilt ran through my naked body. Manfred and I go back a long way. We have been friends and done things together for years. Now his wife lies warm, sweet and unclothed in my bed. I have cuckolded him. Even as I think these thoughts, I want to lie with her again.

The conflict between working for hours in the cold, shoveling the snow away from the car, or joining Julie under the duvet, warm and sweet smelling, she returning my advances with ones of her own, accepting me, loving me, reducing me from a living thinking human being, into a part of herself, was in the end no conflict at all.

I slip under the duvet. I feel her skin, warm and soft like velvet against my own cold flesh. She stirs and wraps herself around my body, absorbing the coolness from mine. Our body temperatures become even. Then together they rise. Now no longer warm but hot. The heat is unstoppable. With breathless utterances we settle once again into deep exhausted sleep.

I awaken to Julie's strident voice.

"Jack! It's been snowing. I can't even see out of the window. We have to get back to town." I sit up in the bed and look at her. She has not dressed. Her breasts and her wide hips beckon me; she is a beautiful dream standing near the stove, in the muted day light from the snow-covered glass. I open my outstretched arms I want her to come to me.

"We have to get back to town Jack, or there will be Hell to pay for the both of us. Get up and get dressed!" Of course I knew Julie was right. It had been an absolutely wonderful night, but it was over. We had to get back to reality. I climbed out of bed and reached for my clothes. Like Julie's, they were scattered around the cabin floor after last night's frenzy to disrobe.

"I'll put some coffee on the stove while you go and dig out the car to get it ready to leave." She said, obviously concerned about the unknown consequences of our illicit night together. I dressed in my warm winter clothes then opened the cabin door. A wall of snow crystals fell into the cabin. It was then that I felt the wind pushing the snow to its will. The wind had filled the porch almost to the roof. It would be difficult to even get outside, let alone find the woodshed at the porch end where the snow shovel would be. I struggled up the pile of snow at the door, bringing large amounts of it to collapse inside the cabin.

"My God how much snow is out there, Jack?"

"I don't really know, Julie. The wind has made snowdrifts; it might just be deep right here on the porch." I knew I had spoken an untruth, but I didn't want to worry Julie any more than necessary. I crawled on top of the snow under the porch canopy until I reached the woodshed. Fortunately the door opened inwards so after finding the hasp, I slipped down inside. There was an axe, a broom, the splitting maul and wedges, but no shovel! I tried to think of where it might be. I began to panic a little. I would be in a bad state without one. Even if I couldn't dig the car and lane out, I would have to clear the porch to keep the stove supplied with wood to keep us warm. I made my way around the cabin to see if the shovel was hanging on the wall out back. It wasn't!

I made my way back to the cabin door. It was still open because Julie hadn't been able to close it on account of all the snow that had fallen inwards. Now the cabin had lost most of its warmth.

"There is no Damn shovel out there Julie!" I said angrily.

"Don't you carry one in your car trunk in the winter?" She said accusingly.

"No! Only if I know there is going to be a snowfall and I didn't know about this one."

"You should have come prepared Jack. You should know anything could happen here in the high country."

"Don't jump on my case Julie. Being nasty won't help us."

"Nasty! I'm not being nasty! If I were you would sure know it. I don't care how you do it, but get this snow out of the way and get the car started. I have to get back before Manfred gets home or the crap will hit the fan. I'll tell you this for nothing, Jack most of it will hit you in the face." Julie was beginning to really get under my skin.

"Listen, you stupid bitch! I can't get to the car without a shovel, let alone dig it out and drive down the Goddamn mountain, Manfred or no Manfred."

"So. Now you have got round to the insults have you Jack? Just because you are too stupid and ignorant to have brought a shovel with you, you are passing the buck to me!"

"Who do you think you are, calling me stupid and ignorant? Who was it came up this Damn mountain to play house while your husband is away?" My words must have really angered her. She reached for the cast iron skillet hitting me on the arm with it.

I lost my temper good and proper. I took the skillet from her hands bashing her on the head with it. I must have hit her much harder than I intended. She fell to the cabin floor and lay still, bleeding profusely from her head.

"I'm sorry Julie." I said. But she did not answer. I lifted her onto the bed, but I think she was already dead. I knew I had to get down the mountain somehow to face the music.

It took me four days to struggle down Mount Bastion crawling most of the way over deep snowdrifts. When I made it down to traveled roads someone picked me up and took me to the hospital then reported the matter to the police. I have lost both my feet to frostbite as well as all the fingers on my left hand, and two on my right. My murder trial begins next Monday. The prosecution claims I took Julie up there on Mount Bastion, for the sole purpose of committing murder. I have a feeling; soon I will pay an even higher price for my night of passion.

TSUNAMI.

WITHOUT WARNING, the stylus shot off the side of the seismology drum and jammed. Five seconds later, Al Madson's chair shot from beneath him. The room shook violently. He lay on the floor unable to stand. Furniture traveled around the office at will, cabinets emptied themselves of their contents, sliding and bumping into him and his free-floating desk. At the same time an awesome rumbling sound rose from deep within the earth drowning out all other sound. He knew that this was a massive earthquake. Likely the big one that the experts had been talking about for years; the one so long predicted; the one that they said could happen. Massive earthquakes happened to other people, in places like Japan the Middle East or South America, but not here in British Columbia.

The evening had started quietly in the Vancouver Island Seismology office, the only sound being the soft hum of the computer's electric motor and the almost imperceptible scratching sound of the seismograph stylus moving gently over a graph-covered drum.

Al Madson valued solitude. He tended to choose the night shift for the quiet it afforded him, so working alone; he dressed in rumpled tweed suits and wore old scuffed shoes. The first minor quake on this particular shift occurred offshore north of Vancouver Island.

Small quakes were a common occurrence at sea; the number two registered on the Richter scale meant that only rarely were they felt on land. He recorded the event in his log. *At two forty one. Oct 2nd 2008 a deep disturbance sixty miles north of Port Hardy.* He determined that the second quake's epicenter to be northeast of Campbell River. He entered the disturbance into his log at *two fifty nine on Oct 2nd 2008.*

Once again the stylus swung from side to side over the graph indicating another two point five. He determined the epicentre to be very close, just east of Swartz Bay, north of Victoria, British Columbia's Capital city.

He recorded the submarine quake, but felt there would be minimal or no damage. Through his training and experience, Alf knew it would be highly unlikely that a Tsunami would occur; it required a quake of over seven on the Richter scale to generate one. Within minutes the graph showed another two point five, with an epicenter deep below the entrance to Puget Sound across the international boundary in the State of Washington.

Al traced the series of disturbances and noted that all had occurred deep below the fault line that ran down the eastern coast of Vancouver Island, into Puget Sound and beyond into Seattle and Tacoma. This was highly unusual.

Checking the seismograph he saw that several minor aftershocks had occurred registering two point eight. He determined the epicenter about seventy miles above the northern tip of Vancouver Island in open water.

There were now five recorded disturbances on the coastal fault line.

By five a.m. he had recorded ten deep submarine quakes along the fault line. It was the highest number of disturbances he had witnessed on one shift since coming to work at the Seismic Center.

The clock read five twelve am when the big one began.

The seismology station was built on bedrock in the form of a cube of reinforced concrete. The contents were hurled and shaken within it, but the structure remained intact. Darkness enveloped the windowless station as the violent shaking continued.

Bruised and scraped, Al tried to prevent further injury to his person as the wild motions continued. They stopped just as suddenly as they had begun. In the pitch black, Al searched for the door. Emergency lighting equipment lay smashed on the floor. Al searched for the door, finding it blocked by a filing cabinet. Using his feet he slid it away and stepped outside.

In the pre-dawn light over the Victoria landscape not a single electric light could be seen. Soon lights from fires began to flicker in the darkness quickly becoming a multitude of infernos. Al assumed they were fed by ruptured gas lines. Light from the fires revealed downed trees, power poles, with useless wires hanging dangerously. His car lay crushed under a huge fallen tree.

From his vantage point, he could not know that in downtown Victoria, all of the old brick and stone structures including The Parliament building had disintegrated to rubble. The Empress Hotel reduced to smoking debris. Survivors staggered aimlessly among the wreckage searching in vain for help.

In Nanaimo, the downtown core had vanished into a gigantic sinkhole created by the collapse of a maze of abandoned coal mining shafts and tunnels. Broken water mains filled the crater drowning those surviving death by crushing.

The City of Vancouver suffered the big quake so long predicted. Brick buildings were the first to fall. Gastown and the downtown East Side became rubble. West End high-rise apartments waved like fields of wheat. Some fell, spilling glass, furniture and humans into the streets and alleys. Building after building collapsed, killing residents in them and on the streets below. Skytrain tracks fell like dominoes. Industrial buildings collapsed onto their contents and burned after falling onto their own furnaces.

Power and water had gone, the refineries on the banks of Burrard Inlet burned in a fireball that illuminated the blacked out city. Burnaby Mountain slid en masse into Burrard inlet with Simon Fraser University still sitting atop. The massive water displacement caused a wave that inundated Port Moody, dousing the fires. The returning mass of water washed the damaged buildings and their occupants back into the landlocked sea that had been the inlet.

Houses in West and North Vancouver slipped and rolled downhill self-destructing. In Richmond and Delta, homes built on delta mud sank in fluidized ground. At White Rock, houses tumbled down the steep slopes to the beach, spreading fire among the wrecked homes as they fell. Survivors fled to the beach for safety. Roberts Bank Superport sank completely out of sight in the liquefied seabed.

At Vancouver International Airport, aircraft collapsed to the ground as landing gear gave way with the violent shaking. Tons of glass fell from windows in the terminal buildings killing workers preparing planes for the morning flights. A fuel truck driving along to fuel a jetliner, struck the lowered wing causing both tanker and aircraft to explode in a fireball engulfing the entire terminal too quickly for the early passengers to escape.

Ground transport halted. With the bridges all down there was no way to leave Sea Island. Richmond became isolated when the Massey Tunnel collapsed and flooded. The mud flats at Boundary Bay had liquefied; the railway trestle and much of Highway 99 sank into oblivion.

The massive earthquake felt all the way from Alaska to Southern California caused thousands of landslides and rockfalls. At Lytton in the Fraser Canyon, both sides of the canyon collapsed plunging into the river, creating a humungus dam of trees and rock debris. The village of Lytton disappeared. Bridges on the Coquihalla highway slipped from their supports and fell. Rock falls of gigantic proportions severed the Hope to Princeton highway.

Al Madsen knew there was nothing more he could do here at the station. The equipment was wrecked and there was no power. Since he could not drive his car, he would walk to try to get to his family.

The quickest way would be along the shoreline road. The first light of dawn brightened the horizon revealing the extent of the devastation. Confused people desperately searched for help. When Al reached the beachfront path his heart skipped a beat. There was no water visible, just empty seabed.

He remembered his training. The first sign of a Tsunami can be a drawdown in the seaward direction that can be as great as five hundred feet. He recalled his instructor saying that in the great Tsunami at Hilo in Hawaii, children had gone to play on the exposed reef; they all perished when the Tsunami roared in. Tsunami's resulted from seismic disturbances causing a rise or fall in the water column. This was the initial formation of the Tsunami wave. There had just been such a disturbance he could only guess that it had occurred along the entire length of the submarine fault. The result could be a Tsunami of gigantic proportions wreaking havoc on the entire coastline.

He realized that he alone could not warn the populations of low-lying coastal areas. Al broke into a run to reach his family in an effort to get them to higher ground. Knowing that Tsunami waves were really shock waves able to travel at speeds up to five hundred miles per hour he had very little time.

Deep in the Strait of Georgia, the fault line had ruptured along much of its length. Vancouver Island had lurched twenty feet closer to the mainland. The tectonic plate diving downwards as it moved east. Massive water displacement had occurred. The shockwave, traveling west, bounced off the island coastline and rebounded to follow the wave traveling east towards the mainland. In effect, two deadly Tsunami waves surged silently towards the heavily populated Lower Mainland.

Vancouver Island's eastern coastline suffered little damage, marinas and waterfront homes bearing the brunt of its force. A ferry at Swartz bay, preparing for its first departure of the day sat on the seabed when the drawdown occurred. The surge of the incoming Tsunami tipped it on its side hurling it high onto the shoreline rocks.

The shock wave began to climb the seabed as it rose to meet the Mainland. Fraser River silt, stirred to the consistency of thin porridge, began to move pushed by the Tsunami and becoming part of it. The water level began to rise dramatically up the seabed as it approached the land. When the shock wave hit the land the wall of water had reached sixty feet in height traveling like an express train with a second wave following a mile behind.

The Lower Mainland had all its services severed. Only minimum radio contact existed, all transmission towers having been felled by the quake. No Tsunami warnings had been transmitted. The wave roared towards Delta and White Rock. The heavily populated Tsawassen bluffs took the first impact; the waterfront homes were smashed in a millisecond. The water, still energized, climbed the bluff creating death and havoc.

Further south past Point Roberts, the wave bore down in the direction of White Rock. South and north of the bluffs, the wave roared over the shore crossing the flat farmlands every house and barn was leveled and carried away in the wall of debris filled water. At the mouth of the Fraser River, Ladner and Steveston disintegrated into shards of pulverized lumber. Fishboats were picked up and carried in the wave. Lulu Island and its inhabitants disappeared under the churning sea.

The airport on Sea Island was submerged. Disabled aircraft were driven like leaves smashing into the burning terminal while others were carried along with the crest breaking apart as the wave progressed. Logs from the booms moored in the river rose skywards and burst open. The wall, now a mixture of mud, water and logs hurtled upriver, the height rising with the narrowing terrain. In Queensborough the wave reached eighty feet in height.

In English Bay the wave, rising rapidly, roared in unhindered. Six freighters riding at anchor rose with it. The surge lifted them high above the shoreline and deposited three of them in the West End jammed between high-rise concrete apartment blocks. Another was driven into False Creek demolishing the remaining parts of the fallen Burrard Street Bridge ending up on the old Expo 86 site where it became lodged; bow first, in the Science Centre. The remaining two were carried on high into Burrard Inlet tearing a section out of the Lions Gate Bridge deck still swinging from the quake. The forward movement of the wave took the ships crashing into the Second Narrows bridges; the south tower of the Road Bridge keeled over onto the adjacent Rail Bridge isolating the North shore. The two mangled freighters, now that their progress had been halted, sank by the bridge piers.

The surge moved up the narrowing inlet until it hit the dam created by the collapse of Burnaby Mountain and Simon Fraser University. The dam absorbed the Tsunami's energy then the second wave struck, climbing over the dam creating a huge salt lake that covered Port Moody, low lying, Coquitlam and Port Coquitlam.

Down in White Rock, people escaping the inferno that was the hillside; now stood dazed and terrified on the beach. Screams of the doomed; announced the wall of water and mud bearing down on them from the sea. The narrowing of the terrain caused the crest to rise over forty feet. The humans on the beach were swept away like dust, into the Little Campbell River channel.

A mile to the south, the American town of Blaine disappeared beneath the first wave soon to be followed by the second. The wave energy spent itself close to the Langley outskirts, then the billions of tons of water began to return to the sea. Carrying with it trees, houses, cattle and battered humans in a reverse wave that stripped the valley of anything that floated or rolled.

In the Fraser River, at New Westminster, the wave contained by the two high banks, rose even higher. The old brick buildings in the lower town, reduced to rubble by the shaking were swept away. A ship tied at the Fraser Surrey docks wound up in the industrial park near the Port Mann Bridge. With its energy diminished the wave slowed; the second wave catching up with it. The mass of water and debris stopped then began its wild rush back to the river mouth. Scouring the banks and riverbed of anything that would move, it returned to the demolished Patullo Rail Bridge, which acted like a strainer and forming a dam of logs, railcars and floating ships containers.

To the north, the wave entered Howe Sound, climbing as the Sound narrowed. It aimed for Squamish, built just inches above sea level. In seconds the town was inundated as the Tsunami rolled up the Squamish River slowing only upon reaching Brackendale.

In Vancouver's West End the water began to recede, leaving a freighter with its bow lodged in a concrete apartment block, with its stern sitting on its props on Davie Street. At the unglazed windows, survivors peered out at the devastation that surrounded them. At street level, cars floated towards English Bay bumping and grinding against each other. Human bodies, smashed furniture trees and fences mingled and drifted seaward. Some concrete structures had broken at ground level and leaned grotesquely against others still standing.

In the flatlands of Delta, death reigned supreme. Richmond was a vast field of devastation. The hillside at White Rock burned. Down below, mud and debris were many feet deep everywhere. In Semiahmoo Bay, human bodies floated seaward with dead farm animals and shock killed fish.

Prince Rupert was spared major damage. The westbound shockwave traveled unhindered at high speed towards Japan across the Pacific.

Upon arriving at his house Al Madsen found it had collapsed.

"Diedre," he yelled, "Diedre are you here?" Hearing no reply he made his way over the demolished furnishings to the bedroom. Diedre was not to be found. A weak muffled cry came from under the debris atop the beds of the children. Bare handed he began to claw at the debris. With his hands torn and bleeding, Al found his youngest child Sarah unharmed but trapped. After he had calmed Sarah, he wrapped her in a blanket, laid her on the lawn, then went to search for Diedre. In what had been the kitchen he found her lying face down under the overturned refrigerator. Diedre had bled to death!

In communities all along the coast survivors struggled to make sense of everything that had happened in an instant to the world around them. Each within his own small area could recognize the scope of the disaster. Death and destruction lay before them in profusion that until now seemed unimaginable.

Those on higher ground dealt only with the aftermath of the violent shaking; those at lower levels, within the Tsunami's reach, reaped a double dose of carnage, those at even lower levels perished. Untold tens of thousands had been wiped from the face of the earth. Some lay buried forever in mud; others were strewn smashed and broken by the wreckage hurled at them. Then the merciless wave had swept them to oblivion back into the sea. Others, their lifeless bodies snagged in trees or debris, hung drying in the air like macabre laundry.

There was no electrical power, no clean water ran from faucets, no telephones worked, even cell phones were useless, the transmitting towers were now crumpled piles of twisted steel on the hilltops. All streets and roads were impassable. Vehicles had been rendered useless except as shelter of the most rudimentary kind. Dense smoke from burning buildings and the massive fuel fires, burning unchecked, at the Burrard Inlet refineries fouled the air. At the international airport, fuel depots had spilled and ignited along with aircraft and the terminal building. In addition, smoke along with the low cloud caused near darkness over the entire area.

The time now was seven a.m. Again a violent aftershock traveled the length of the fault registering at five on the Richter scale in San Francisco. Buildings that were teetering before, now fell spilling the occupants to their deaths on the streets below. The Granville Street Bridge, previously weakened, succumbed to gravity and dropped into False Creek.

Eighty miles to the southeast, Mount Baker, the long dormant volcano, responded to the violent earth movements deep below it. A long sealed fissure opened allowing magma to begin to move through cracks upward to the peak. New pressures caused by the downward thrust of the tectonic plate forced the magma upward creating heat that softened the surrounding rock allowing even more of it to rise. At the surface deep under the massive glacier, heat began to melt the ice forming a lake under the surface of the north facing glacier. Below, the earthquake survivors had too much on their minds to comprehend the changes taking place far above them.

In the Fraser Canyon, the riverbed ran dry below the massive earth dam. Above it the Fraser's water began to back up to form a deep narrow lake along the Fraser and Thompson River canyons. As the water level rose, it saturated the banks and bit-by-bit they collapsed, sinking to the bottom with trees and vegetation rising to the surface.

In the cities and towns on the coast, panic reigned. In the absence of emergency services many survivors felt it was each man for himself. Suddenly, they had no leaders. They had no law. There remained only, the primal law of survival. Some were heroic in rescuing others while others took the opportunity to become base stealing food and water. Survivors with a criminal bent recognized these basic things would be the currency of survival. The injured and elderly would be their first victims.

Seismology stations in Alaska and California were fully aware a major seismic event had occurred, yet no news from these areas had been heard. The airwaves were silent. The entire infrastructure had been destroyed. News flashed around the world telling of an earthquake, in the magnitude of nine that had occurred on the West Coast of Canada, but no information from the area had been received.

In Ottawa, federal disaster officials tried to reach their British Columbia counterparts to assess the extent of the damage and to find out what assistance was immediately required. They tried in vain. The most westerly telephone anyone could reach was located in Kamloops. Two hundred miles or so from the coast, Kamloops could offer no information other than rail traffic west of them had been blocked. The Coast Guard office in Vancouver along with their vessels had been swept away. The time, ten a.m.

Ottawa ordered a military plane to fly from Edmonton to report on conditions in the quake zone. At noon the plane circled the Vancouver airport and determined that due to the debris field it would be impossible to land an aircraft. By radio they described the area as a war zone.

By nightfall, survivors in the Lower Mainland had made preparations to find a safe place to spend the night. Some had emergency rations and were able to eat and drink clean water. Others had none. Many lay trapped in basements. Still others found themselves trapped in high-rise apartments unable to descend due to jammed steel emergency exit doors and inoperative elevators. As darkness enveloped the blacked out city, looting began with food and drink the main targets, the uninjured and able bodied taking what they could and stockpiling it.

The Province at this point was ungoverned a fact which did not go unnoticed by the criminal element within the quake-damaged area.

Above them, magma climbed higher inside Mount Baker. The lake forming under the huge north-facing glacier grew. Steam mixed with heavy cloud went undetected.

The Fraser riverbed in Hope lay bare and empty; the citizens had got off lightly, but higher up the canyon, the dam that had been the village of Lytton, quickly filled with water.

In the absence of any type of authority, Al Madson felt that he should bury the remains of his family in the garden. He and his child Sarah had to go on somehow. The garage that had come through relatively unscathed would be a temporary home. Dragging bedding and the remains of the food from the kitchen he made it as comfortable as possible for them. Taking his old backpack he cut holes for Sarah's feet so that he could safely carry her in his forays for food and water. Like the other survivors, he wondered what the government might be doing to help them.

In Ottawa, the Prime Minister called an emergency cabinet meeting reaching a decision to send in military forces. Troops would be airlifted by helicopter into Victoria and Vancouver. The Victoria contingent had instructions to both assist survivors and establish a military government if the civilian elected authority had failed. The Vancouver area contingent was to restore law and order and assess the quantity and type of aid most urgently required.

The first chopper set down on the lawn of the Legislature building. General Stadniki, in charge of operations, ordered a tent erected and a flag unfurled. He declared himself the Provincial Premier on October fourth 2008. He would establish military style government in concert with Ottawa. The chopper crew reported that the Victoria airport runway would be fit to land cargo planes after some initial cleanup.

The Vancouver contingent did an air reconnaissance of the International Airport. They reported lots of heavy equipment would be needed just to clear one emergency runway, also that all access to the airport had been severed, inaccessible, other than by water. General Stadniki ordered landing craft, bulldozers, men and fuel flown in immediately.

The refineries burned unchecked. It would be years before any fuel could be refined at the facilities. Flying it in would bring the price to incredible levels.

Ottawa swiftly implemented a plan. Everything would be airlifted to Victoria, and then dispersed as required. Landing craft crossed the straits then made their way through the wreckage-strewn marshes to the airport dyke; a bulldozer rumbled over it and began the mammoth task of clearing the main runway.

The Fraser River had drained of its water flow to the point where it was tidal. Many bodies would remain and decompose where they lay. On the White Rock tidal flats, thousands of bodies were rolled and turned by the ebb and flow. Logs, with their greater weight, pressed corpses into oblivion deep into the mud.

In Steveston, canneries and the fishing fleet were gone, the land swept clean of human endeavor. People trapped in high-rise buildings tied bedsheets to make ropes, some tumbled to their deaths. The weak and elderly found themselves being robbed of their meagre water and food supplies.

The military issued orders that looters were to be arrested and summarily shot.

By now the outside world, via television, were aware of the plight of West Coast earthquake and tsunami victims. Equipment and supplies were assembled in many countries, but due to its location locked in by water and High Mountains, delivery of the aid to the rugged West Coast was difficult if not impossible.

In Vancouver's West End, able-bodied men were conscripted to assist the soldiers in rescue work. Refusals under martial law resulted in being shot by firing squad. Realizing that the military meant business, they quickly volunteered.

Heavy rain fell. The drinking water problem eased.

Atop Mount Baker, a deepening and widening lake formed below the surface ice. Magma crept up to the peak. Pressure, relentlessly pushing upward, created even more heat.

A deep aftershock occurred. Millions of tons of water behind the now leaking earthdam in the Fraser Canyon suddenly burst from the bedrock with the aftershock vibrations. The entire structure began to move. A wall of water, rock, trees and crushed houses two hundred feet high rushed down the containing canyon walls. Residents of Yale heard a thunderous roar. All were swept away. Death instant. Downriver the wave scraped the town of Hope from bedrock and sweeping it part way up the mountain before the wall of water turned to the west and the widening valley.

At Mount Baker's peak, the shock waves loosened the glacier free of its grip on the mountain. Tens of millions of tons of ice, snow, water and rock debris began to move over the bedrock, down the north-facing slope at breakneck speed. Freed now of the crushing weight of the glacier, magma, ash and steam shot skywards. Lava melted even more ice as it fell. Mount Baker's volcano was reborn. The cauldron of elements transformed into an avalanche, cascaded down the North Slope to the valley floor.

The American town of Sumas vanished under the avalanche traveling at the rate of an express train. Seconds later, the town of Abbotsford B.C. ceased to exist as the wall of destruction crossed the valley floor continuing to Mission City leaving in its wake a debris trail that blocked the entire valley. The wall of water hurtling down from the Fraser Canyon met and crashed into the avalanche debris re-energizing it, together the two powers rushed seawards. When the mass reached the flatlands, weakening it spread out. Richmond and the airport once again became inundated. The apocalyptic flood rendered useless the work already done. The City of Vancouver cut off once more from all but sea borne aid.

The news that over sixty troops had been lost at the airport along with two super-transport planes costing many millions caused the government to reassess its plans by The Prime Minister. His advisors considered a new plan; it would be the most radical act in Canadian history. Yet possibly it might be the most humane. Input from officers in the field would colour the final decision.

Advisers asked for complete reports on the Lower Mainland's situation regarding fresh water and food supplies, transportation and epidemic possibilities. All agreed the situation to be grave. There were still considerable numbers of survivors on the higher ground. There seemed to be no way all the people in need could be helped, many more would die over the winter months of cold or starvation. All the farmland had been rendered non-productive due to salt saturation and debris. Transportation by any other means than air or water was impossible. Sanitation too, posed real problems. The medical officers felt that major epidemics could be expected; the sanitation infrastructure could take many years to replace or repair.

The Prime Minister, in a pamphlet dropped to survivors by helicopter, outlined a radical solution for all the areas of concern. Under Martial Law normal human rights are suspended. I therefore order an evacuation of survivors out of the area. All Survivors! In order to accomplish this I render all property rights invalid. The western portion of British Columbia will revert to the Crown. All of it! The population will be moved by ship to Prince Rupert and then by train to military bases for temporary housing, unless they have relatives they can go to elsewhere. There are thousands of unburied corpses trapped and unreachable, military personnel will burn all buildings after the evacuation. This plan will create conflict clear across the Nation. I, personally for the greater good, will accept total responsibility for the action. We will use whatever force necessary to remove those who refuse to budge from their property. Citizens who hide from the troops in defiance of the order will perish under the scorched earth policy."

The government moved to split the Province in two parts. A line starting at the International Boundary below Princeton would head north leaving the communities east of the line and Prince George unaffected. The line would then turn west to Prince Rupert. Other than existing aboriginal communities, inside the line would be a no go zone. Vancouver Island too would be divided. All the damaged towns on the East Coast would be torched after evacuation. The British Columbia Capital and the new government would be transferred to Kelowna.

. Ships arriving from overseas were conscripted to serve as people carriers, taking survivors north to Prince Rupert, where trains could whisk them inland. With the scorched earth policy they had nothing to go back to.

In Victoria, Al Madsen reported at the Esquimalt docks with little Sarah sitting in his backpack. They would go to his parents in Saskatoon. He would build a new life, a clean break from his old one.

By January twenty fourth smoking rubble and memories were all that remained of Victoria and Vancouver and other communities. The Big One, and the tsunami, changed everything and yet, history repeated itself. The two governments granted huge tracts of land to the railways to reconnect east and west. As people returned to work on the projects, the government sold flood-plain land to them for homebuilding.

FLIGHT 926.

I am an observer of souls. Unseen, but seeing all.

Bert Adams had begun to perspire profusely before takeoff on his first ever flight. He was filled with apprehension. A few minutes into the flight Bert's head had begun a severe pounding headache, maybe a migraine he thought. His left arm began hurting and he wondered if he had strained it carrying the luggage from the car to the check in counter. A constricting pain gripped his chest so severe he wanted to cry out, but he could not. His vision blurred and his upper body flopped sideways into the aisle still holding his wife Edith's fingers in a viselike grip. He hung like a rag doll with his safety belt locking him in his seat position, The happening created a ripple effect spreading through the ether like a pebble hurled into a still pond; a ripple that affected everyone on flight 926 and beyond.

"As an observer of souls I know these things."

The day had started well enough, for Bert and Edith Adams. They had risen early in the July Okanagan morning with the sun like a golden ball making its appearance over the mountain peaks beyond Kelowna. Bert had not slept well, being far too apprehensive about his and Edith's first flight. Coupled with nervousness as well as his great fear of heights, was the great anticipation of seeing his grandchildren in Montreal for the very first time.

"I will make us a hearty breakfast Bert. We don't know if we will be able to eat between here and Montreal. How about bacon, a couple of eggs and the last of the mushrooms?" Edith had asked.

Was it the heavy breakfast, or a high state of nervousness that caused Bert to perspire so much on the drive to Kelowna from Naramata? At the time of boarding flight 926, Bert was red faced and soaked in his own sweat. Feeling ill but not wanting to say anything to Edith, afraid she might make a sudden change in their travel plans.

Once he and Edith were seated in 1A and 2A he began to calm down a little. The feeling he had just experienced reminded him of similar ones in World War Two. He had seen enough bloodshed and destruction to last him a lifetime. He remembered swearing that he would never leave the Okanagan Valley if he ever made it back. Until today he had been true to his word. Gripping Edith's hand and with his eyes closed Bert remembered coming home from the war a changed man.

Borrowing the down payment from his father, he bought an orchard in Naramata. The orchard provided everything that he and Edith needed for their simple lifestyle. Other than trips to Kelowna and Osoyoos he never had a yen to leave it. Their daughter Evelyn married an engineer and moved with him to Montreal. Now there were two grandchildren he had never seen. Only they possessed the power to draw him from the valley for the first time since 1945.

Edith Adams, a chubby five foot two with graying hair, wearing makeup more suited to a younger woman, let out a loud scream upon seeing her husband slumped over the seat arm. Instinctively she knew that this was serious.

Stewardess Marjory Thompson, busy preparing the in flight beverages, looked down the aisle from her workstation. She saw the passenger in seat 1A hanging grotesquely over the seat arm, while the female companion in 2A waved frantically as she screamed for Marjory to assist.

Upon reaching the passenger she quickly ascertained that he had no pulse. She pushed the passenger into the upright position.

"Hold him up!" She ordered Edith. Then hurried to the flight deck.

"It looks like we have a heart attack victim in seat 1A captain." Reaching for his intercom mike, Captain Morse, a handsome, clean shaven and tall brown eyed man at fifty eight years of age, pressed the button and asked,

"Do we have a doctor on board? Or any other medical people who can assist a passenger in difficulty?" Next Morse radioed a message to the Edmonton control tower requesting an ambulance and medical persons to be standing by on flight 926's arrival. From further back in the cabin a man stood up and took a bag out of the overhead bin. Almost at the same time a young woman arose and followed the man up to row A.

"I am a doctor. Doctor Vale from Kelowna."

"I'm Nurse Trimble from Kelowna General," said the woman. Working in the confined space the doctor released the victim's seat belt and he and the nurse carried Bert Adams and laid him flat on the floor by the exit door. Despite C.P.R. and emergency oxygen, Adams could not be revived.

"Let me administer the last rites? I am father Bob Cranshaw, a priest." The words came from a man who had been closely observing the frantic efforts to revive Adams. Since the two medical helpers could do no more, they stood aside as father Cranshaw spoke the words of the rites. When he had finished, the co-pilot who had emerged from the flight deck and Marjory Thompson, moved the body against the fuselage by the exit door. Marjory covered it with a canvas cover from the beverage cart. Mrs. Adams still fastened into her seat wailed a sorrowful and confused lament.

In an instant her life had drastically changed. She knew she could not just leave her husband's body in Edmonton and carry on to her daughter's home in Montreal as arranged. All existing plans had to be scrapped and new ones formulated almost immediately.

The ripples from Bert Adam's demise spread outwards into the ether, affecting the lives of many who did not even know him. As an observer of souls, I am well aware of those whom the ripples touch, affecting them in a myriad of different ways.

For instance Captain Henry Morse, in whose hands the lives of the passengers on flight 926 were temporarily entrusted, had left his home in Kelowna this morning without a word of goodbye to his wife Janet. They had been together for twenty-five years. He felt that their lives were becoming stale, since he had been reduced to captaining intercity flights and he spent almost every night with her. His annual medical two years ago had forced him from the international flights on larger aircraft where he had ample opportunity for philandering with pretty and willing young female flight crew. If Janet ever suspected him of infidelity she had never voiced it.

Just two years away from retirement and the final commercial flight of his aviation career, the body of the passenger lying dead behind the flight deck wall caused him to think of his own mortality. It brought to mind his relationship with Janet and the thought of retirement without her if she too were to suddenly exit life like the unfortunate soul on the deck behind him. Janet so far as he knew had always been true to him, the thought of which brought pangs of guilt and remorse at his philandering.

As flight 926 reached altitude on its path to Edmonton, Morse made the decision to greet Janet with flowers and a new respect on his arrival home tonight. He would reaffirm his love for her, and would be much more of a friend to her than he had been of late.

Invisible, soundless, imperceptible ripples rolled gently through the ether affecting the lives of the others they touched.

Co-pilot Sandy Wilson, aptly named for the shock of reddish hair atop his well-shaped head, mindlessly brushed a toast crumb from his uniform pants while sitting in his flight crew seat. The daily 926 flight to Edmonton had become routine, but on this day the events left him disturbed; there was a body lying on the floor in the main cabin. It was far from a routine flight. It clouded the warm thoughts of waking up alongside Maria Vargas just two hours before flight time. They had played love games until the early hours, with Maria an eager and willing partner. He didn't love her. Sandy knew that, but his fiancée Beverly, insisted upon waiting for marriage before giving herself to him.

Maria was convenient and discreet, not looking for marriage but she fulfilling his sexual needs relieving him of the need to press Beverly unduly. Sandy knew he was two timing her, but strangely it was not until now that he felt any guilt about it. A ripple of remorse passed through him. He had seen the face of the woman in seat 2A, wife of the dead man on the floor. Inexplicably he saw in her, the look that Beverly might wear if she were to know the truth about his spending his nights with another woman. It must stop. He made the decision to call Maria tonight and break it off. Philandering would be his past, not part of his future.

Stewardess Marjorie Thompson bravely went about her duty seeing to the needs of her passengers. She tried not to look down at the body draped in the beverage cart cover as she made her many trips up and down the aisle. She had been trained to handle all kinds of aircraft emergency situations. This was the first time she had experienced a death on her watch. Despite her training to remain calm and assist the passengers in any given crisis Marjorie, beneath her calm exterior, felt deeply disturbed by the passing of Mr. Adams. She did her best to offer comfort to Mrs. Adams in between her in-flight duties.

Toward the rear of the plane, Doctor Julian Vale stared blankly at the pages of his book. He had been unable to help the passenger up front. It did not concern him unduly, for death, healing and suffering were his chosen lot in life. His thoughts were much further afield than the passenger on the floor. His mind took him to the city of Atlanta and the medical convention there. He had told his wife the convention would be a bore for her it being mainly about cancer treatment, besides there was nothing much in Atlanta that might interest her.

"Stay home with the kids, you will be much happier." He had told her. To his hidden delight she bought his line. At this moment Dr. Vale's mind was many miles away slowly undoing buttons and holding a warm and willing body next to his. He turned and looked at the nurse who had assisted him with the now dead passenger.

Nurse Trimble acknowledged his look bringing her eyes down to read her magazine. It was all going to plan but for the incident of the death in seat 2A, but given the situation no one could possibly know that she and the doctor were having a torrid affair. It had gone on for several months, mostly secretive coffee break meetings and necking and petting in his car after hospital rounds. Enamored of the doctor, Anne Trimble fully expected that after their clandestine weekend in Atlanta, Julian would want to leave his family and be with her.

She had a feeling that once Julian had bedded her, he would find her so irresistible there would be no turning back. But for now they would continue the agreed upon charade of not knowing each other until they reached Atlanta. The voice of stewardess Marjorie Thompson, asking, tea, coffee or juice, interrupted her thoughts of passionate lovemaking with Julian.

Sipping his scalding coffee, Julian Vale glanced at the man sitting across the aisle from him. The man in his forties, well dressed and groomed, sat with an open briefcase upon his knee like a desk. Julian wondered if the man was a doctor like himself and also going to Atlanta. The thought made him realize he must be very careful not to be spotted with Anne Trimble in and around the hotel. But then he realized that had the man been a M.D. he would have stepped forward when the call came for assistance. His thought caused him to reinforce his need to be careful in Atlanta; after all he did not know all the other doctors in the Okanagan valley. If there were others at the convention it could possibly lead to an embarrassment at a local medical function at a later date.

Across the aisle, the object of Julian Vale's concerns, shuffled the papers in his briefcase with one hand while holding his coffee cup in the other. Harold Wyman's flight was taking him home to family and his head office in Edmonton. He had spent a lonely week in Vernon investigating a fraud case for his company, International General Insurance. Harold was onto every fraud trick in the book and saved I.G.I. a great deal of money each year. The trip to Vernon would save his company just under $400, 000 for which he would receive a bonus. As the ripple in the ether passed through him, Harold made an instant decision to greet Allison, his wife, with an enormous bunch of flowers, take her out to the finest restaurant in Edmonton and spend the weekend together before reporting to head office.

Stewardess Marjorie Thompson passed a miniature bottle of scotch and a glass containing ice to the military officer seated in 3A shoulder pips indicating his rank of Major. Neatly groomed hair thinning on top, matched his handlebar mustache and eyebrows adorning a stern but sad face. Rene Arsenault, a career soldier had served in the Canadian army since the age of eighteen. His compassionate leave now over he was returning to camp at Petawawa, leaving his grieving mother in Penticton following his father's funeral. Rene felt little regret at his father's passing, they had never seen eye to eye, but he felt a great sadness for his mother now alone at the far end of the country. Seeing the unknown man seated just ahead created a wish that he and father had better understood each other he made a resolution that he would keep in closer contact with his mother. In his melancholy he declined to get into conversation with the woman seated next to him.

Leaning over him, Stewardess Marjorie Thompson passed a diet coke to Marlene Sansey. Middle aged yet not appearing so, Marlene, the head representative for Smart Girl Cosmetics in the Okanagan Valley was a living-walking ad for her company's products. She dressed well with clothing that complemented her youthful shape and always had her hair carefully styled and groomed. Marlene had twenty-five reps working under her, all chosen for their looks and sex appeal. She encouraged her underlings always to be sales conscious and to have a cosmetics sales party at least five evenings per week. On arrival in Edmonton she would transfer to a Toronto flight for the semi-annual sales convention.

At forty-two, married and childless, Marlene and her husband Frank, a real estate lawyer, enjoyed a lifestyle with no financial worries. She encouraged her underlings that they too could live like her and Frank if they pushed hard for the maximum sales parties.

She had a sudden premonition that she would win the coveted beauty consultant of the year award at the convention, allowing her to put aside the disturbing feelings she had experienced watching the medical people in their vain attempt to save the dead passengers life.

Marlene felt her hair being tugged from behind. She felt instant annoyance; it had just been styled for the convention. She turned to see a harried young woman trying to control her restless infant. A ripple or wave of compassion and understanding crossed Marlene's mind, instead of protesting, she smiled at the young mother.

Tony Young, with her heart and mind in turmoil, returned a resigned and sad smile. Her baby Joel began to cry inconsolably adding to her abject misery. This morning at six thirty her marriage as she knew it, ended. Her abusive husband, a constant drinker, had taken his fists to her for the last time. She had become afraid that he might hurt the child and perhaps give her a serious injury. She remembered the tearful call to her father for help and how he had sent her an airline ticket to go home to Winnipeg. She had left the house with only the shabby clothes she wore and carrying the baby with one extra diaper and a bottle of formula. A neighbour, who was aware of her situation, had driven her to the Kelowna airport promising not to tell where she had gone. Stewardess Marjorie Thompson brought a heated bottle for the baby, bringing a temporary lull in the crying.

Across the aisle a tall man in his fifties, balding save for a wisp of a comb over, watched as the baby suckled on the bottle while the mother tried to sip her coffee without spilling it on the lively youngster. Father Cranshaw, the priest, who had delivered the last rites to the deceased lying by the exit door, was minus his clerical collar. Had it not been for the unfortunate event of the man's demise he could have traveled incognito all the way to Regina. Despite his reason for travel, Cranshaw considered himself first and foremost a priest and had felt duty bound to offer the last rites to the unfortunate fellow traveler.

His diocese had ordered his transfer to Regina without notifying his congregation of his leaving. The diocese felt it would be much less of a scandal were he to suddenly disappear, rather than facing up to the several allegations of child molestation with young boys in his church. It was the third such move for him, but he saw nothing wrong in touching the boys. He felt it had nothing to do with his vow of celibacy and wondered what awaited him in his new parish. As a non-detectable ripple surging through the ether momentary passed through his body, a heretounknown pang of guilt and shame crossed his mind.

"Thank you miss," he said as Marjorie Thompson handed him an orange squash.

Directly behind him in seats 5A and 5B. Lana and Ernest Sokowitz chatted excitedly. A computer specialist, Ernest had created a dramatic increase in sales in the Kelowna office. The stocky fellow whose crew cut hairstyle revealed a chubby round face with a permanent smile etched on it. Needing to feel comfortable, Ernest traveled in a sweatshirt and jeans. As a reward for his sales performance he had been offered the manager's position in the Mississauga office near Toronto. They were to overnight in Edmonton with Lana's parents, before continuing on to Toronto. Lana, a natural blonde had unusually pretty good looks and she dressed well. Ernest adored her and he often told her so. Lana wondered what unexplainable wave like force caused both her and Ernest to seek out the others hand at exactly the same moment. As she sipped her coffee she wondered what their new home would look like feeling full of anticipation about meeting her parents and two sisters again.

She glanced at stewardess Marjorie Thompson as she brought a tray containing two wineglasses and two small bottles of white wine to the couple sitting directly behind her.

Alan and June Bolton were in a world known only to them. Married only fourteen hours they were totally besotted with love. They had spent their first night of betrothal in the Kelowna Grand tearing themselves from between the sheets in order to catch flight 926 connecting with the plane to Jamaica. Tonight they would love the night away on the island paradise to the sound of a tropical breeze playing through swaying palm trees. They each gazed into the limpid eyes of the other as they sipped the wine and willed the hours away, when once again they would lie as one. The ripple, as it passed through them, counted as nothing. Love was everything.

Across the aisle, Anne Trimble swished the last of her diet Pepsi around her glass casting discreet but envious glances at the couple so obviously and blatantly in love. It troubled her to see the couple express their love so openly while she had to hold her feelings for Julian Vale at bay until they reached Atlanta. Younger than Julian by a number of years, Anne felt proud of her looks. She had been able to attract Julian's amorous attentions, to her that was proof enough of her looks and charms. She felt that she could set her cap at anyone, but she had set it at him. This weekend in Atlanta she would win him totally. She looked furtively up the aisle at Julian seeing only the back of his head.

Across the aisle and one seat back, a nondescript man in his fifties stared at the seat back in front of him with a morose look upon his face. He had noticed the girl across the aisle, it was hard not to, she exuded an air of confidence and from where he sat the shape of her breasts were in profile, and a strong but pleasant perfume lingered in the air around her.

Jake Allcroft was in no mood to make a move on the girl, nor was he in a frame of mind for small talk with anyone else. Flight 926 for him was, in an odd sense, an errand of mercy. A call from his sister informing him of his mother's impending death from lung cancer was his sole reason for being here. He hadn't been home in twenty years never having felt the need. Growing up to adulthood in the family home, life with his parents had not been easy. His father, a mean and cruel man, had made life a misery for his sons, and their mother had never stood up to him in her children's defence. Frankly Jake never expected to make a trip like this but felt some healing might come to him from it. Right now, at this moment, he had no idea what he might say at his mother's bedside. There came a ripple flowing in the ether and as it passed through Jake Allcroft he decided he would tell her that he loved her, it was possibly the last thing he could do for her before she died. If she went to her grave without hearing his admission, Jake knew he would feel bad for the rest of his own life, after all, had he too not been selfish in his own attitude to his parents.

Flight 926 had been airborne for some time and nearly half way in the flight. Marjorie Thompson, after consultation with Captain Morse in regard to possible turbulence, began to serve the luncheon trays. Mrs. Adams still overwrought, waved her tray away and requested,

"Just a glass of water please? What will they do with Bert's body when we arrive in Edmonton miss?"

"An ambulance will take the body Mrs. Adams. The medics will inform you where the body will be taken, and our flight desk at the airport will assist you in any travel plans that need to be changed, and any other matters you may need help with. Captain Morse has notified them by radio as to what has taken place on the flight. I will bring you a glass of water in a few moments."

Dr. Julian Vale looked with disdain at the tray the stewardess placed before him. Vale was a staunch believer in abstaining from food between main meals, especially this kind of food. The tray contained a wrapped sandwich made the Lord only knows when. A bag of oil rich potato chips and a strip pack of unidentifiable cookies. He planned to have a proper meal with Anne Trimble on arrival in Edmonton, not eating again until he and Anne had exhausted their passions at the hotel in Atlanta. Vale believed wholeheartedly that hunger enhanced his sexual performance.

From the tray the stewardess had placed before him moments ago, Harold Wyman Nibbled on the potato chips. He would reserve his appetite for the fine dinner he would enjoy with his wife Allison. Harold knew Allison well; she would have prepared a meal to welcome him home. If she declined his invitation to dine out, he would still have a fine meal at the house. Each had a healthy respect for the others feelings, this Harold felt, made their marriage a good one.

Still unable to pass the body on the floor without looking down, Marjorie Thompson carried two more trays along the aisle. She placed one in front of Marlene Sansey, the other before the priest Cranshaw.

Sansey, utterly conscious of her body shape and her pressing need to maintain it took a single bite from the chicken sandwich, chewed it slowly, leaving the balance of the food on the tray. She glanced nervously at her watch, slightly worried about missing her connecting flight. With only thirty minutes between them, any delay of flight 926 could be a minor disaster. If she were to walk in part way through the seminar it would detract from the thrill of receiving her expected award.

The tray placed in front of Tony Young and her infant was cleaned off in a matter of seconds. Tony had not eaten since yesterday. There had been nothing in the house and she had no money. She saved a cookie to soothe her child and glanced around her at the other passengers leaving their meals uneaten. Tony wished she had the courage to ask for an extra sandwich, but her self-confidence had been beaten down. She still suffered the trauma of running away like a thief in the night. Dressed in her old wrinkled and soiled clothing she felt shame and yet she knew that the shame was not hers. Unlike the other passengers, hers was a flight for survival. She was a refugee in her own land. Tony knew that dressed the way she was, people in the airport would look down on her. They would see a woman with unkempt hair wearing a much-stained dress, worn out shoes and no self respect. They would not see the once proud and pretty girl whose love and concern for the safety of her child exceeded everything.

"Could I get a bottle of warm water for the baby miss?" she asked as Marjorie Thompson passed her seat carrying two trays. Marjorie leaned over and whispered,

"I can warm up some milk for you." Gratitude gleamed in Tony's eyes.

Father Cranshaw ate from his tray in silence, mulling over the Bishop's words, telling him, not asking him, to pack his bags and be on the morning flight.

"We will tell the congregation that you were urgently called away in Gods service to a much needier parish." It wasn't the truth, but then neither was it an outright lie, but it was the way things were done. At times Cranshaw wondered if he had chosen the right calling. He had to move often and make new relationships and get to know the church councils in different parishes. On the up side, he did have the opportunity to develop relationships with the young boys of the church. But he never understood the fuss when one would complain about his touching them. After all he felt he was showing love to the boys not sin or violence, and the activities seemed perfectly natural to him.

The trays placed before the newlyweds, the Boltons, were quickly emptied. Both were ravenous, having forgone breakfast in order to spend every second in bed before racing to catch flight 926. Sustenance for them was not a high priority. The airline taking them to the Caribbean would feed them before they arrived to begin their marathon of passion.

With her passengers taken care of for the moment, Marjorie took two trays to the cockpit and came back with one for herself. Sitting in a jump seat she joined Captain Morse and Sandy for her break.

"Have they given us chicken again Marjorie?" Sandy asked with an air of disdain.

"Yes. It's the same as the rest of the week. You would think the caterer would vary the menu once in a while. But I suppose the passengers don't realize it's the same darn thing everyday."

"We are going to have to start carrying tin lunch buckets like construction workers in order to get some variety." Captain Morse ventured. Marjorie responded,

"You know I really don't feel like eating with the dead guy lying on the other side of the wall."

"How is his wife handling it Marjorie?"

"As well as to be expected. How are you going to handle the situation when we land?"

"I will have the passengers stay buckled in until the medics have taken the body away. We can't have them stepping over a corpse as they deplane. Have any of the other passengers freaked out Marjorie?"

"No. None of them seems unduly disturbed, but there is a young couple who are behaving like they would like to join the mile high club. They are all over each other."

The fifteen-minute break ended all too quickly and Marjorie returned to the main cabin to collect the luncheon trays. Captain Morse's voice boomed over the intercom,

"Ladies and gentlemen we are beginning our descent into Edmonton International. We expect to be at our arrival gate in thirty minutes. When the seat belt sign comes on, we request that you keep your seat belt fastened until I have turned the sign off. As you know we have had an unfortunate incident this morning and the seat belt sign will remain on until the doorway has been cleared and it is safe for you to deplane. Thank you for flying with us today and we hope you will be flying with us again soon."

Marjorie walked down the aisle asking if anyone needed any further beverages. Rene Arsenault asked for another Johnny Walker scotch and water. Accustomed to drinking at any time of day he happened to be in the officer's mess, he didn't care if he was tipsy. He would not be reporting for duty until Monday in Petawawa.

A distinctive change in the tone of the engines announced the beginning of the long slow descent. Julian Vale began to fidget in his seat. It would not be long now before he could hug and kiss Anne when they arrived in the anonymity of the terminal building. After lunch in the airport dining room, he and Anne would be able to sit together on the plane to Atlanta. It would be the longest time they had ever had together without some kind of interruption. It would be the prelude to their checking into the hotel room, and the wild abandon he felt would follow.

The seat belt sign flashed on. Marlene Sansey nervously checked her watch as Marjorie stepped down the aisle checking to see if the passengers were properly buckled in.

"How long is it likely to take to remove the damn body from the plane? I have an important connection to make." Marlene said haughtily.

"It shouldn't take long madam." Marjorie replied reassuringly.

"Well I hope not or your management will hear about it." Marlene snapped.

The newlyweds gazed wistfully at each other. Nothing could break the spell they were under. It seemed the world around them no longer existed; they were all alone in the universe. A tropic isle awaited them with warm winds, swaying palms and an eagerness to please each other that knew no bounds.

Tony Young managed to change her infant's diaper on her knee and did her best to straighten her hair. Tony at last felt much safer. In a matter of hours she would really feel safe and secure, back in the home of her parents. Tony knew that this was only the beginning of a long struggle to raise her baby alone. She would have to get a job to support her and her child and then there was the matter of a child minder. She could not expect her mother to take on the job permanently. The body lying on the floor made her realize that had she not run this morning, she too may soon have been just as dead as he.

A loud grinding sound indicated the landing gear being deployed. Jake Allcroft having had a complete rethinking of his relationship with his mother, could not prevent a tear from forming, knowing that it would be only a matter of hours before he could tell her what was in his heart. How he regretted staying away for so many years and only coming to see her at these her final hours. Mild panic struck his heart thinking of the possibility of not getting there in time to tell her. The body lying at the exit door brought home to him the fragility of human life. The thought brought forth a gush of tears from eyes that had not shed them since his youth.

Feeling comfortable sitting next to her husband. Lana Sokowitz looked out of the tiny window at the outskirts of Edmonton down below. She looked forward to being with her family again and it would be in just a few minutes. The body at the exit door caused her to think of her father in a different way. She knew he was struggling with the effects of diabetes, and while she had never given it much thought, suddenly she realized that one day she would get the call to return to the family home for a funeral. From this moment on she would see her father in a very different light, and she would let him know that she felt he was precious.

A puff of smoke from the tires announced to Edmonton that flight 926 had arrived. After taxiing to the terminal building, silence enveloped the aircraft until the ground crew opened the door. Ambulance personnel stepped inside and proceeded to place the body on a stretcher.

"I have to go with him." Mrs. Adams yelled.

"Our terminal people will take you Mrs. Adams." Captain Morse advised, "Please remain seated and we will take care of you when the other passengers have gone."

One by one the passengers went on their individual way. None of them knowing Bert Adams, but each of them affected by him in different and mysterious ways through the waves and ripples sent through the ether by his leaving this place of mortals.

I know these things. I am an observer of souls. Unseen but seeing all.

THE NEST.

I CLIMBED OUT of the bath and dried myself. I brushed my hair and then I looked at myself in the full-length mirror. I turned to see my silhouette. My breasts are still firm and perky; and my bottom is not out of proportion with my body. Since I am alone in the house I say out loud,

"You are still a good looking woman Brigitte Wright so why on earth would your husband choose to wander." I turn to see myself from the other side and basically I am pleased with my reflection. I turned and looked at my back over my shoulder, my waist goes in and my hips curve out. Even by magazine model standards I am a good-looking woman. I turn to view myself from the front. My auburn hair frames what I consider a pleasing face, my breasts are even in size and do not sag and my hips and thighs are as much as a woman wants them to be, and that men profess to admire.

So why then does John feel the need to be with other women? I have no proof that he does yet, but all the signs are there. The secret telephone calls from female so called clients of his law practice. The evening meetings that go on until the early hours of the morning and the weekends away at what he calls legal seminars. The most compelling feeling I have of his infidelity, stems from the fact that he comes to me less and less.

He claims that he does not wish to disturb me when he comes in late, despite the fact that I have made subtle suggestions that I want to be disturbed. It was such spontaneity that spiced our relationship for the first few years of the marriage. Now it does not exist. While John has certainly provided a beautiful home for us, sometimes I feel like a prisoner in it. I want more than pleasant surroundings. I need love and companionship. I need to feel desirable sexually. I need to feel that John and I are a team doing things together, not just two people who have breakfast together on weekday mornings.

Sometimes I wonder if the fault is mine. Maybe I am not exciting enough for him to want me in the way I need to be wanted. At other times like now, as I look at my reflection in the mirror, I know in my heart that it is not the case. I am a sexual woman and a pretty woman in every sense of the word. I recognize admiring glances when I am out shopping and then I know the problem is not with me. It is obvious that John seeks the charms of other women for reasons of his own.

I reach for my bathrobe, put it on and go to my bedroom. It used to be our bedroom, until John's late homecomings started him going to the guest bedroom so that he would not disturb me. At least that's what he said, but the fact is, it has become a permanent situation. I found it most hurtful and I would lie in my bed hearing him come home. I would wait and hope that he would come to me and we could rekindle the closeness we once shared.

I went to my dressing table and took out my very best lingerie. I had recently been in one of those shops that sell seductive garments, in the hope that by letting John see me wearing them he would take me, as he once used to. I had chosen black ones to contrast against the whiteness of my skin. Slipping on the lace bra I looked at myself in the mirror and I felt pleased with the result. Next I pulled on the black-laced thong panties, and finally the sheer black three quarter length housecoat.

Out of the bottom drawer I took an erotic book I had bought, then went into the guest bedroom to await John's arrival. I put on a single bedside lamp and lay reading and waiting for the sounds of his homecoming. It was just after one in the morning when I heard the front door close. I lay in what I thought was a seductive pose. John crept quietly into the room and saw me.

I hoped he would fling off his clothing and come to me and make me feel like a woman again.

"What the Hell are you doing in my bed?" He demanded.

Instantly my feelings of anticipation and warmth vanished. His nine-word sentence said it all. He did not love me anymore. He did not find me attractive anymore. All my efforts to make myself sexually appealing had been in vane. John just stood there as I rose from the bed. Anger choked my throat. I could not speak and say what I wanted to tell him. I picked up a table lamp tearing the plug out of the socket and threw it at his head. I had always been good at softball and I didn't miss my target.

"What the Hell is the matter with you Brigitte? Why are you so god-damn angry and why are you not in your own bed?"

If John had come to me even at this point and tried to console, and make advances, I might have forgiven him and become lost in lovemaking. But he didn't and I had a gut feeling that he had just spent all his energies in the arms of some other woman.

I stormed back to my own bedroom, in anger I tore off the sexy garments and got into my pajamas. I began to cry. Instinctively I knew our marriage was over, but this time I did not blame myself for its failure. The fault was all John's and I felt if the son of a bitch was trying to lay the blame on me he had bitten off more than he could chew. He was a lawyer, I figured when things got really nasty he would try to keep the house and my car for himself.

I had always trusted him and I knew that all of our possessions were in his name. I had a feeling that when the time came for divorce, I would be kicked out with nothing, and the new trophy wife would step in and get everything. As I wept the night away, I resolved that it would not happen. I didn't know how I would prevent it, but I also knew that I would, no matter what it took.

I was up and about in the morning when John came downstairs.

"What the Hell got into you last night Brigitte? Why did you throw a lamp at me?"

"You have another woman don't you John?" I asked. "You are late home every night and gone most weekends. Who is she, what is she like, is she much younger than I. Do I know her?"

"You are crazy Brigitte. I'm working very long hours to get the law practice off the ground and into the big leagues."

"I don't believe you John. What is her name?"

"I don't have to listen to this Brigitte. I will get my breakfast on the way to the office."

"Do you want a divorce John?"

"Well I will tell you this Brigitte, if you keep on with your accusatory and unreasonable behaviour I might just ask for one. Goodbye."

I knew immediately that it was just a matter of time before the marriage came to an abrupt end. I assumed John had already got his plans underway and that I had better get on with plans of my own. I thought the first thing I should do, would be to find out for sure what John was actually doing on those late nights. I couldn't face eating breakfast so I dressed and took the car in order to see a private detective agency.

"Round the clock surveillance will not come cheap, Mrs. Wright." Ex cop Mark Sturtze said. "But if you really want to know what your husband is up to, it will be worth the cost."

"There is a lot riding on the information Mr. Sturtze, I will pay the fees so get on to it." I told Sturtze the pertinent information on John and he said he would get on the case right away. He was as good as his word. Three days later he had news for me and several photographs.

"Her name is Wanda Preston, Mrs Wright. She lives over on Banks Street in an apartment rented by your husband John Wright. For the last two nights, we observed your husband go to the apartment after his office closed at six and he did not emerge until after eleven. On the first night we observed your husband and Wanda go to the Raging Bull steakhouse for dinner, we were able to get these photographs."

"Show me." I said. I almost choked. Wanda could not have been more than twenty-one and she was beautiful. Even in my anger toward her I could see that. I paid Mr. Sturtze his five hundred per day in cash. I knew now that my marriage was doomed; the rest was up to me. I had to protect the investment in my side of the marriage to John. But how? I knew it would be difficult, if not impossible, to get a lawyer to represent me against John. His company had a good reputation and for a smaller law firm to go after him could mean economic suicide.

I thought of shooting him. I knew John had a revolver in the house hidden in the back of the liquor cabinet. But I knew I could never get away with it. I am no fool and ballistics experts would point their fingers directly at me. I had to come up with something different, something unique. Something that would not lead the authorities back to me.

I racked my brains over the next several days but came up with nothing. On Thursdays I usually did some yard work, since John had always claimed he was too busy for that kind of thing. I went into the tool shed for my rake and heard the buzzing of insects. I looked up and to my horror I saw a wasp's nest bigger than a watermelon. Yellow jacket wasps crawled all over it, coming and going through a hole in the base. They must have been building the nest since spring but I had never noticed it before. It hung from the peak of the shed almost down to the level of the door top.

I held my breath and walked under it to the outside. In the safety of the open air I turned to look where the insects were getting in to the shed. I saw a steady stream of them walking in and out of a gap under the eave. I would have to get John to do something about it next time he was at home, but then I remembered he was afraid of them. Allergic, he said. It was at that moment I realized this was the answer to my prayers.

On Saturday morning I asked John to get the lawnmower out of the shed.

"It seems to be jammed I can't get it out." I said. It was a warm late September morning and John was wearing his shorts and a short-sleeved summer shirt. He went to the back of the shed where I had purposely trapped the lawnmower in with our bicycles and other things. When he bent down to try to free the mower I knocked the nest down with a broom and grabbed the door and held it shut from out side. I could hear the buzz turn into a frenzy of angry wings and then I heard John start yelling. I held on to the door handle with all my strength as John tried to get out. His screams only lasted for about ten minutes and then the only sound was the wasps. I left the shed until darkness fell when I knew the wasps would have quieted down. I shone the light on him, his arms face and legs were a mass of swollen stings, and his eyes were wide open in horror.

"Accidental death," the coroner said.

I didn't crack a smile at the reading of the will, which he hadn't yet changed. I played the part of the bereaved widow and got the house and the cars, his life insurance and the widow's pension benefit from the company group insurance plan. I am set for life financially, but my revenge at his infidelity and scorn, was the icing on the cake and the cherry on the top, was evicting Wanda from the apartment my husband had installed her in.

THE FISH TANK.

I SAT IN the prisoner's box. It was not a new or unusual experience for me; I have claimed this seat on many occasions. I have a long list of break and enter convictions, a couple for assault and battery and one for murder. The murder conviction netted me twenty-five years, but with time off for good behaviour, I was out in fifteen completely retrained in criminal activities. I suppose you could say I am a slow learner, because here I am back in the prisoner's box again. Just minutes ago the jury handed in their guilty verdict. Murder in the first degree.

It is so easy for me to be angry with the jury, for their decision will have a dramatic effect on my life and freedom from here on in. Having said that, I did kill the son of a bitch in a planned cold-blooded murder. As far as I was concerned, he deserved it. My lawyer tried his best to suggest it was an unfortunate accident, but the fact that I waited outside the bar with a colt pistol and shot him in the forehead when he came out, obviously swayed the jury.

What really ticked me off was the prosecutor saying that I was an incorrigible career criminal. He knew very little about me and yet he had the audacity to suggest I should receive life without any possibility of parole. At this point I didn't know if the judge would accept his recommendations and act upon them. The way I see it; I had made a few mistakes in my life, but then who hadn't. But life without parole seemed pretty darn savage to me, after all; the guy I bumped off was not one of society's darlings.

Always in the past there was a day somewhere down the road when I knew I would walk free again. Frankly the thought of dying inside the Pen scared me a little. I looked up as the Judge entered the courtroom. He sat down and put that stupid little black cap on. What a dumb ritual.

It's like a kid's game. Anyway he asked me to stand to hear my sentence. I felt like telling him to get stuffed, but I didn't I kept my trap shut.

"Matthew John Bodine! After hearing all the evidence presented to the court and viewing the list of your prior convictions it is the courts decision that you be incarcerated for life with no possibility of parole. Because the court feels that past incarcerations have taught you nothing about being a useful and productive citizen. You seem to feel as though you should be allowed to wander freely among society, doing as you please without regard for others. Since the state in its wisdom has banned capital punishment I am recommending to the penal system that you are a candidate for the F.I.S. programme. The Final Incarceration System."

The Judge banged down his gavel and walked out of the court. The swine didn't even look at me. He probably went back to his chambers and had a couple of belts of good scotch then a big fancy dinner and home to his mansion in the country. I don't think anyone should have so much power. Yet the little jerk with the black cap had ordered me put away for life in this F.I.S. thing whatever that was.

I have been in quite a few jails in my life but I have never heard of this one. Then I thought to myself, maybe this is one of the more modern prisons where I can have my own T.V. and computer. Possibly they have a golf course and horse riding stables, weekends in the town with day passes. I could handle that, I figured maybe I could get a girlfriend by mail and have her come to the F.I.S. for conjugal weekends.

The bailiff grabbed my arm and escorted me out of the courtroom and downstairs to the cells. He put me in a holding cell with three other guys. "What did you get?" one of them asked me.

"Life with no parole. But I get to serve my time in one of those luxury pens, the F.I.S. the judge said."

The other guys just looked at me and grinned. One of them said,

"Luxury! You call the Fish Tank luxury? Have you just crawled out from under a rock, man?"

"What do you mean?" I asked, "I have never heard of it. What is this Fish Tank as you call it?"

The guy, who had spoken to me, turned to his buddies and they all began laughing.

"What a sap! This jerk won't last ten minutes in the joint," he said.

"So tell me what kind of a place is this Fish Tank, are you saying it is not one of the new luxury prisons?" They began roaring with laughter again. I figured at this point the best thing I can do is to keep my mouth shut. When they realized that they couldn't bait me anymore, one of them began to explain.

"We have heard of the F.I.S. or Fish Tank. No one gets out of there alive. Because of that very fact, details are sketchy. The guards know about the place, but they are instructed not to talk about it. But you know how it is, some of them do. As a result of massive public outcry about hotel like prisons and what they claim are unrealistic sentences for major crimes; the Feds built the fish tank for what they term as incorrigible criminals. I have been told that the Fish Tank is located up in the arctic tundra two hundred miles from the closest settlement. I have also been told that because of the design of the Fish Tank, escape from it is absolutely impossible. There are no prison guards there; the place apparently doesn't need any."

"No guards! I ask. How can they run a prison without guards?"

"The inmates have to look after themselves. It is apparently a completely democratic facility. The inmates make the laws and rules themselves and they police them too. Since escape is out of the question and there are no guards to enforce the rules they have to make them work. It is just like the society outside, but this society is comprised of killers, child molesters and serial rapists. Outside society has washed its hands of them and within the Fish Tank they are a law unto themselves."

"You guys are having me on. How can it be? It just wouldn't work."

"Well according to the guard who told me about the place, it does work. Guys in the Fish Tank, who do not toe the line on the rules of the joint end up dead. Since they are all in there for life without any chance for parole, as far as the outside society is concerned, their sentence has been completed when the helicopter hauls the bodies out."

"Helicopters? What helicopters?"

"Once a week a helicopter lowers the week's food supplies into the Fish Tank and hauls the bodies and the garbage out."

"I don't believe you. Helicopters? Dead bodies? What the heck kind of building needs a helicopter to service it?"

"Well you will find out soon enough when they lower you in. The Fish Tank is apparently built like an ant's nest. The top of it is a huge dome with one access hole where the helicopters bring the prisoners and supplies lowering them two hundred feet down into the Fish Tank using steel cables. The cons load the cage with the dead and the trash and up she comes and that's it for another week."

"What if someone gets sick down there?"

"Nothing. Remember society has washed its hands of the Fish Tank occupants. You are stuck there until you die, be it illness, freezing to death, or violence by your peers. Only corpses make the trip back to the surface."

"The more you guys tell me, the more I think you are pulling my leg." Stunned I lay down on the empty bunk and began to ponder what I had been told. If it was true, it was a pretty scary concept. I stayed in the same cell for four days then the guards came for me.

"It's Delivery day for you Bodine," one of them said. They put leg shackles round my ankles and handcuffed me behind my back. "Well we won't be seeing you back here again Bodine, you have bought yourself a one way ticket."

"Where are you taking me?"

You are going to the airport Bodine, but you sure as Hell aint flying to a tropical paradise." The guards hurled me unceremoniously into a windowless paddy wagon and slammed the door. I rode in pitch dark until they opened the door alongside a small airplane. Another guard led me up the steps into the plane and chained me to a wooden seat. There was another prisoner seated across the aisle from me while the rest of the cabin was filled with cartons of groceries.

The plane took off and I noticed a look of genuine fear on the face of the other prisoner.

"Scared of flying?" I asked.

"No. I'm scared of what happens after landing. We are going to the Fish Tank you know. The name is Briggs, Chester Briggs."

"I'm Matt Bodine. They tell me this Fish Tank is a pretty rough place, what have you heard?"

"Nothing good Matt. Nothing good. I am not a strong man; I figure I won't last much longer than a week in there, according to the stories I have heard. The way I figure it is that the courts have sentenced me to death. But since the death penalty has been abolished they are going to let the cons do it."

"What the Hell did you do to qualify for the Fish Tank Chester?"

"I raped and murdered a twelve year old. Then I robbed an elderly couple and the guy died when I roughed him up a bit. The old bastard of a Judge figured he would cleanse society of me permanently. How about you?"

"I put a bullet through a guys head to get my second murder conviction."

The plane landed and we were hustled out. The guards took off our restraints and at gunpoint ordered us to empty the plane and pack the groceries into an iron cage. When we were done the plane taxied away towards a parked helicopter.

"Get in the cage!" The guard ordered. Since he was packing a Smith and Wesson we quickly complied. We both noticed that the cage door had no lock and the guard saw us looking at the door.

"Yes boys, there is no lock; you have the choice of jumping out on the way, or descending into the Fish Tank." Off in the distance the helicopter fired up its engine. It hovered over the cage while the guard hooked a hanging cable to it. Within seconds we were airborne with the cage door swinging open and shut. It was obvious that Chester was terrified of heights. It was freezing cold, made even colder with the wind whistling through the mesh cage. Far below us a huge dome rose out of the flat frozen tundra. We could see the hole in the top that we had been told about. The helicopter hovered over the hole and we could see men just like ants far below. Chester suddenly made his choice, he leapt from the cage and hurtled down and splattered atop the dome.

I decided that I did not wish to end my life this way; I would rather take my chances in the Fish Tank. Suddenly the winch whined into action and the cage dropped deep inside the dome. At the first glance I could tell that escape was impossible. The cage hit the floor with a thud, and within seconds men were throwing me out and grabbing the cartons of groceries. It was empty in no time, and then some other men brought four bodies and bags of garbage placing them on the cage floor. They had no sooner finished than the cage rose rapidly up to the hole high above. I noticed a man clinging to the bottom of the cage. When he was about a hundred feet in the air he let go and crashed into a crumpled heap on the floor, it was an obvious suicide. Some of the cons standing around laughed and then turned their attention to me. One stepped up to me and hammered me with his closed fist. In hindsight I should have thumped him back.

"Here's another pretty flower for one of you guys," he said. From that point on everything went down hill for me. I wandered away from the centre of this gigantic cavern; the entire prison was one massive circular room. Against part of the wall, some inmates lay on their blankets. Others were curled up on the concrete floor sleeping without blankets. Many of the inmates were obviously suffering from malnutrition. I soon discovered that the strongest men in the Fish Tank claimed most of the food and blankets at the expense of the weaker ones. Food and blankets were in fact the currency of the Fish Tank.

A number of the prisoners looked terribly abused and lay beaten and cold. Over the next week, several starved to death buying the ticket to get out of the Fish Tank. It is only now that I realize how I had used and abused the weaker ones in society when I lived outside this Hellhole, how wrong I had been. It occurred to me that this terrible place was a miniature model of the world outside, where the strong and powerful control the lives of the poorer and weaker. A world where the rights of others are usurped by the greedy and done so with the suggestion that it is the right thing to do. A world where violence is an acceptable way to change opinions and gain for oneself the property of others.

I have become very weak now, having had no food since arriving. I am not likely to survive here more than a day or two longer. If I were to be granted another chance at my freedom I would live my life differently. I would respect the rights of others and their property; I would cease my meanness and become a kinder person a more generous person, a more honest person. But I realize it is too late now. I should have made the decision long ago. I hear a voice calling my name, I wearily open my eyes.

"Give me your blanket Bodine you won't be needing it anymore."

I clutch the blanket tightly to myself, I saw the wooden club coming to my head. There is agonizing pain for just a few seconds. In an instant I knew my debt to society was paid, then darkness envelopes me. I am getting out.

SHEA.

"I KNOW YOU will not believe my story Doctor. I am fully aware that it is bizarre, but I believe it to be true. I am seeking your help because no matter what I do I cannot get my head around the incident."

"Perhaps you should allow me to decide whether I believe your story or not, Mr. Danforth. I am the psychiatrist after all. Please tell me what it is that concerns you to the point that you have come to see me?"

"I recently had an experience, out on the highway, which stretches beyond the normal into the world of the unexplainable. I have no experience with spiritualism or the occult; I have never believed in ghosts and goblins. I always felt that people who did were odd. Of course I never voiced my opinions for that would be cruel. I am a placid, easygoing kind of person who has respect for the ideas and beliefs of others, but I am entitled to my own opinions. Having said that, the encounter with Shea has shaken my beliefs to the core. I have begun to wonder now if we humans can accidentally receive some kind of communication waves out of our normal range. Can we intercept the thoughts and suggestions from beings unlike ourselves? Can we be contacted by spirits of the long departed? My experience with Shea has opened a Pandora's Box of questions and doubts and I am in a state of terrible confusion. Did it really happen? Or did I have a momentary blackout and dreamed it? The physical evidence suggests the latter, but my mind insists that the encounter with Shea was real."

"As a psychiatrist, Mr. Danforth, I hear many odd stories as you can imagine. However some of the stories are real and traumatize the patient. But the imagined stories can produce the same effect. Psychiatry is not an exact science, often there is no right or wrong answer to a patient's questions and so it is my job to help the patient to understand the reasons for his or her distress. It would probably be best if you were to begin at the beginning and give me some personal background. What do you do for a living Mr. Danforth?"

"I have a very ordinary job, Doctor. I am a driver. I drive big rigs between major cities. And have for a number of years and that's why I find the incident with Shea so disconcerting. It makes me wonder should I be driving at all. I have a strong sense of responsibility toward the traveling public and momentary blackouts could spell disaster. I suppose that is the most compelling reason for my being here in your office."

"That is a commendable attitude, Mr. Danforth and that in itself suggest that you are not suffering from mental illness. If you were, you would probably have no concerns of the results of your actions. Do go on."

"It was two weeks ago Doctor. My buddy and I were instructed to haul two loads of frozen blueberries to Saskatoon. Together we loaded the palletized berries in two forty-five foot reefer trailers. We fueled up our tractors at the terminal, collected our paperwork and we were ready to go."

"What are reefers Mr. Danforth?"

"It is slang for refrigerated trailers. Any way, my buddy Hank's Freightliner is a little bit faster than my Kenworth so Hank always drives ahead. We usually run the road about two miles apart so I never hold him up. We both have radios so we are in contact, and if Hank feels like stopping to eat he pulls over and when I catch up we go and eat together. It's a system that works for us. It's the same when we need to rest, I pull in behind him and we climb into our bunks."

"Do you drive long hours between rests? What I mean, Mr. Danforth, is do you get enough sleep? A tired mind has been known to make people hallucinate. I am not for a moment suggesting that this happened to you. But it is a possibility, were you very tired when the incident that concerns you occurred?"

"No Doctor in fact it was within an hour of waking. It was morning, already daylight, around seven o clock. There were patches of ice on the road so we were driving according to conditions. I could see the top of Hank's trailer about a mile ahead and then it began. I had this very strong feeling that something was wrong in my head. It wasn't like a headache there was no pain; it felt like the thoughts of another was trying to get inside me. It was strange and powerful. At first I thought,

My God! I'm having a stroke. I pulled my foot back off the throttle and placed it on the airbrake pedal. I figured if I was indeed having a stroke, I didn't want to have it at fifty-five miles an hour. I just let the rig slow down easily. I checked for a wide spot where I could pull over without being a road hazard. The strange feeling in my head intensified. By now I didn't think it was a stroke. It was more like a warning or a premonition. I checked the dash gauges but nothing was wrong. I saw a wide spot where I pulled over to try to figure out what was happening to me.

I idled in and stopped. I pulled the button to set the parking brakes and closed my eyes. I tried to think logically. I had no chest or arm pain so I ruled out a heart attack. I spoke out loud. I had not lost the ability to speak and both my arms and legs felt fine so I ruled out stroke. And yet the powerful feeling increased. I lay my head down on the steering wheel with my eyes tightly closed. I can remember thinking, God; I hope I don't die in this tractor on a deserted highway. Then I heard Hank calling me on the radio, but I didn't answer."

"Under the circumstances, Mr. Danforth, would it not have been wise to let Hank know you were having some difficulty?"

"It did not occur to me Doctor. Whatever was going through my head had more or less taken over. Besides, what could Hank have done anyway? He might have had to go ten miles to find a place to turn around."

"What happened next, Mr. Danforth?"

"I felt compelled to lift my head from the steering wheel. I opened my eyes and that is when I first saw her."

"I do not understand. You speak as though it were a woman standing by the roadside, and yet how could there be a woman there in the middle of nowhere?"

"I told you Doctor that you would not believe me. Shea was a female wolf. The biggest wolf I have ever seen in all my travels. The wolf sat on the gravel in front of my tractor. It seemed to not fear the big idling rig. The animal was mostly black with tinges of grey around its ears. It had huge eyes that seemed to be staring up at me through the windshield; they were not angry or savage eyes, but pleading eyes. I turned the engine off and silence surrounded us. I would have thought that the killing of the engine might have spooked the wolf. I felt quite safe six feet off the ground in the cab, but I sensed no danger from the wolf below sitting on its haunches in the gravel. I had the oddest feeling it was trying to communicate with me.

With our gazes locked, I heard a voice deep inside my head. I strained to hear, and then faintly I heard the words,

"I am Shea. I am Shea."

"I just about jumped out of my seat, Doctor. Instinctively I knew the wolf was speaking to me and was telling me its name. By now I figured my mind had cracked, although I had never heard of mental illness striking so quickly. I found myself asking, is Shea your name? The voice in my head answered, and I knew it was the wolf speaking to me.

"Yes my name is Shea. Tell me your human name?"

"My mother named me Gerald." I replied mentally.

"I ask you to help me Gerald human. Do not be afraid of me; I will do you no harm."

"Even though I felt foolish at answering an animal, I responded by mentally saying how can I help you? We are of a different species; we have always feared each other."

"We are all children of the soil human; there is a common thread that runs through all living things. There is a connection between you and I, Gerald human, but until this moment you have never recognized it. You the greater part of your species are unaware that we, the children of the forest, are much more than teeth fur and feather. Wee are living, thinking beings, concerned with much the same things as you humans. We bear young, we need food to sustain us, and we need a place to live just as you do.

"So, how can I help you, Shea?" I asked again.

"By now Gerald human you will have realized that I have contacted you in a way that is highly unusual for your species. It is only of recent time that you have begun to think that species other than your own have a similar intelligence. Humans have begun to accept that Dolphins and Whales living in the domain of the sea have feelings and independent thought. We have always known this. We animals have always been able to communicate between ourselves, the one exception being the humans. You hold yourselves apart from us; you do not feel a connection between us. The history of our two species tells us that you fear and revile us, and you try to kill us without good reason."

"I have to tell you doctor, I am not an educated man, and the wolf definitely seemed to have a point. But it scares me to think that I am listening to the voice of an animal. This is such a bizarre situation, I cannot possibly tell anyone of my experience. I would sound just as crazy if I told them I saw a U.F.O. in the road."

"The wolf's voice spoke to me again from inside my head."

"Follow me Gerald human and you will see. I will not keep you long from your journey."

I grabbed my jacket and stepped down to the ground. Shea did not seem to have any fear of me, and strangely I had none of her. The wolf loped across the meadow, and I followed as quickly as I could. She turned several times to see if I was following. I remember thinking at the time that no one would ever believe this; they would think I had been on drugs or drink. I followed Shea into a large clump of trees. There I received the shock of my life. All manner of wildlife sat in a circle and Shea led me to the middle of them. Predator and prey sat quietly looking at me with no apparent animosity toward me or each other. Then the wolf spoke again.

"Children of the forest. This is Gerald human. He has come to hear our united voice. Gerald human I have chosen you to hear us, and to take our message out to the human world. We, the children of the forest and field, have come to this gathering place in peace and harmony, so that you may understand without any doubt that we can communicate between ourselves. The fact that you are here tells you that we can communicate with humankind. Many times we have tried to tell the humans of the damage they are inflicting on the earth and how it adversely affects us. Our attempts to communicate have always been blocked out. We have chosen you, Gerald human, as our spokesperson."

The wolf looked around, and the assembled animals nodded agreement.

"I said I would not keep you from your journey for very long Gerald human and I will be true to my word, but on behalf of the assembled company, I ask if you will tell the other humans to respect us and tell them that the animals of the field and forest can communicate with them if they will only accept the concept."

"Doctor. I couldn't believe it when I heard myself saying that I would. Me! A transport driver becoming the spokesperson for the animal kingdom? It was ridiculous and yet I said it."

Shea led me out of the circle and out of the trees to my waiting rig. I climbed up into my cab and the wolf sat watching me. I heard her voice inside my head again.

"We are depending on you Gerald human. You are now our voice in the human world."

She turned and loped off across the field to the trees. She was a magnificent animal. I watched her until she reached the trees then she turned and looked back at me.

My head had cleared and I could only hear the sound of the wind whistling round the tractor. Then I heard the radio came to life.

"Breaker. Breaker. Gerry, what's your 10 20. Have you hit the ditch? Over"

"The 10 20 is code for what is your location, Doctor. I picked up the mike and said no I had just pulled over and had been out of the cab for a few minutes. I could not tell him what had just occurred. Nor have I been able to tell anyone else since. That is why I am here talking to you, Doctor. If I am to believe what I have told you, and I think I do, I have a huge responsibility on my shoulders. But should I carry out that responsibility, the world might think me a madman. Should I fail in my responsibility, I may have missed the greatest opportunity humans have ever known to understand and listen to the wisdom of the other beings inhabiting the world."

"As a psychiatrist, Mr. Danforth, my job is to separate fact from fiction. The fact is you stopped by the roadside maybe because you were tired. Possibly an overactive imagination temporarily took over your mind. My suggestion to you is that you to try to forget the incident and get on with your life. I do not think for a moment you are suffering from a mental condition of any kind. You just had a vivid dream. Good day."

I left his office unconvinced. I knew Shea had spoken to me. I know that I went with her to the circle of animals within the trees. On the way back from Saskatoon I had stopped at the place where I had parked before. I saw both of our tracks in the thin layer of snow, coming and going to the trees. There was no way the psychiatrist could explain this away as a dream or a momentary blackout, the tracks were real, not imagined. Shea was real. And so was the quest she had given me.

I had no idea where I should begin. I am a trucker, not a philosopher or great orator. As I drove along toward home base, I remembered Dan Littletree. Dan worked on the truck terminal dock loading and unloading trailers. He was a quiet individual, friendly when spoken to, but mostly he did his work without any fuss and his loads were well put together, never shifting out on the road. Dan was a First Nations man who had left his reserve years earlier to come to the city to work. He had short braids of jet-black hair and dark eyes to match. He had a square jaw that had received its share of punches from racist whites over the years. So far as I could tell, Dan held no grudges for the occasional discrimination he encountered, he seemed to accept that such behaviour was just a part of life.

This of course is my interpretation of Dan. It was entirely possible that he harboured deep resentment but kept it to himself. I knew that First Nations people had a different approach to nature than we whites, so I decided when I got back to base I would take Dan aside and discuss with him my encounter with Shea. I had a feeling that Dan would not think me a fool, even if he did not understand what I had to say.

My backhaul was frozen meat and after I had delivered it, I dropped my trailer at the terminal and went to look for Dan. I found him in a trailer, building a general cargo load bound for Winnipeg.

"Hey Dan how's it going?" I yelled in greeting. He looked at me and grinned recognition. "I know you are busy right now Dan, but there is something I need to talk to you about. Can I buy you a coffee when it is your break time?"

"Sure Gerry. I'll see you in the lunchroom in fifteen minutes."

When Dan came in for his break I found it hard to begin telling him about Shea, so I began by asking him some questions.

"Have you ever heard about people communicating with animals Dan?" He looked at me oddly but didn't answer. "I don't mean chatting with a dog or a horse, we all do that, but communicating with the animals of the forest. Wild animals that we don't often come into contact with?" Dan sipped his coffee and looked at me.

"Why do you ask me these things Gerry?"

"You are a First Nations man Dan, and I believe your culture has a better understanding of the secrets of nature, than those of us who have come to live in your ancestral lands. On my last trip to Saskatoon, I had an unusual experience that I do not fully understand." I took a deep breath and said. "I met a wolf. She was a large black wolf with tinges of grey around her ears and she spoke to me."

I stopped talking to see his reaction. His eyes narrowed, but he remained tight lipped. I thought he might have laughed at me, but he didn't and I was encouraged. I told him everything that had happened out on that lonely stretch of highway. He listened without interruption.

"Do you think I am crazy, Dan? Could I have been hallucinating?"

"No Gerry. I don't think you are crazy. I have some distant and unclear memories of my grandfather speaking of such things. But as you know our culture has suffered grievous harm and loss over the last 100 years. A lot of the old beliefs and practices have been virtually lost. My people were very close to the rhythms of nature back then but I have little knowledge of such things; I have become an urban Indian. There is not enough time to properly deal with your revelations Gerry; I have to get back to work. But I will tell you what I will do. If you want to come with me to the reserve on the weekend, I will take you to see some of our elders."

Dan Littletree and I arranged to meet real early on Saturday morning when we would take my car and travel north. We arrived at his reserve around noon and we immediately went to see an elder named Annie Crowfeather. Annie was old her face heavily wrinkled. Despite her advancing years, she insisted that she cook and we eat with her before beginning to talk. Over a mug of a special tea she had prepared, I began to relate my story of meeting and talking with Shea.

Annie listened carefully and respectfully to me and by watching her face I knew I had struck a hidden chord in her memory.

"There was a time, Gerry, when our people knew of such things. The children of the forest were respected and revered. Both they and our people knew that some of them must give their lives to sustain us in the winter months. We asked their permission to take one or two of them for our food and we thanked them for giving us their lives. I have been told that there was a form of communication between us. The children of the forest went about their business just as we did, living free, raising their young, and dealing with the seasons. Sadly our way of living has been disrupted. Many of the old ways have been lost.

I believe your story of speaking with Shea, Gerry. For as I speak, long hidden memories of talk of a huge she wolf, black with silvery ears comes to mind. I believe it was said that this wolf was the leader of the forest animals and birds. She was wise and gave good advice to them. She taught them how to hide and blend in for safety from the peoples from afar who wanted only their skins, fur and feathers. You said her name was Shea. Gerry?"

"Yes. That is the name she gave me when she first called to me on the highway."

"Let's go together to see Michael Running bear. He is almost a hundred years old now but he is still sharp and wise. I will ask him if the name Shea means anything to him."

We rode in my car to an old log building that stood alone among some Aspens. Michael shared the cabin with his daughter now an elder herself. He sat in a high-backed chair with a blanket over his knees. The furrows in his face were like a ploughed field, and his hair was reduced to a few grey wisps. Annie approached him and asked,

"Does the name Shea mean anything to you Michael?" His eyes opened wide.

"Shea is the leader of the forest people! I have not heard the word Shea, since I was a child. Why do you ask about her now?"

A shiver ran down my spine. The evidence that I had both seen and spoken with Shea was conclusive. Shea, had chosen me to represent the animals and birds and I felt deeply honoured. But I still did not know how to bring what I knew to the human world. I thought that driving a big rig was a heavy responsibility, but it was miniscule compared to what I knew I now must do. I knew there would be massive opposition from all sides to the concept of birds and wildlife with thoughts and feelings. There was the fur industry, wildlife management, game farming, just to name a few. These groups had financial resources I could never dream of. I had a feeling that I would be laughed off the stage the first time I made a speech. I felt that Shea had made the wrong choice in me. But again, maybe she hadn't. I believed her, where most would not have. Somehow Shea had known that. It added strength to my resolve. I would do my utmost to be the voice of the forest inhabitants.

We said goodbye to Michael Running bear, dropped Annie Crowfeather off at her house and started on the trip back to the city. Dan Littletree sat silently in the passenger seat. He had little to say. It was obvious to me; this morning's events had shaken him to the core. He was torn between the culture he had chosen to follow and the one to which he was inextricably tied. I found myself torn between the culture I had always known and the one I had come to know only this morning.

We were traveling south. Suddenly a motorist pulled out to pass from behind a tanker truck. We hit each other head on at high speed. I knew I was dead. Dan and I walked together out of a dark tunnel into brilliant light. Death had been painless it had come so quickly. But I did have one regret. I could not carry out the quest that Shea had set me. She had placed her faith in me to bring our people and the children of the forest closer together. I had failed her due to the careless act of a fellow human.

THE IMMIGRANT CHILD

I was not put on this ship of my own free will.
I did not choose to have both my parents die.
I did not choose to be here in this place.
I had no say in the choosing of my guardians.
I have no choice other than to stay where I am bid.
I have no knowledge of what happened to my siblings.

I CAN REMEMBER vividly the times I wrote each of those lines, even though it was so long ago. Time itself has a way of healing the wounds of the past. Perhaps healing is the wrong word to use, for in reality the wounds never fully heal, there is always a scar to remind one of them. As an adult, I am pretty well over the injustices of my childhood, indeed for not to, would have meant a life of misery. I am a man who has found a measure of happiness despite my harsh beginnings. I have become a writer of note. I have a deep well of resources within me to draw upon. I say I have become a writer, in retrospect I have always been a writer. It began the day the authorities herded me aboard the children's emigrant ship. I can recall clearly finding a pencil and a sheet of paper and writing the words,

"I was not put aboard this ship of my own free will."

The words were a silent protest over events of which I had no control. I kept my sheet of paper and added other memories to it. What had started as the silent protest of an orphan child became an obsession to record my triumphs, tribulations, my rare joys and deep emotional feelings. Paper was very difficult for me to come by, so I learned very early to write in exceedingly small print. I could squeeze five of my own lines into one of regular lined paper. I kept every piece of paper that I wrote on, right through to adulthood. I suppose one could say it was a diary of sorts, but it was a diary with a difference.

I stopped writing when I gained my freedom from my guardians at the age of twenty-one. But I did not destroy the mass of loose papers that represented my life thus far. I kept them in the bottom of my suitcase, where they lay undisturbed until I was thirty-five. I was living in Vancouver at the time and I had a chance meeting with a man who claimed to be a writer. In the course of our conversation, I happened to mention my own almost forgotten writings. His eyes opened wide.

"Do you know what you have there my friend?" He asked. "You have all the resources and research for a fact based novel."

I thought deeply about what the man had said. And over the next few weeks I mulled over the seed of an idea he had planted in my mind. I had never married. The battered ego I had gained in my younger days never really recovered and so I tended not to seek the company of women. This meant of course that I had plenty of time to write undisturbed after my job as a helper on one of the city's garbage trucks.

I retrieved all the papers with the miniscule writing from the lining of my suitcase. I could hardly believe how small the words were that I had written so long ago, and I knew I would have to buy a big magnifying glass. I also had found out that if a publisher were to read the re-write of my experiences, I would have to learn to type. I went out and bought a used Underwood machine. It seemed very complicated and I quickly found out that a single simple mistake meant throwing out the entire page and starting over. Rather than begin my story under these learning conditions I practiced by copying the pages out of books and magazines. It was well over a year of practicing before I felt confident enough to begin my own work. I began with my earliest memories.

I was the second child in the March family, my parents called me Winston. I had an older brother named Ryan. Eventually a sister came along and our parents named her Caroline. We lived in England in an industrial area of filth, smog-laden streets and all around poverty, although I have to say we children never felt poor. Our parents provided tolerably well for us; they both worked in the mills and so while we were often alone as children, we were well fed and taken care of. Ryan always had the job of being our protector when our parents were at work and he and I developed a special affinity for each other. We both loved little

Caroline although we didn't really understand why she didn't like playing tin can football or cowboys and Indians with us in the narrow back streets.

Mother got the sickness first. She became very thin, coughing terribly; sometimes blood came up from her lungs. Dad took care of her when he was home from the mill and we children did what we could when he was away. We had no idea of the seriousness of mother's complaint and we were shocked beyond all belief when dad told us she had died in the night.

We all followed the funeral cart to the cemetery where they put mother in a big hole in the ground and covered her coffin with soil. I had never seen dad cry before and it set us all off. Dad never fully recovered from mother's death and it wasn't long before he too began to cough like she had. When he became too ill to work, some people came to the house and took him away. Other people took us to a place they called an orphanage. We didn't like it there. Ryan, Caroline and I were separated into different parts of it. One day one of our keepers came and told me my dad had died.

"You are an orphan now," they said.

It wasn't long after that when the orphanage people put a big label on my jacket. Ryan and Caroline and I with a large group of other children, were marched down to the docks and put aboard a big ship. The only thing they told us was that we were going to loving homes in Canada. I didn't know what or where Canada was and I didn't like being on a ship surrounded by water. I remember I was afraid of the water and stayed back from the ship's rails. It was the first night aboard that ship that I wrote my first line.

"I was not put on this ship of my own free will"

It seemed appropriate that those few words should be the start of my story.

Obviously I cannot tell you the story in its entirety; you will have to buy the book if you want to know every detail. But I will be as brief as possible and give you the general outline, a sort of verbal synopsis. We were fed decent food on the ship, but that was a short-lived pleasure. After I don't know how many days, we were removed from the ship in a place called Montreal. The last time I saw my sister Caroline, she was on the dock, crying. The stern faced woman in charge of my group refused to let me go to comfort her

"Stay in line Brat." She said to me. I will never forget her; she seemed like a messenger from Hell and the memory of her harshness is seared into my mind.

Ryan stood away from me with a group of older boys and he gave me a final wave goodbye as his group was marched away. I never saw my brother again. The group of girls containing Caroline were all crying loudly, as they too were marched like cattle to the slaughterhouse away from their siblings. Children do not necessarily understand death, but I remember desperately wanting to be wherever mum and dad were at that moment. Then it was time for my group of younger boys to be herded off the docks to a waiting train. The stern faced woman was in charge of us but she gave us no comfort, we were simply human livestock. At nightfall we were all given a cheese sandwich, which I remember was all dried out around the edges. At a station far down the line, I and four other boys were removed from the train and handed over to another equally stern faced businesslike woman. She looked at the label on my jacket,

"You will be going to the Fritz farm. You had best mind your manners and do the work assigned to you. I will come out to the farm in a year's time to see how you are doing. The woman grabbed my shoulder and pushed me toward a couple dressed in rough durable garments that I assumed to be farm clothing.

"This is Winston March, Mr. and Mrs. Fritz, see that he gets some schooling and religious instruction."

Dieter Fritz said nothing to me, but pointed to a farm wagon. He climbed onto the seat and Hilda Fritz joined him. They had no words of welcome or even words of explanation. I sat in silence, looking at their backs, until we reached the place where I was to spend my life until I became twenty-one years of age and had the freedom to leave.

I won't go into any great detail about my life there at the Fritz farm; suffice it to say that the first year of adjustment was very difficult for me. I secretly managed to continue with my recording the daily events of my life. The Fritzes were very religious and I was drawn in to their particular style of worship. I cannot recall love of any sort being a part of it; mostly it was about Hell fire and damnation. I was expected even at my tender age, to become a farm labourer doing heavy manual labour. The Fritz's had consequences for non compliance, some times it might be a strapping with a length of harness, at others denial of a meal or two. In retrospect I don't think the Fritz's were evil, they just didn't have a clue about the needs and wants of children.

I remember at the end of my first year with them, they received a note saying the orphan placement inspector would be coming by the following week. They took me into town and had my hair cut, and bought me some better fitting clothes. On the day the inspector came by, she found me at the kitchen table washed, scrubbed, working with some exercise books a bible in front of me. She left with the erroneous assumption that all was well with me at the Fritz farm. It was an annual charade that continued until I reached the age of twelve years.

Then as far as the orphan placement agency was concerned they were finished with me. But unfortunately I was not finished with them. I was obliged to work for the Fritz's until I reached the age of twenty-one as my repayment to them for my upbringing and education. They were supposed, under the contract, to give me some small remuneration each year, but Mr. Fritz said he would hang on to it for me until the end of the contract.

I found it difficult to obtain writing paper during those years of labour with no pay, but when I did school work I was able to get a few sheets out of my exercise books unnoticed. As my twenty-first birthday approached, Mr. Fritz tried to talk me into staying on at the farm. I knew I had been an invaluable source of cheap labour for him.

But nothing on earth would have made me stay. I have to be fair about it; Mr. Fritz did give me the money I was owed and I walked off his farm for the last time. There was a whole new world out there. I was twenty-one and I wanted to see it. All of it.

Work was plentiful in those years and I traveled doing short-term jobs then moving on. Finally I ended up in Vancouver working on a garbage truck. One day as I was looking through the handwritten account of my early years, I began to wonder if I might be able to find out what had happened to Caroline and Ryan. Any knowledge of them had ended on the Montreal dock nearly twenty years ago. I was thirty now and Ryan would be thirty-four and Caroline would be twenty-seven. I tried for months but I found doors slammed in my face every time I made inquiries. The secrets of the orphanage children, it appeared, were intended to remain secret.

But I digress. I went to work on my story day-by-day adding more pages, until there were two hundred and fifty pages of materiel neatly typed and ready for a publisher to read. I contacted the fellow I told you about, Bob Reimer, the man who made the suggestion that I write the story in the first place. He gave me the name of an editor with a book publishing company. I wrote to him. But in his reply he said personal stories like mine were a dime a dozen. I was crushed. I had worked so long on the project and to have the work rejected without him even so much as glancing at it really hurt my already damaged ego. Bob said,

"Look Winston. If you really believe your work is good and worth reading, take the manuscript to his office and slap it down on his desk in front of him. He can either have you thrown out of his office, or open the work and read the first page. What have you got to lose, he has already hurt your feelings he can't do it twice?"

I thought about it for a few days as my anger rose. Finally doing as Bob had suggested. I went down to the publishing company and asked to see Frank Moore. I had to wait a while to see him and when I entered his office I slapped the manuscript down in front of him. He seemed shocked.

"This is not a dime a dozen story, Mr. Moore. Open it!" I demanded. To cut to the chase, he began to read it and he kept on reading it. After looking through several pages he raised his eyes and said,

"You are right Mr. March. This is not a dime a dozen story; however I must say that your approach is highly unusual. Leave the manuscript with me and I will be in touch shortly.

Within six months The Immigrant Child was on the bookshelves in stores clear across the country. I received many letters from people who had similar experiences some of whom were transported on the same ship as me. Then one day I received a letter that turned my life completely around.

Dear Winston, At last I have found you. I bought the book The Immigrant Child and I knew after the first page it really was you, my always-beloved brother. I have searched for you for a number of years but always came to a dead end. I am married now with two small children. When I read to them at bedtime I always think of you and how you would try your best to read to me. Life has been hard for both of us; your book tells me this. I have some sad news to impart though. I found that our brother Ryan ended his life at his own hand. I was able to obtain a copy of the coroners report. According to his friend, Ryan constantly failed in his quest to find us, and he became so despondent he chose not to continue living. Please come to see my family and I as quickly as you can? Caroline.

I went the same day and bought a ticket on the evening train bound for Winnipeg. I sent Caroline a telegram telling when I would arrive. I could not sleep on the journey; my heart was bursting with joy and anticipation. There was no mistaking Caroline as she waited for me with her children. She was crying, just as she was the very last time I saw her on the dock in Montreal. We clung to each other like shipwrecked sailors. We must have been in a clinch for five tearful minutes. We did not speak; our mingling tears said all that needed to be said. Finally we separated and Caroline placed her little daughter in my arms.

"This is baby Caroline. And this is my son Winston March Abercrombie. Meet my husband Brian."

And so you see that my life has changed. Holding my sister in my arms was the first time I have been close to a woman since my mother last held me. It was a revelation for me. I am no longer afraid of women and soon I will marry Janice. The Immigrant Child has after all these years found love again.

"Don't forget! Buy the book if you want to know all the details. You will find it on the best seller's shelf at any bookstore."

THE ARMCHAIR.

In appearance it was no different than a thousand other armchairs of its type. Thickly upholstered arms, with a wide soft seat and back and standing on four stubby feet. But this was a chair with a history; this was the chair that would lead to my ultimate downfall in the eyes of society. This was the chair responsible for putting me in this dreadful place.

The cell door slams shut and I hear the guard locking it from the outside. I look around the dreary cell and see another prisoner lying on the bottom bunk. I decided that since we were to be close companions for God knows how long, I should speak to him.

"Since we are to be here in this cell together for a long time, I should introduce myself. My full name is Antonio Luigi Dipalma. But everyone calls me Tony. I am here because of a great miscarriage of justice. I am not the kind of person I was portrayed to be in the court that sentenced me. Twenty years! I am given twenty damn years for something I didn't do, nor had any knowledge of. The justice system was out for blood, anybody's; mine was the blood they chose to spill.

I have heard that almost everyone coming to prison claims to be innocent of the crimes they are sent here for. I would suppose it is a form of denial brought on by the shock of actually being here. But in my case it is not a denial of that nature, it is a real and genuine denial of any kind of guilt. I have led the life of a good citizen; I have hurt no one; I did my job proudly and well until the day the police came to arrest me."

"So why don't you tell me about it?" The inmate said rather curtly.

"You might well ask what happened to me. Since you are to be my cellmate, you might as well know the whole story. Who knows? You may be the only person to actually believe me.

It all began with a phone call from my local Freemont police office. They said they had been trying to trace me and was I Antonio Luigi Dipalma. I told the officer that I was indeed he. You have a brother by the name of Marcel Dipalma? He asked. Yes. I told him. But I haven't seen Marcel for a number of years; we had sort of drifted apart after dad died." The officer said,

"The San Francisco police have the body of a Marcel Dipalma in their morgue, we have been asked to inform the next of kin. His building manager discovered his body and they are investigating the circumstances of his death to see if it was from natural causes, or if foul play was involved. They want to know if you can please go to positively identify the body." I was shocked for a few moments, then I said,

"Yes I could go to the S.F.P.D. morgue. If I jump on the Bay Area Rapid Transit train I can be there this afternoon." He thanked me and offered condolences for my loss.

They pulled Marcel's body out of the refrigerated cabinet on a long tray. He had aged since I had seen him last but there was no doubt it was he. I signed a proof of I.D. and they handed me an envelope with the things they had found on his body. They asked me about disposal of the body and would I take the responsibility. I was surprised; I had not thought about such things, but we had no other relative to handle it, so I agreed.

I looked in the yellow pages and chose a funeral home with a small ad; I thought they might cost less than the ones with full pages. They tried to sell me all kinds of crap, but I told them I wanted a simple cremation and no fancy service. It was not as if Marcel and I had been close. Thinking back even as kids we were distant and had different agendas. I took the B.A.R.T. to Oakland and to the address the cops had given me for his apartment.

I checked with the manager and explained who I was. I had the apartment key from the envelope, so I let myself in. It surprised me. Somehow I thought that Marcel would have had nice furniture, but it was just ordinary. A gigantic armchair dominated the room. The chair was aimed at a medium sized television set in one corner and a well-worn sofa lay along the wall. Next to it a smoker stand, still full of stinking butts, leaned against the sofa arm. On the coffee table, a pizza smeared plate shared space with three empty beer cans and last week's newspaper.

I walked into his bedroom. The bed was unmade and the dresser drawers were partly open with socks and underwear hanging out. A table lamp sat atop a small filing cabinet. This is what I wanted to find. If I were to take care of Marcel's affairs I needed pertinent information. I removed the file folders and took them into the living room I sat in the big armchair where began leafing through them.

It appeared Marcel had a car parked under the apartment block, a Buick according to the service papers. I found a small life insurance policy; if the premiums had been kept up to date it would cover the cost of his cremation. There was a simple hand written will. Marcel apparently wanted me to have his car, the television and the big armchair. For some reason the word armchair was underlined.

I almost missed it by throwing it out with the other junk papers but I found there was a sealed envelope with my name on it. It read,

Dear Antonio. I presume if you are reading this I will already have passed on. There is a lot about me you do not know. We never did see eye to eye on anything, so I never told you about myself, or what I was doing. I have known for some time that I would not live to a ripe old age and I didn't even want to share that with you. By the way I hope you are sitting in my big chair as you read this letter. Several years ago I was involved in criminal activities. To be more specific, I was an accomplished cat burglar. I made a fair living at the expense of my victims. It may sound like I am proud of my career of crime but that is not the case. As I approach the end of my life I have sincere regrets, but alas I cannot make amends.

But to get to the seat of the matter, I want to tell you about how one night an incredible opportunity came my way. Quite by coincidence I discovered that I had entered a hotel with a jewelry fabricators convention happening. Someone inadvertently had left the safe unlocked. I scooped everything up, and left as quietly as I had come in. Back at home seated in my big chair, I looked at my haul. I could not believe the value of the score I had made.

According to the next day's papers, I had pulled off the biggest value heist in the history of the country. They also said that almost all of the gems were identifiable. I began to get scared. There was no way I could take them to my usual buyer. This stuff was so hot; the city was crawling with detectives looking for a lead. I could not sell them, and I certainly couldn't take them back. I had only one option I would have to ditch them.

I could not bring myself to just discard them they were priceless and irreplaceable. I sat in my chair and tried to think of a place where I could hide them, a place where if the police suspected me, after searching everywhere, they would not find them. Since I had already a reputation as a burglary suspect, they did come several times and search my apartment as I sat in my chair and watched them. Of course they left empty handed, and it was two years before they gave up and left me alone. The stuff remains sitting hidden today, I have never ever taken it from the hiding place since the day I hid it. I am truly sorry Antonio that you were the one I had to unburden myself to, and despite what you have learned I hope you will think kindly of me as you sit in the chair. After using it for a while you will realize how comfortable the chair really is. Yours, Marcel.

I read the letter several times. It was hard to accept that my own brother was a criminal. Both of our parents would have been terribly ashamed of him had they known of his criminal activity. I locked up the apartment and went down to the parking garage, where I found the Buick. It was a nice one, two tone green, almost new. I drove to the funeral home and finalized the arrangements. When I got home I arranged to have the chair and T.V. delivered to my place and then I called the charity people and told them to clean out the rest of the stuff from Marcel's apartment. After the cremation I collected from his life insurance, and my life was starting to get back to normal.

I pulled out his letter one day and read it over and over. I had a feeling Marcel was trying to tell me something. Then it struck me! The chair, he kept referring to the damn chair. I turned it over, it was just a normal chair, nothing different about it. Since it really didn't fit my décor and I had only brought it home because he had specifically requested it, I decided to pull it apart. With my big kitchen knife I made a cut in the upholstery on the seat back. I slashed it along the top and down both sides and pulled down the cloth like a flap. I tore out the stuffing, and that was when I saw the metal box fastened inside the wooden frame. I found my screwdriver and removed the box. I could hardly believe my eyes at the gems inside. I thought to myself. Now what? They do not belong to me nor do I want them. Like Marcel, I became scared. Just holding the box scared me. I took the box and hid it under my mattress, and then I struggled out to the trash with the wrecked chair. The truck wouldn't pick it up until Thursday but I didn't care, I wanted it out of my house.

I agonized for more than two weeks over what to do about the gems, they were not mine. Finally I decided they would have to be returned to their rightful owners. I thought it best if I had the police come here, then I could explain in the comfort of my own home. I called the Freemont police department and told them that I had found some jewels that I believed were stolen property. It was only minutes later when my front door crashed into the house, and the cops were all over me. In seconds I was lying on the floor in restraints. They asked where the jewels were, and I told them they were under my mattress.

Before I could tell them any thing, I was hurled into a paddy wagon and whisked off to the Freemont lockup. An hour later the San Francisco P.D. were interrogating me. No one would believe a word I said. They charged me with grand theft and set a date for a trial. No matter how many times I told them about the chair, they didn't believe me.

There is no evidence the chair existed they said. I told them about the letter and they said produce it. But I had discarded it the same day as the chair

The district attorney told the jury that I had been the jewel thief and that I had concealed both my involvement in the burglary and the jewels, until my conscience could no longer deal with the enormity of my crime. So the judge sentenced me to twenty years in the penitentiary. And that's my story, so what is your name and what are you in here for?"

"You sure yap on a lot for someone who has just moved into my space. You will get to know my name soon enough greenhorn. I'm serving life for murder if it is any of your goddamn business. The top bunk is yours, don't talk to me or disturb me or you will wind up looking like a plate of hamburger. Just so that you know, I don't believe your goddamn story either.

THE STAIRWAY.

I SPEAK SOFTLY of the stairway for there are few that would believe of its existence. Even fewer who might believe I discovered it and saw the stairs with my own eyes. I had always laughed at stories of the occult and goblins and such, believing them to be the product of over active imaginations or a reason to control others through fear. Having discovered the stairway for myself, I have been obliged to change my mind.

I have no idea how I came to be the one to learn of and witness the stairway's existence and the horrors contained therein. It is possible, even likely that there are others. I am not by any means a man devoted to any religious sect. There are so many of them, each with conflicting views of historical events or legends that I tend to discount all of them as a result. But now, there is no doubt in my mind of the powers of evil. The stairway has compelled me to both believe and fear them. In a world filled with checks and balances, I am now grasping for an acceptance of an opposite to the forces of evil. Surely there must be one? But I digress, hear me out and let me tell you about the stairway.

The story began innocently enough in an old and seedy part of New York, an area long past its heyday, an area of crumbling brick buildings where the poorest of the poor lived, an area of high crime and low morals. I went into the area on business for my employer a moneylender. I don't remember the particular case at the moment; there were so many and it was my job to shake down the ones behind in their payments.

Even though I had been in the area many times in the past, I had never noticed the small bookstore on the corner of Roberts and Madson St. The sign over the window had almost weathered away and it blended in with the old brownstone house it sat beneath.

The letters of the sign, once proudly displayed in gold leaf, were now barely readable, the gold swept away by many seasons of neglect. I wondered how on earth a bookstore could survive here given the pitiful economics of the area, unless they sold comic books or dealt in illicit substances using the bookstore as a cover.

My curiosity got the better of me. I have always been an avid reader and I thought that if the bookstore was for real, they might just have something different than the run of the mill bookstores on Staten Island.

I paused to look in the window; a row of books lay in an odd method of display, dust covered, and looking like they had not been disturbed in years. There were no new titles, no shiny colourful dust jackets, in fact no real invitation at all to enter the store and browse. But my curiosity was aroused so I pressed down the latch and pushed the heavy door inwards. The unmistakable smell of musty paper and backing glue hit me full in the face. The blast of odourous air was cold, much colder than the air in the street, which was odd, for it was a late October day.

A bell on a metal spring jangled annoyingly with the opening of the door then jangled again as I closed it behind me. No lights were on and my eyes struggled to see in the semi darkness. As they adjusted to the dim interior I could see bookshelves around the walls and a row of shelves in the centre with books on either side. A small counter lit only by the light filtering through the dust-laden window sat near a door at the rear of the store.

It appeared that I was alone. I assumed the bell would have alerted the owner that he had a prospective customer, so as I waited I began to scan some of the titles. None of the ones I looked at were familiar to me, and the books appeared to be very old. The sound of the scraping of un-oiled hinges, on the door at the rear of the shop startled me, the figure of a man stepped into the store. Once again I felt the icy blast of cold air. My immediate thought was that he must have been working in the back yard and left the outside door open.

I looked at the man's face. In the dim light he had a look of the essence of wickedness, his eyes were narrow and piercing under bushy brows that came to a point. His nose was hooked and resided over thin lips shaped in the form of a snarl. On his head a cap pulled well forward suggested that he was hiding something under it. As his thin lips formed the words,

"Can I help you?" They revealed teeth that were dull grey and appeared sharply pointed. I felt a great feeling of uneasiness, a foreboding, a sense of evil in the air, but nothing to base my ill feelings on. In my work I often found myself in a position of some danger of assault from irate and intoxicated deep in debt clients, but this was different, this was a feeling I could not explain.

"I just stepped in to have a look around." I answered. He did not reply but with an odd flourish of his gloved hand suggested that I look over the shelves. I began to examine several of the books but they all dealt with matters of the occult. Meanwhile I could feel the piercing gaze of the storeowner upon me. I did not need to look for I knew he could see right into me. Uneasily I moved to another shelf and removed a book, his gaze never leaving me for an instant. I had become quite uncomfortable so without looking at the book and needing an excuse to leave, I said,

"I will take this one. How much?" In a deep grating voice he said,

"There is no charge. Take it home and if you don't like it, bring it back and I will replace it for you."

"I cannot expect to come in and get a free book the first time in your store. How much?"

"Take it. There is no charge." His commanding voice took me by surprise and I felt exceedingly uncomfortable, almost a mild fear. It didn't make sense but the feeling was very real, so gripping the book I gladly left the store. Out on the street I felt an intense feeling of relief. I immediately began to question my feelings as they did not seem logical. The fact was, the storeowner had given me the gift of a free book. I should have been feeling gratitude. I slipped the book into my briefcase not looking at it until I was home at day's end.

The book's cover had a coating of heavy dust. Edges of the gold leaf pages were grey with years of accumulation. I wiped it clean and sat down to see what I had grabbed in my haste to get out of the odd bookstore. It had a fine maroon leather cover, embossed with black letters that I did not recognize. Now I wondered if in my haste I had chosen a foreign language book. The inside pages had pictures of devils, goblins, acts of bestiality, vampires and other occult matters. Like I said earlier, I did not believe in such things, but this compilation fascinated me even though I could not understand the text.

I returned the book to my briefcase deciding I would take up the offer of a replacement, next time I was in the area, for one that I could read. Three weeks later I found myself on Madson Street, and remembered the book in the bottom of my case. The store looked as though no one had been through the door since I was last there. The same annoying bell clanged as I entered and closed the door behind me. There was again the same sensation of coldness and foreboding as I waited for the proprietor to come in from the back. The squawk of dry hinges announced his entry. As before, he had a look of utter evil on his face, but I quickly told myself that the man couldn't help how he looked and that I was being discriminatory in thinking that way.

"You have returned Mr. Moore. I knew you would," he said icily.

"How do you know my name? I never disclosed it to you."

"I know much more about you, Mr. Moore, than you think. You live on Staten Island, you work for the City Finance Company as a collector and you are a non believer in either the forces of good, or its counterpart."

"How do you know these things about me?"

"I make it my business, Mr. Moore, to know many things about many people. It is my quest to reap the fallen and the ones about to fall, into my domain."

"I do not understand sir. Who are you and what has any of this to do with me. I just came in to buy a book?"

"I knew you would come in, Mr. Moore. I arranged it. As for my name it does not matter. I am a servant of Lucifer. The books all around you are literature of praise for him and his ideals. You have come to the stairway entrance that leads to his seat of power. Allow me to show you."

He opened the door wide revealing a long stairway descending deep into the earth under the store. Burning torches hung on either side of the walls. The stairway was so long and steep that it narrowed until it disappeared, much as looking down a long section of railway track. Just for a moment I thought I heard the screams of the damned from very deep down the stairway.

"This stairway, Mr. Moore, is one of many, where the spirits of darkness come up to enter into the upper world to go about their business of reaping the fallen and falling.

Come, I will show you the rewards you can expect to receive if you come to Lucifer's side. Since you are not committed to either Lucifer or his counterpart he is giving you the opportunity of a preview so that you can make up your mind which way you want to go."

I had no inclination to go down this stairway but I found myself following, much afraid, but unable to stop myself. It was as if invisible hands were drawing me along. As I followed down the stairway, I happened to glance at the dust-laden steps where his feet had just been. The prints were of cloven hooves. I did not understand how such a thing could be. Momentarily I stopped and turned to look at my own footprints and the cleats on my shoes were visible in the dust. I quickly glanced at his feet. There were shoes on them but hair such as on a sheep or goat showed under his trouser cuffs. We stopped at a window in the wall many hundreds of steps below the bookstore. In a chamber of rock, lit by flaming torches, hundreds of bodies writhed in a multitude of agonies in a pit below a chair. A naked yellow goblin, with a face of utter vileness, such as I had seen in the book I had taken home, sat high above them presiding over their torture.

"Such a position can be yours if you swear allegiance to Lucifer, Mr. Moore. You could have a position presiding over the fallen."

"I would never seek such a position. Why do you even suggest it?"

"Do you not exercise your power over the debtors to your employer now? Do you not gain pleasure from their suffering? Sign Lucifer's contract and he will guarantee you such a position for all eternity.

"No! I do not enjoy the suffering and poverty of my employer's clients. I just do my job. No more, no less."

"It is surely just a matter of degree, Mr. Moore. The goblin before you is doing just that of which you speak. Come, let me show you a different view." I could feel the heat rising as we descended deeper into the earth. He showed me several more horrific scenes making the same offer of immunity from suffering if only I would agree to become Lucifer's servant. My heart was filled with fear at the horrors I had witnessed on the stairway. I knew I had to get away.

I turned and ran up the stairway, step after step, with my lungs bursting for air, my heart pounding as though it might burst inside my chest. After what seemed like an eternity I saw the door to the store up above me. I leapt over the last step into the store and found him waiting for me. I had no idea how he had gotten here before me, or why he wasn't out of breath like me. He placed a contract and a pen before me.

"All you have to do is sign here, Mr. Moore." I took the pen hurling it across the room and fled out of the store into the clean autumn air. Safely across the street, I turned to take a final look at the bookshop that housed the stairway to Hell. The bookstore was not there. A simple brownstone house sat on the corner identical to all the others on the block. I felt my head; it was still soaked in sweat, my clothes were cold and clammy as I came out into the cold. I was panting from racing up hundreds of steps. I pinched my wrist as hard as I could to make sure I was not having a bad dream. A new bolt of fear struck me as I realized that I was wide awake and fully conscious. I went home in a state of terrible upset; there was so much I didn't understand.

When next I opened my briefcase, I saw the strange book. In my haste to leave the shop I had omitted to return it. But I now knew that the shop did not exist, and yet I knew it had existed, and that I had been into the depths below me seeing with my own eyes the horrors contained therein. Now the book sits on my shelf taunting me, reminding me that it is the only tangible evidence of what I have just told you. I want to dispose of the book of unspeakable satanic acts and rituals, but I am held back by the fear of what may occur if I did. After considerable thought I decided to take the book and discuss it with the minister of a church. I placed the book in my briefcase and went to the large church not far from where I live. As I stepped inside the church the acrid smell of burning reached me. The smell became stronger as I proceeded down the centre aisle, and my hand felt hot. I looked down and my briefcase burst into flames. I dropped the case and stood back. In a matter of moments my case burned to a cinder. Oddly the smoke did not rise into the air of the church but followed the floor to the door, and then disappeared under it.

As I said before, I have come to believe in the powers of evil and I have chosen to live my life differently. I am now searching for checks and balances and the power of the forces of light.

DENNIS.

I AM DENNIS'S cousin. I am telling his story for him. In his anguish and remorse, he finds it difficult to speak about his life and what happened to finally bring it crashing down about his ears. Dennis was born mentally impaired; it didn't show for the longest time. As a baby, everything had seemed quite normal, but when he tried to walk and talk it became apparent that something was wrong. He did learn to walk and speak, but his steps were halting and unsure. His vocabulary was limited his speech having a distinctive slur to it.

Dennis seemed to be completely unaware that he was different from the other children at school. He joined in with their games and withstood the insults by children who were intolerant of his slowness. Some of the more cruel children called him Bonehead, or Retard. But Dennis had no comprehension of the meaning of the words the children used, so he rarely became upset or angry with them. He never really graduated primary school, but because of his large size the authorities deemed it best that he move on to secondary school. Dennis suddenly found himself in a new and different environment. His fellow pupils were much more boisterous and loud and he had begun to understand the cruel names they called him when the teachers were not in earshot. The children tended to shut him out of group play and loneliness began to creep into his life.

Dennis quietly and imperceptibly began to withdraw into himself. I was a year older than he and when I saw him standing off alone in the schoolyard, I would join him and try to cheer him up, but it was to no avail. The constant stream of verbal abuse and insults weighed heavily upon him and he sank into a sort of depression. The school officials did not seem to notice Dennis's decline. It appeared to me that they had reluctantly taken on the role of glorified babysitters and so long as he was quiet and did not disturb classes they tolerated his presence. They made no extra effort to teach the slow learner in the midst of their other pupils giving him paper and crayons to draw with, while the other children worked on Math and English.

Dennis survived the unhappy period at secondary school but at age fourteen the real tragedy struck. After an evening at the movies a drunk driver killed both of his parents

When the police came to the house and found Dennis alone, watching television, they called social services to deal with him. They quickly decided that Dennis was unable to function and live alone in the house, so they forcibly removed him to a group home for the mentally challenged. Once again there was a drastic change in his environment. The insults and name calling ceased when he found himself among others of his ilk. Once he had overcome his grief at the loss of his parents, Dennis found himself coming out of his shell.

Over the next four years, Dennis learned a number of life skills and the group home arranged for him to apply for a cleaning job at a fast food restaurant. He got the job and Dennis applied himself with pride and gusto.

"Be sure to get the corners clean," the manager told him. Dennis never forgot the advice nightly going down on one knee in each of the corners as he said,

"Do a good job on the corners Dennis." It was simple mundane work, but Dennis loved the job. It gave him a sense of worth that he had lacked before. The fact that he was bringing in some money of his own, after paying part of his wages to the group home, gave him a sense of pride that urged him on to better things. In consultations with the home and social services it was decided that Dennis be allowed to go out to live by himself in the outside world. He had learned how to handle money, take care of his room, personal cleanliness, appropriate dressing and elementary cooking, and he had mastered the bus system.

The social worker found him a furnished studio apartment close to the bus route and Dennis proudly moved in. He had a bed, a kitchenette and two comfortable chairs. I had a good job at the time and I bought Dennis a small T.V. I only saw Dennis once a month. I, of course, had my own life to live and it now included girlfriends. Dennis had never expressed an interest in girls and I assumed he had none. But like they say, still waters run deep.

It wasn't until I went to visit Dennis in prison prior to his trial, that I learned that he did have an interest in girls.

"I didn't mean to hurt her Alan," he said tearfully. "And now there is no one to clean the floors and the corners will get dirty." I tried to calm him down and tell me what had happened. Start right at the beginning I asked him.

"There was this girl, she moved into the room next to mine. I often saw her going to work as I was coming home from my job in the mornings. I never spoke to her, I was too afraid and shy. She was a very pretty girl, I thought that she would not want to talk to me because, well you know why, I'm different. I began to think about her a lot and tried to get home as she was leaving for work just so I could look at her. But she never seemed to notice me. I began having dreams about her; she looked soft and warm like my mother used to be. I wanted her to lie down with me and hold me and stroke my head and give me kisses.

I knew she wouldn't want to do that with me. She was pretty and I am retarded, not like other boys. And I know that boys like me don't get pretty girls like Amanda. I got her name off the mailbox, that's how I know it. Well, my dreams of lying with her got stronger. One morning, as she went to work she left her keys hanging in the door lock. I took them into my room thinking about what I should do with them, because people should not leave them in the lock like that, in case bad people get them and steal things.

I thought and thought. Then I decided to go to the hardware store and get an extra key made. I put the new door key in my pocket and gave the others to the building manager."

"Why did you do that?" I asked.

"So that Amanda could get back into her room."

"No. Why did you get an extra key, Dennis?"

"So I could look at her room when she was out. I started going in just after she had left, and climbing into her unmade bed. Sometimes it was still warm from her body and I would undress and lie in the warm spot. It felt nice, like my mother's bed and sometimes I went to sleep in her warm place."

"Did you not know that you should not be doing this, Dennis?"

"Sort of Alan. But I wasn't hurting her. And it felt to me like she loved me by giving me her warmth to lie in."

"So what happened Dennis?"

"One morning she came back and saw me lying in her bed. She screamed. I don't like loud noises so I jumped out of bed to ask her to be quiet and to tell her I would not hurt her. When she saw me naked, she screamed even louder. I got frightened, so I grabbed her throwing her onto the bed, and covering her mouth and nose. She kept on struggling so I pressed harder. After a couple of minutes she lay still and quiet.

"I didn't come to hurt you," I said. But she did not answer. When the police came, they told me she was dead. They say that because I had a key to her room, it was premeditated murder, whatever that is.

"What is an electric chair Alan? I did not mean to hurt the pretty girl. I just wanted her warmth."

I fear for Dennis's life. We live in the State of Texas, renowned for executing those convicted of murder.

KIBBLES.

I'M MIKE Dewson. The idea was mine, but my brother Jeff went along with me in planning to murder Hank Stark. After we had killed him by smashing his skull with the pipe, we stripped him of his clothing and rammed him headfirst into the big meat and bone grinder. His skull slowed the grinder down considerably, but it didn't stall it. The rest of his body went through all right and then we added some condemned for human consumption, beef and pork, along with the chicken plant waste. When we had a vat full of the grindings, we turned on the mixer blades and added water, fish oil and spoiled bran and rice. While the ingredients mixed into a smooth paste, Jeff went to throw Hanks clothing into the burner chamber and I started up the kibble-making machine.

The kibbles were made by being forced through small indentations in a big drum then superheated and cooked, as the drum slowly turned. After which the cooked, dry dog kibbles fell onto a vibrating tray then sent along a conveyer to the bagging area. It usually took about an hour for a batch of mixture to be turned into kibbles, so it wouldn't be long before any trace of Hank Stark had been turned into high-grade dog food and stored in a large hopper before being bagged, ready for the shipping department.

I prepared another batch of meat products in the grinding machine to be sure it was completely cleared of any human remains. Then I mixed in the dry products and continued on with the kibble cooking. Jess and I were the only two workers on the midnight shift; we had worked together at the plant since we had left high school. It had always been a good place to work, until Hank Stark had been hired on as plant supervisor eighteen months ago, when the dog food company's ownership changed hands. Plant morale had plummeted since he came on the scene.

Stark seemed to delight in baiting and insulting the workers. What had formerly been a relatively happy place, despite the foul smells of rotting meats and mouldy dry products, had turned into a place of discord. With the lowered morale, came lower productivity and Stark's attacks on the staff increased tenfold. While there was no organized plan by the staff to slow down, it just happened of its own accord. Stark took the position that it was an attack on him personally and he reacted with savage verbal attacks on all of us.

He was so sure that Jess and I were not pulling our weight; he would show up at one or two in the morning expecting to find us napping. Of course he never did. Jess and I had worked the graveyard shift as a team for years. We had a system that worked for us and we produced enough kibbles on our shift to keep the bagging and shipping department busy till noon. Even this did not please Stark; he always found something to complain about before going home again. One night we were so angry at his outburst we decided to load so much meat and waste in the grinder at one time that we jammed it up solid, burning out the motor. We spent the night in the lunchroom, waiting for the maintenance guy to fix it on the day shift. Stark went ballistic; there were no kibbles ready for the day shift to work with. He came at us like a wild man and said,

"You two bastards have done it on purpose." With tongue in cheek I told him,

"We were trying to get the production up, Mr. Stark. You keep telling us you want more."

It was the only time we did it, but he treated us even worse after that. We organized a delegation to go over Stark's head to upper management, and tell them what was happening to the moral and consequent reduction in output in their plant. The staff elected me as spokesman and three of us went to the plant offices.

"I will not have insubordination in my plant," the new owner told us. "Hank Stark was hired to run the plant efficiently and I believe he is doing a good job despite the lazy staff he has to work with. Production could be doubled with the right workers; perhaps it is time for us to consider replacing you."

It was painfully apparent that we would get no satisfaction here, so we left with a decision to meet their indifference with our own. When Stark found out that I had gone over his head, he came after me like a mad dog. He swore he would get enough on me to fire both Jess and I. Jobs are scarce in this area so we gritted our teeth and put up with his abuse as best we could.

There were minor acts of sabotage in different areas of the plant that would never have happened under the original management. But they were acts of utter frustration, as opposed to acts of sheer vandalism. We lived and worked with these appalling conditions for about a year under Hank Stark, and then came the final straw that broke the camel's back.

Our sister Madeline was to be married the second Saturday in June. Jess and I were scheduled to have the weekend shift, so we asked Stark if we could exchange the Saturday shift with one of the day shifts just for this one weekend, in that way we could attend the wedding and reception party.

Stark's face twisted into one of demented delight.

"I have been waiting for a chance to get back at you two Dewson bastards! No I will not allow it. You will work your assigned shift, or I will can the pair of you"

We loved our sister Madeline and we both wanted to be a part of her big day, so that's when Jess and I began planning for Stark's demise. We began by spreading a rumour everywhere we could, that Hank Stark had a clandestine romance going on, and that he planned to leave his wife for her and run away to New York. The word spread all over the community to everyone but Mrs. Stark and Stark himself.

It was two weeks before the wedding when Stark strode into the plant at one in the morning. The machines were running and he seemed terribly disappointed that he still had not caught us shirking. I nodded at Jess and we put our plan into action. Jess came up behind him and brought a length of two-inch pipe crashing down onto Stark's head. He was dead in seconds. Together we tore off his clothing and shoes. Then I turned on the empty grinder and we forced him into it headfirst. We took his car keys from his pockets and Jess burned his clothing. When we had turned him into kibbles, I drove his car to the Greyhound depot with Jess following where it was abandoned. Then together Jess and I drove back to the plant to resume work.

On Monday morning when Hank Stark didn't show up for work, the day shift told us there was a gleeful attitude in the plant. By Wednesday, when there had been no word from him, most of the community was aware that Hank Stark had intended to run away to New York with his girlfriend. Almost everyone thought they knew what had happened. The morose and depressing attitude in the kibbles plant vanished almost overnight. Production took an immediate upswing and the plant owner grudgingly agreed that things were better without Hank Stark. He asked me as a long time employee if I would take over the supervisor's position at foreman's pay. I said I would, but only on the condition that the plant is run democratically and that the workers are treated with dignity and respect.

Reluctantly he agreed. And so a new era began. Madeline had a beautiful wedding and our entire family had a great day. The police investigation was only a cursory one, given what the community knew about Stark's plans to run. The kibbles plant became a happy place again. By using ideas the plant employees came up with, kibble production soared. So who says that crime doesn't pay?

AUCTION BARGAIN.

MYRA AND I had always enjoyed going to auctions. In fact much of our home was furnished with auction purchases. We began frequenting them even before we were married; I suppose Myra got the auction bug from me. I took her to her first one when on a date and she became fascinated at being able to determine a value on a particular item, to stick to it and not get drawn into the auctioneer's game of price elevating.

We were on a motoring holiday in western Pennsylvania when we had decided to stay in a motel in a small town. We noted an auction barn on the edge of town with a sign out front proclaiming, Auction tonight 7pm. After we had checked into the motel, we went along to see what kind of merchandise would be going on the block. We found the usual junk and a few decent items of furniture. Myra spotted a carton of miscellaneous items with a nice, dust covered, rosewood box in the bottom; it was quite small and looked as though it might have been a sewing box.

"I wouldn't mind having this if it goes at a reasonable bid. I would go as high as fifty dollars," she said.

"Let's go have an early dinner and come back here later." I replied. We found a small town, style restaurant, serving simple country fare meals. After watching the evening news on the motel T.V. we returned to the auction barn. The place slowly filled with locals who gave us more than a passing glance. The auctioneer, in his obligatory cowboy hat, started the proceedings off at seven fifteen. The carton Myra wanted to bid on was number twenty-five in the sale catalogue. We watched the other items go at very reasonable prices and Myra said,

"There is a good chance I can get the carton for very little money."

"Let's hope so." I replied. Finally number twenty-five came on the block. The assistant held up the carton as the auctioneer announced,

"Number twenty-five, a carton of odd items from the old Schumacher place. Who will start the bidding at ten dollars?" The auction barn was strangely silent. "Five dollars, who will give me five for it." Again there was no response. "Two dollars folks for this carton of goodies?" Myra yelled,

"Two dollars."

"All right folks two dollars I'm bid, who will give me four?" He did his best to get a raising bid, but the barn was silent. Finally he gave up and saying, "Sold to the lady in the blue dress for two dollars." He banged down his gavel and went on to the next item.

"I can't believe I have bought a rosewood sewing box for only two dollars, Neil. Maybe no one else looked in the carton and saw what was in the bottom." The box was the only thing we were interested in, as we paid for it we noticed the people looking at us and the auction barn went silent as before. We left taking the carton out to the car.

"That is the oddest sale I have ever been to," I said to Myra. I opened the rear door of the car and placed the carton inside. I don't know how I managed it, but I trapped my fingers in the door as I closed it. I yelled out with the sudden pain and Myra had to come around the car to re-open the door releasing my fingers. I had flattened three of them and I knew they would go black with bruising. I could feel every heartbeat in all three fingers. Gingerly I started the car. As I was leaving the parking lot I had to make a hard right turn. My sore fingers slipped off the steering wheel, and I scraped the side of our Chrysler on the gatepost. I became angry; the car was almost new and I knew without stopping to look, it would be a costly repair. I parked in front of our motel room and got out to survey the damage done to both doors and the rear fender.

In order to get away from my cursing at this misfortune, Myra took the carton out of the car. Heading toward our motel door she must not have seen the curb falling headlong hurting both knees. The carton went flying into the wall and the saucers and other ceramic pieces smashed, leaving only the rosewood box intact. I helped Myra into the room where I sat her on the bed; both of her knees were skinned and bleeding. I soaked one of the towels with cold water and placed it across her knees. Then I went outside to clean up the broken crockery. I picked up the pieces using my good hand, noticing the damaged side of the

Chrysler again. When I went back inside I spoke to Myra, I shouldn't have said it I know, but I was angry.

"Your goddamn box has cost us two scraped knees, three flattened fingers and at least a thousand bucks to fix the Goddamn car!"

"My Goddamn box! What do you mean my Goddamn box? Don't blame me for trapping your fingers and scraping the car. It was you, too stupid to pull your fingers out of the door before you closed it. It was you behind the wheel, when you carelessly damaged the car. Don't you dare try to pin the blame on me for your failings Neil Hartford?"

"Who else is there to blame Myra? It was you who wanted the bloody box in the first place. If it hadn't been for you we could have been resting with a gin and tonic, instead of wrecking our holiday over a junky old box."

"If the holiday is wrecked it is through your stupidity. You never were too bright Neil. I knew that even before we got married."

"Then you are the stupid one Myra, for marrying me, knowing that. The fact is Myra, I thought that I might be able to teach you a thing or two and shed some of my brightness upon you. Until today I thought I had succeeded, but obviously I was wrong."

I had never before spoken to Myra this way. I knew that what I was saying was not true, mean yes, but I didn't seem to be able to help myself. Myra had never spoken cruel words to me before either. And I thought that maybe we were more tired from traveling than we figured.

"Let's get some sleep," I said. "I think we must both be overtired"

"I don't know where you are going to sleep, Neil but it isn't with me in this bed."

I tried to apologize and make amends, but Myra would have none of it. In fact she refused to speak with me anymore. She took the rosewood box into the bathroom and began cleaning the dirt and dust from it. She accidentally knocked the water glass onto the floor where it broke and then she stepped onto a jagged piece and ripped open her foot. When I glanced through the open door I saw her bleeding profusely and sprang to her aid.

"Stay away from me" she hissed. I knew she was still furious with me, but I also knew I had to help her. I sat her on the toilet lid, picked up her foot and she ceased protesting. I pulled out a large shard of glass from the ball of her foot and went to get a band-aid from the first aid kit we always carried in our suitcase. I washed the wound and dried it with toilet paper, then put on the band-aid pulling the wound together. When I backed away from her, I felt a sharp cutting pain in my left heel.

"I don't believe this!" I roared. I lifted my leg to look at my foot and found that the base of the water glass had sunk jagged edges up, deep into my heel. I looked at Myra expecting help and sympathy but I got nothing but an icy stare. The rosewood box sat on the washbasin. It seemed to taunt me, so I picked it up and flung it into the room.

"That's it Neil. Behave like a three year old; take out your childish anger on the box.

I didn't think she deserved an answer; I felt more like slapping her face. Myra got into bed while I tried to tend to my wound. When I was finished I hopped into the room attempting to get in bed with her, but she would have none of it.

"After the things you have said to me tonight, I don't want you anywhere near me, sleep on the floor, or in your precious bloody car! Take your pick." I hopped around getting the spare blankets out of the closet and lay on the floor. It was hard, uncomfortable and cold and my fingers and heel throbbed. A shaft of light through the drapes shone directly onto the rosewood box. It seemed to glow in the light and it annoyed me. Every time I opened my eyes my gaze went directly to the box. It occurred to me that until we had bought the box we were having a good vacation. Myra and I hardly ever disagreed and now we were at each other's throats. And what about the string of mishaps. Were they the fault of the box? But how could they be? It was just a sewing box. Since I could not sleep anyway I got up to have a good look at the damn thing. I placed it on the dressing table as I put on the light. The box had a brass band where the hinges should have been, but there were no hinges nor was there a keyhole to unlock it. It was a sealed box. But why? What was the point of such a box? I couldn't figure it out at all, so I decided I would try to sleep again. As I hopped past the bed to my blanket on the floor I stubbed my right foot on the bed frame. I hit it really hard and I wondered if I had broken a toe. I yelled out at the top of my lungs. Myra sat bolt upright and smashed her head into the reading lamp. She began to bleed from her forehead.

"You bastard." She screamed at me. "You did that on purpose."

"Like Hell I did! I stubbed my toes on the bed foot. "Don't you think it's about time you started taking responsibility for your own actions instead of always blaming me?"

"I don't always blame you! But maybe I should. You always seem to be close by when things go wrong."

"There you go again, blaming me!" We ended our verbal sparring as I got back under my blanket. Now both feet throbbed along with my hand and my emotions were in turmoil. This was the most appalling time Myra and I had ever experienced. My thoughts returned to the accursed box. It was beyond coincidence that so much had gone awry since we had acquired it. I had a feeling of bad vibrations coming from the box; I couldn't put my finger on it, for it made no logical sense. How could it be? But the feeling continued and I could not get it out of my mind. Sometime just before dawn I got up and hobbled out to the car with it and put the box in the trunk. I felt a strange sense of relief with it out of the room, my anger toward Myra calmed down and I realized how wrong and cruelly I had behaved to her. I knew I had to apologize to her and the sooner the better. I sat on the bed edge and began to speak softly to her.

"Darling Myra, forgive me my cruel behaviour and my foul uncalled for words. I do not know what came over me." Myra opened her eyes and responded,

"I too was cruel and nasty Neil, I will forgive you if you will forgive me?'

We sealed our agreement with a kiss and I climbed into bed with her.

"You might think me crazy Myra, but I believe the sewing box exerted some kind of influence over us. We have never been accident prone, nor have we ever quarreled to the extent we did last night."

"No I don't think you are crazy, Neil, but it does seem a little absurd that a small wooden box could have any sort of power, it is just a sewing box after all."

"But it isn't a sewing box, Myra. There is no lid. It is sealed, kind of like a coffin." I have no idea why I said coffin but now that I had, the thought stuck with me. We managed to sleep for a couple of hours and awoke about nine. We got dressed and decided we would go for breakfast at the same place we had dinner last night. As we got into the car Myra said,

"Why do we always have to eat in the places you want to?" I could feel my anger rising again,

"We don't, and if you don't like the place we were at last night pick somewhere else. I get tired of your whining and indecision Myra."

"There you go again with the damned insults Neil. You can be so childish it is beyond belief. Forget the damn breakfast. Turn this piece of junk around get our belongings from the motel then let's get out of here."

"What do you mean junk! We picked this damned car together, you didn't think it was junk then."

"Well I do now. I wanted you to get one of the new Fords, but I let you have your childish way so that you wouldn't weep all over the upholstery." I tried to think logically instead of continuing to fight.

"Myra. Think about this. We are close to the damn box again, and we are fighting like we did last night. Remember how we both calmed down when I took the box outside?"

"I don't see how that had anything to do with it."

"Neither do I, Myra. But it is a fact. Let's try something. We will leave the car at the motel and walk for breakfast and we will see if our demeanor changes."

"It sounds pretty stupid to me, Neil but just to humour the child in you, I will."

I parked outside our room and we set off to walk to the café. We were only fifty feet from the car when Myra said,

"I'm sorry Neil. I don't know what got into me." We hobbled hand in hand up the road like a couple of lame horses.

"Do you see what I mean now, Myra?" I am totally convinced there is something evil about that damn box; something that affects those near it. Do you remember how last night nobody would bid on it and how the people looked at us as we left with it? I am positive now that they knew something we didn't. After breakfast let's go back to the auction barn and ask a few questions." Despite the discomfort we walked to the auction. The man in the cowboy hat and his helper were inside. They looked at us walking in lame but said nothing.

"We have come to ask a few questions about that box we bought last night. Where did it come from, why is there no lid for it to be opened and has there been any rumours about strange powers coming from it?"

"The Schumacher box you mean? I don't really know much about it, except that it keeps showing up in the salesroom. We must have sold it five or six times now. We don't ask why, we just try to sell it again."

"Who are the Schumacher's? Why would a box from them keep showing up here?"

"Willy Schumacher sent it here with a bunch of other stuff after his wife died, that's about all I can tell you. But if you want to know more, go see his brother Wolfgang. He runs the town funeral parlour. It's directly behind the auction barn on the next street."

"Thanks." I said. I was determined to find out more about the previous owner of the box so we hobbled over to the funeral parlour to talk with his brother Wolfgang. He looked at me strangely when I asked about the box.

"Willy and his wife were constantly at battle. It had been an arranged marriage that had never worked. They had virtually no friends; no one could stand to be around them constantly yelling at each other. Hildeguard swore she would never leave him in peace, not even after death. She became ill and she died. I did the funeral service and cremation for her. Hildeguard wanted her ashes scattered at sea, but Willy said no. The tale is that he had the box made for her ashes so that it could not be opened. I personally set no stock in the story that Hildeguard's spirit stays with the box wherever it is. But others believe it and some say her meanness is passed to those who are near to it. I deal with death on a regular basis and the story seems like a cock and bull story to me. Tell me why are you asking me these things?"

"We bought the un-openable box last night at the auction barn; we were the only bidders. Within minutes of taking possession of it, we started having accidents and fighting with each other. It seemed to us the people at the auction knew something about the box that we didn't." The funeral director looked at me wryly.

"I have to be truthful. We have been waiting for someone from out of town to buy the box and take it away from here. Several owners of the box have met with tragic accidents; others have ended up in divorce. Where is the box now?"

"It is in the trunk of my car back at the motel. What do you suggest?"

"Take it back to the auction barn very carefully, or better still where do you live?"

"Why."

"If you live near the sea, take it there and set the spirit free, by putting the box in the ocean. Try talking to the spirit and tell it what you intend to do. There is a good chance you can travel in peace until you get there." I looked at Myra and she shrugged,

"Why not? We have nothing to lose but the two dollars we paid for the darn box. But we stand to gain our sanity and our health."

We decided to abandon our touring holiday; we both knew we would be more comfortable at home to nurse our wounds. Back at the motel I opened the car trunk and I spoke to the box, making sure no one could see or hear me talking to an inanimate object and appearing to be a little unbalanced.

"Hildeguard" I said, "I am going to take the box, containing your ashes, to the sea, as I understand this is what you wanted. It is quite a long journey from here and I want to be sure you don't cause me a major car accident, or have Myra and I fight all the way home. Suddenly the vibrations from the box ceased. We packed our bag put it in the trunk with the box and we had an uneventful trip home.

Before we went to our house we went down to the beach. I tied a rock to the box and hurled it off the pier into the sea. Since then we have often wondered if our auction bargain was an elaborate hoax, or if our injuries and fighting were as a result of Hildeguard Schumacher's spirit. I don't suppose we shall ever know.

NORTH SEA

"HANG ON guys!" Skipper Briggs yelled at the top of his lungs. Briggs was only marginally older than I, he was a competent skipper, tough and decisive, but with a dash of compassion and good humour thrown in. I and the other crewmembers of the trawler North Sea clung desperately to the handrails around the wheelhouse as a mountain of dark green saltwater towered above us. We had abandoned our quarters below deck in favour of the relative safety of the wheelhouse in case the North Sea began to lose the battle with the storm. We were very much aware that if she were to sink, we would have no chance to get to the life raft from below decks so had elected to share the wheelhouse with the skipper until the storm abated.

My name is Grant Wilson but everyone just calls me Wilson. Twenty-eight years of age, unmarried and I am told, a fairly good-looking fellow. I have never had any problem getting girl friends but none ever really got under my skin until connecting with Nancy.

In one sense it was even more frightening here in the wheelhouse where we could see the savagery of the ocean, than it had been below, where we could only feel the movement of the ship in the troubled sea. The North Sea's wide sturdy bow plunged into the base of the gigantic wave like a sharp knife into fish flesh. I felt that the end was close for us as the wave's utter height blocked out the light of the dawn. The North Sea took on a vertical position as she tried to climb the monstrosity. The crest of the wave suddenly broke and the trawler was completely engulfed in a wall of water. How she managed to climb the wall I shall never know. But suddenly we were atop the wave looking down at least sixty feet into the chasm of the next trough. The North Sea's keel began to change from the vertical to the horizontal position, then like a child's see saw, she began to lean forward sliding off the crest and plunging headlong bow first into the chasm below. Our feet went out from under us, but we clung like grim death to the handrail.

The North Sea dove into the deep like a harpoon. It was suddenly black dark. Any second now I expected the wheelhouse windows to cave in under the pressure. Instinctively I took in a deep breath; I knew that in seas like this there would be no real chance of surviving in the water, but the will to live was alive and well. Like a cork held under water and then released, the North Sea's deck pressed against my feet as she shot up from the deep, into the light and air of the cavernous trough. A new fear hit all of us in the wheelhouse. A collective groan filled the little space. The sound of the North Sea's engine slowed then stopped. I knew it was the sound of a death knell in a storm such as we found ourselves in. We were about to be engulfed by the next wave with no power to fight back.

"Wilson!" The skipper roared. "Get below and drain the intake and exhaust protectors!" I wondered why he had chosen me to go below, but Briggs was the skipper and I had to do his bidding. I released my grip on the handrail and staggered to the wheelhouse door. I knew I had but seconds to get from the wheelhouse to the door of the crew's quarters. I opened the door, and the high walls of water, fore and aft of the North Sea, seemed eager to swallow me into their toothless jaws. I chose my moment. I leapt down the five steps from the wheelhouse, raced across the narrow deck and hurled open the door. As soon as the door closed behind me, I heard the water outside crash into it. The deck under my feet began to rise to a vertical incline. I slid across it and slammed into the front bulkhead. I crawled uphill to the companionway and made my way down to the crew's sleeping compartment. With the deck pitching wildly, I managed to lift the hatch over the engine. As I went down to the engine deck I could feel the North Sea being violently lifted, it was a sensation like being in a fast moving elevator.

I found the crescent wrench hanging on the u-shaped air intake pipe and quickly took out the two-inch plug to drain out the trapped water. While it was draining I undid the plug for the exhaust. When they were both empty, I replaced the plugs and pressed the auxiliary engine start button. With my heart in my mouth I listened as the engine turned, then after what seemed an eternity, she spluttered into life and slowly gained her running speed. I climbed back up to the crew's quarters and picked up the intercom.

"I will stay down here skipper in case we have to do this again," I yelled into it.

"O. K. Wilson." I heard him yell back over the din in the wheelhouse.

I made my way to a lower bunk and sat down on the edge. I began to think. Why had skipper Briggs ordered me to see to the engine? Jess Warnock normally looked after the mechanical things aboard the North Sea, why not him? Then I wondered if the skipper had found out about Nancy and I, and sending me out on deck in such appalling conditions were perhaps a way of breaking the triangle. Had I been swept away he could be considered blameless in my demise and Jess would still have been able to restart the North Sea's engine.

But if he did know, it must have been Nancy that had told him and that didn't make sense. She told me herself the last time we were together, that she had come to hate his offhand treatment of her and his roughness toward her when he wanted his marital rights. She said that she could hardly wait until the time that she and I could get away from Grimsby and begin a new life together. The fact is, the fault we haven't yet done so, is mine.

I felt that I didn't have quite enough money saved for us to start over in a new place and the only trade I know is fishing. To move away from the coast and move into a different line of work was just a little scary for me. I love Nancy, there is no doubt in my mind about that and I have always felt that she loved me. Then I wondered if she had told the skipper about us why would she have done so? Possibly he had threatened her and she had let it slip out.

We had always been very careful not to be seen coming and going to our clandestine meetings and it seemed unlikely that someone else had ratted on us.

The North Sea gave a tremendous lurch throwing me across the cabin. As I lay on my back on the deck, the porthole went dark with seawater. We were under the surface again. But this time the engine did not stall. I wondered how long the sturdy little ship could take this battering and how long it would be before some of the welds would begin to split with the strain of twisting and pounding against her hull. The skipper's voice came over the intercom.

"Are you O.K. down there Wilson?" I crawled over to the mike and replied,

"Yes skipper I have taken the odd bump, but I am all right."

I wonder about his concern for my well being, is it genuine? Is the skipper disappointed that I didn't get swept over the side? Could it be that he hopes I will sustain a fatal injury down here? Could it be that he is totally unaware that his wife Nancy and I are lovers and that his concern for me is genuine? I wish I knew. I have strong guilt feelings about the situation. Skipper has always treated me fair and square and I am cuckolding him. He pays me well enough, certainly the full going rate for a deckhand, but still I feel I do not have enough savings to take Nancy away from him and run. After a while the skipper's voice comes on the intercom.

"The weather looks like it is beginning to calm down now Wilson, see if you can get a pot of coffee going down there. If you can get the Goddamn pot to stay on the stove give the wheelhouse a shout when it is ready and I will send Jess down to bring it to the wheelhouse. By the way make it strong. We need it with a bite this morning."

The skipper's voice does not sound like he is gunning for me; possibly I have it all wrong. Maybe he knows nothing of Nancy's infidelity, or of my involvement in it? It just might be that he sees me as his deckhand trustworthy enough to be sent below in a violent storm to start the crippled engine of his ship in grave peril. I get the coffee pot and fill it with fresh water and put the ground coffee in the strainer. Then I light the propane burner and set the coffee pot on it. I set up the slide guards and hold the lid down with one hand while steadying myself with the other. I begin to think again, now that I have time on my hands waiting for the pot to boil. I see my reflection in the mirror behind the stove, I see a handsome fellow with a dark complexion black hair and brows and I remember that Nancy always looks at me in an admiring way when we are alone.

Guilt once again begins to rear its ugly head. If skipper knows nothing of Nancy and I and he trusts me implicitly to defend his ship against the storm, the shame is all mine. How can I be so disloyal? How can I go behind his back and be with his wife like a thief in the night and yet I do? The truth is that it was I who coaxed Nancy to lie with me to forget how unhappy she had become. In retrospect I should have suggested that she seek counseling to help her deal with the situation and kept my distance emotionally. But I chose the other route and created an explosive situation.

Face it. I said to myself, you have only heard one side of the story, hers. The skipper might have his own reasons for behaving toward her like she said he did. Maybe she had been unfaithful with others that he knew about and I did not. It could be too that she was lying about the skipper. It was entirely possible that he was a good husband and provider, kind and gentle in the bargain. Perhaps the stories she told me were designed to make me want to comfort her while the skipper was away.

The coffee began to perc and when it was ready; I poured myself a cup and called the wheelhouse on the intercom.

"Coffee is ready when you are," I yelled into the mike. In a minute or so I heard the sound of feet outside the door then it opened, and Jess stepped inside soaked to the skin.

"Son of a gun! I sure didn't time that wave right," he said, spitting salt-water out. The waves are not quite so high now. I think we are over the worst of it. I will need an extra cup we are one short in the wheelhouse." I handed him a cup and he jammed it into his pocket.

"Open the door and tell me when to run. I don't want to drop the damn stuff."

I did as he asked and he darted off to the wheelhouse. I returned to my thoughts and the feelings of guilt. Perhaps I should act like a man and tell the skipper what has been going on behind his back and take my licks whatever they might be. But then I think what purpose would it serve, three lives could be ruined. I certainly could not expect to continue working on the North Sea afterwards and the knowledge of Nancy's infidelity would more than likely split the marriage apart. Who knows how the skipper would handle the news, he might just go off the deep end and try to take my life.

The storm abates at last and cook comes to prepare breakfast for us. I offer to take the skipper's meal to the wheelhouse and I pluck up the courage to speak with him.

"Why did you choose me to go to restart the engine skipper? Why did you not send Jess?"

"I have come to know my crew pretty well Wilson. While Jess is a good man at mechanical things, I felt he could not handle the pressure of going below alone in a storm such as we have just experienced. So in answer to your question I sent you because I knew you could do the job without wavering. Getting the engine running again was vital and I trusted you."

The skipper's words increased the guilt that I felt. If only he knew how untrustworthy I really am. If he knew what I was doing behind his back, what would he think of me then? My feelings of guilt became overpowering. I had to tell the skipper about my misdeeds and face the consequences. We were nearing the fishing grounds and soon we would be busy as beavers trawling for our catch. I had to tell him now.

"Skipper," I said. "You will probably want to kill me for what I am about to tell you. I feel terribly ashamed, and I really don't know how to begin."

"Spit it out Wilson, it's just about time to be getting the gear ready."

"It's about your wife Nancy and I skipper." I was in so deep now there could be no backing out.

"What about you and Nancy?"

"There is no other way to say this skipper, we have become lovers."

"Is that all that is worrying you? I have known about you since the first time you slept with her. We have an open marriage Wilson. Where the heck do you think I was when you were with her? We both have our extra partners, it suits us and we tell each other about them."

"Nancy said she was unhappy with you and that's when I began comforting her." The skipper began laughing.

"It works for her every time Wilson, you took the bait on her hook."

"You are not angry with me then skipper?

"Of course not Wilson. Nancy does her thing and I do mine, it works for us. Now go for the crew and get the gear out." I could hardly believe my own ears. Nancy had played me for a fool and the skipper knew about it all along. I no longer felt guilty, now I felt like an idiot. I mustered the crew and we set out the trawl net. The skipper yelled out of the wheelhouse door,

"Go for a coffee break now boys." He walked down the wheelhouse steps toward me. "Come with me Wilson. I want your opinion on the starboard side net hawser, I think it may be wearing thin and we don't want it to break on a full net. We went to the stern and at the top of the net ramp he turned to make sure the other crewmembers had gone below and that he and I were alone. He turned to face me with a wild look on his face. His normally placid eyes were narrowed, and burned with silent anger.

"I have had suspicions that Nancy had a lover, but now I know." With no eyes to see but his own, he threw me onto the greasy ramp. My fingernails tried in vane to dig into the wet ramp and stop me and I slid down into the trawl net, and the last thing my eyes saw was the skipper's twisted smile of revenge as the net dragged me under and down. Saltwater filled my airways. I ceased fighting as all went dark.

THE CAR LOT

IT WAS much like any other used car lot, with a row of highly polished cars facing the street and with eye-catching bunting flying from the spotlight posts. The best-looking cars were always in the front row and the questionable worn out has beens in the back. The small office at the rear of the lot had undraped windows facing the street so that the predatory salesmen could see anyone approaching, ready to be fleeced like innocent sheep. The hard as nails salesmen sat there hour after hour, waiting to pounce upon an unsuspecting prospect wandering into the sales lot, much like a mouse walking unknowingly into a spring loaded trap.

Franco's Used Cars was, I suppose, no different than many other car lots in its approach to taking excess profit from unwary customers. But it was different in that I became privy to what was really going on there. Franco's dealt mainly with Jack Franco's own ethnic Italian community.

Jack Franco aimed all his advertising at his own ethnic people and a goodly number of them believed the tales of him helping out his community with good honest deals on cars and light trucks. Jack and his sales team capitalized on the trust. New immigrants to the community felt safer dealing with one of their own countrymen who spoke the same language. But being new and trusting, it set them up for Jack Franco's special treatment.

Franco's salesmen most often spoke quietly, into their prospect's ears, about the bargain they were about to buy. They would suggest that a buyer from a different ethic group was interested in the car and that he would rather see one of his own become the owner, for that reason that he should move quickly, as the other buyer was coming back later to put his money down. The trust in his countryman and the chance to snatch a bargain from under someone else's nose most often resulted in a sale. More often than not, the car involved had been someone else's lemon or it had been gussied up and the mileage turned back by the two teenage lot boys who worked in a shed behind the office.

It goes without saying that the salesmen and Franco himself claimed to have no knowledge of such goings on. It was explained to customers, who were faced with crippling repair costs, that it was just bad luck or the vehicle had not been driven and cared for properly since leaving the sales lot.

Franco's Used Cars obtained most of its stock of vehicles from the dealer's wholesale auto auction. Jack tended to buy what most of the other dealers rejected. His other stock came from dubious trade-ins by owners dumping the vehicle before it finally fell apart. It did not appear that Jack Franco had any sense of morality in his dealings, the suckered customers paid for his high lifestyle and he apparently believed that this was the American way. Jack owned a large house in the suburbs, he had an unlisted telephone, and he wore the best suits money could buy. With his tight curly hair and rugged European looks, Jack looked the part of an honest and successful businessman.

His complacent world began to unravel the day he sold a clapped out Chevrolet to new immigrant, Mario Conti. New to the country, and to the world of big cars, Mario thought he had bought a magnificent automobile. It was big, shiny with a set of cheap new slip-on seat covers. As his eyes scanned the shiny four-door body, he paid no mind to the blue smoke coming out of the tailpipe.

"They all do that until the engine warms up." The salesman said. Mario paid no mind to the four bald tires showing the cord in places. Had he opened the trunk he would have seen that it held three inches of rusty water and no spare tire.

"There is another guy who badly wants this car; he is coming in later with the money. You had better put at least a deposit on it, or it will be gone. At twenty-five hundred this vehicle will be gone in a shot. The salesman said.

"I pay cash now," Mario answered. The salesman smiled. Once he had the cash, nothing Mario said or did would get him his money back. Mario counted out twenty-five one hundred dollar bills and went into the office to sign the papers.

Proud as punch at his shiny big American car, Mario drove off the lot. He drove very carefully until he got the feel of the car, then he picked up the speed. At the first red light he applied the brakes, and the Chevrolet pulled to the side. He held the vehicle straight by gripping the steering wheel. When he braked to a stop, the water in the trunk shot over the sill into the car and wet all the carpeting. It was then that the engine stopped. Mario cranked the engine until the weak battery gave out. He did not know what he should do next. The people behind him lining up honked impatiently causing quite a traffic jam by the time the police arrived. Owing to the language barrier, Mario had no idea what the policeman was telling him. Eventually a tow truck arrived to tow the car off the highway.

"He doesn't understand English. Take the car to a repair shop." The policeman said. Mario was baffled and confused; having no idea what was taking place. He sat in cab of the truck and rode with him to a repair shop. The shop employees pushed the car inside and began to work on it, while Mario went to call a friend who could speak both languages. When his friend Leo arrived, he began asking about the car on Mario's behalf.

"We don't think the car is worth repairing. It leaks around the rear windows and the trunk fills with water every time it rains or gets washed. The battery is useless and the carburetor is leaking both air and gas. We got the engine running, but the rings and valves are shot, it's amazing that the car runs at all. The tires are bald, there is no spare, and the body has just been painted to cover all the rust spots. While we had it on the hoist we checked the brakes and there is nothing left on the brake shoes. The car is not safe on the road. A rough estimate to make the car roadworthy is a minimum of four grand and that doesn't include any bodywork. You say your friend has just bought the car? Well you can tell him it is the worst lemon I have ever seen. I suggest he have it towed back there and demand his money back."

Mario was heartbroken and angry all at the same time, but given the bad news he and Leo decided they would have the car towed back to Franco's Used Cars and demand a refund. The tow truck dropped the car in the middle of the sales lot. Mario paid him the fifty-dollar towing charge then went with Leo to the office.

"You sold me a bad car." Mario said to the salesman. "I have brought it back and I want my money returned."

"Can't be done. The car is in your name now, besides you signed the contract with the words, 'as is' on it. That means you accepted the car just the way it was when you drove it off the lot. I'm sorry sir but you own the car and whatever problems it may have developed since you took it off our property."

"The problems were there before I bought the car and you must have known about them before you sold it to me."

"I'm sorry sir; the car was in good condition before you took it away and damaged it. If you want to leave it here for us to resell, we can do that for you at twenty five percent plus costs."

"I want to see the boss!" Mario demanded. Jack Franco smiled, he had heard it all on the intercom and he had made two grand out of the sucker in the outer office.

"I am sorry sir. You signed a legal contract with my salesman. As an honest and respected businessman I cannot break the law by tearing up legal contracts. Perhaps we can smooth this out by offering you a two hundred dollar credit for your old car on something you might like better." Leo grabbed Mario's arm.

"Don't go for another deal with these guys, Mario. Take your losses and run."

"But I'm out twenty-six hundred with the towing and shop estimate.'

"I know Mario. But sometimes you just have to take your lumps." And so they left leaving the Chevrolet behind.

Jack Franco tore up the contract Mario had signed and yelled out of the back window to the lot boys,

"Come and get this Chev running again and stick it back in the lineup."

Mario Conti may have just arrived in the country and he may have been a greenhorn car buyer. But he was still savvy to the ways of dealing with men like Franco back in the old country. His car-buying fund had been taken from him and in the code of the old country it had to be revenged. Mario bided his time and at the next meeting of the new immigrants group he told the membership what Franco Used Cars had done to him. It was agreed that a delegation from the group approach Jack Franco and suggest that in the interests of his future business with new immigrants to the community, he give Mario his money back. Franco laughed at the delegation,

"He made a deal with us fair and square. Franco's used Cars will not give him a cent back. The man is obviously a whiner to get you guys to come here to plead for him." At the next meeting the delegation told the assembly what Franco had said. No words were spoken in reply, but heads nodded at each other knowingly. When the meeting ended at ten

P.M. a group of cars left the meeting hall and proceeded to Franco's car lot. Several men kept watch while the others slashed every tire, on every car on the front row.

No one spoke during the operation. Everyone got back into their cars and left as quietly as they had come. The next day the delegation returned to the car lot and repeated their request for Mario to be repaid. Jack Franco was in an absolutely foul mood. He hadn't been able to come up with enough used tires to get his cars back on their wheels, so he had been forced to buy a number of new ones.

"Tell this Mario bastard to get lost. He won't see a plugged nickel. I had vandals in here last night and it is costing me a fortune in new tires."

The delegation left and the word went round that he would still not give Mario his money back. Leo said to Mario,

"Franco has been away from the old country too long. He has obviously forgotten how things work." That night the members met again, but this time they were better equipped. Some smashed in the rear windows of all the cars in the second row while others smeared house paint over all the trunk lids. From the street all looked normal, but from behind, it looked like a war zone. The next day Mario went alone to Franco's,

"I have come for my money Mr. Franco. It comes to about twenty-seven hundred with the towing."

"Get off my property. I have problems enough without you hanging around."

"What a shame about all the damage to your cars, Mr. Franco. It would be terrible if these vandalism attacks were to continue. Are you sure you don't want to give me my money back?" Jack Franco looked at him. Slowly the light bulb in his mind began to brighten.

"You son of a bitch! So you are responsible for all this damage to my property."

"Oh no, Mr. Franco, I have been at home with my family every night and I can prove it. I have just come by to see if you have reconsidered giving me back my money."

"If I did, could I expect the vandalism would end?"

"I don't know, Mr. Franco. Vandals tend to move on after a couple of attacks. All I know is that you have not treated me fairly and to give me back my money would be the right thing to do. Who knows, the vandalism might just stop?"

"And if I don't?"

"I wouldn't like to say, Mr. Franco. I have no control over what may or may not happen. With vandals you never know what they will do next. Some of them even start fires in houses, I'm told."

"You son of a bitch, Mario. You are trying to shake me down!"

"Not really. I'm just following the code."

"What code?"

"You have been away from the old country too long, Franco. Think back about how we handled injustice, how men like you were brought to their knees by the people."

"Do you know how much you and your vigilante friends have cost me?"

"No. But it is not so much as it might cost you if you don't refund my money and the vandals come back."

"You are bluffing. Go to Hell, Mario."

"Fine. May I suggest you order a pair of crutches on the way home ready for tomorrow."

"Crutches. What are you talking about?"

"It is hard getting around without them when your legs are broken. Trust me. Order them tonight."

"You are stark raving mad, Mario.

"No. It is you who is stark raving mad. You could have saved yourself a lot of problems had you just played fair with me. Now all you have to do is give me back my money, and you could save yourself a lot more."

"You are blackmailing me. I will call the police."

"Go ahead. I have an ironclad alibi. But rest assured the code will come into play when you least expect it. Surely you haven't forgotten how it works, Franco."

"No. But this is America. You can't get away with that kind of thing over here."

"Watch us. If I haven't got my money in my hand in the next few minutes, I guarantee you will regret it."

"I'm calling your bluff. I won't be threatened, or shook down by a fresh off the boat immigrant who has no idea how the law works here in America. I'm telling you for the last time, you signed a binding contract. Now get off the property or I will shoot you."

Mario and his friends bided their time until the obvious police surveillance ended and Jack Franco had stopped looking over his shoulder all the time. One night a car parked behind the sales office mysteriously caught fire and burned down the building. Franco was furious and told the police that Mario was probably responsible, but Mario had an iron-clad alibi. He was at home with his family and two guests. Three night's later forty pairs of headlights were popped.

Jack Franco had had enough. He knew he had been bested by a fresh off the boat immigrant. The cost of returning Mario's money was miniscule compared to the damages he had suffered, so he called Mario to come and collect his refund.

"How much to get you off my Goddamn back?"

"Twenty seven hundred dollar." Mario replied.

"You mean you are not trying to shake me down for a small fortune?"

"No. I just want my money back."

"Do you know how much this fiasco has cost me Mario?"

"It has cost you nothing. You have the car back and when you give it to me, I will have my money back." Jack Franco opened his wallet and handed over the refund.

"You may have won over me this time Mario, but you haven't heard the last of me. You have ruined my good reputation in the community. And cost me over thirty thousand in damages."

"Then wouldn't it have been better to give me the refund right away when I asked?"

"Get off the property, Mario but keep your eyes peeled. I remember a different code from the old country, one that keeps people like you in line. From my perspective you owe me over thirty grand, plus the twenty seven hundred sitting in your pocket, plus the commission I had to pay my salesman for your broken contract."

Three days later as Mario came home from work, two burly men jumped him and beat him badly right outside his home. As he lay on the sidewalk unable to move, he felt his wallet being removed from his back pocket. The car refund money was taken and the wallet thrown to the sidewalk besides him. He had no proof, but Mario knew who was responsible. It was a week before his injuries would allow him to return to work and he began to make inquiries about purchasing an untraceable handgun. If Franco's attack upon his person did not go unchallenged he would not be able to hold his head high in the community. Eventually Mario obtained a small handgun and a clip of bullets. He went to the car lot and waited in the shadows for Jack Franco to come out at closing time.

The office lights went out; Jack Franco stepped onto the porch turning to lock the door. Mario seized the opportunity and ran up and shot Franco in the back. After the second shot he went down and rolled over. Mario paused to look at him. Franco pulled a handgun from his belt and shot upwards at Mario hitting him in the chest. Mario emptied his clip into Franco before falling down on top of him. Together they bled to death. Each in his dying moments felt as though they had been avenged. The Chevrolet that was the root cause of the two deaths sat unsold at the rear of the lot. The sign on it read, ONE OWNER SPECIAL $2,695

THE HAUNTED HOUSE.

I of course never believed such claptrap. Folks always said the place was haunted. Don't go there after dark, they said. Hogwash was my usual reply. This foolishness had been passed down through the generations, but I never found anyone who had actually seen one of the apparitions. From my point of view none of the evidence was reliable.

Some people said the ghost was the spirit of a woman who had been murdered in an upstairs bedroom. The story was that she had been unfaithful and because of her terrible guilt, her spirit could not leave the house. Another version of the tales was that the ghost was of a woman who had lost her child and her spirit wandered through the house looking for him. Still others believed it was the ghost of a woman who had died of a broken heart when her husband failed to return from the wars. Some said it was because her husband had abandoned her for a younger woman.

The village folks tended to interchange the stories, depending upon who was listening at the time. So whenever the tales of the haunted house came up I tended to be totally skeptical. One Saturday night my wife and I with ten other couples were at a party at Ruth and Emmet's house, when the subject came up. As usual, it was the women who began talking about it. We guys listened to our wives rehashing the old tales with conviction, that the old abandoned mansion on the edge of town was indeed a haunted house. By this time I had demolished about a half dozen rum and cokes. Full of bravado and male superiority I opened my big mouth.

"Hogwash," I said. "Hogwash and nonsense. I can't believe that a bunch of grown intelligent women can believe such claptrap."

Within seconds, I knew I had stuck my foot in a hornet nest. Now that I am sober I realize in hindsight that I had in fact insulted their intelligence. Words lubricated with alcohol swarmed around my head, even my wife had turned into a hornet. The other guys in the room sat back with their drinks and said nothing; the party had turned into a spectator sport not unlike the lions against the Christians. Big mouthed me was the lone Christian in an arena of savage beasts. I looked to my male friends for support and it was immediately apparent they were actually enjoying watching me being verbally torn to shreds.

The harder I protested the more the hornet's swarmed around my head. Then I heard one voice above the buzzing,

"If you are so damn sure there is nothing to fear at the mansion why don't you put your money where your mouth is, take a sleeping bag and spend the night there?"

Instantly I saw a way out of my torment. I could get these hornet like women off my back and I could get back to talking about golf. So I let out the clutch on my big mouth again.

"If that's what it takes to get a bunch of dizzy ghost believing broads to learn that there is no such things as ghosts, goblins and poltergeists, name the day you want me to do it."

I was proud of my outburst. That last rum and coke had really bolstered my confidence. I would call their bluff and quash the stories forever making them look foolish in the bargain.

"Tomorrow night. The sooner the better." Said the woman whose idea it was.

"Yes do it tomorrow night." The other hornets echoed.

"It's Sunday tomorrow and I have to be at work early on Monday. I will need my rest."

You would think I had hurled hot coals at the women. They shrieked savage delight at what they called my cowardice.

"You are too scared to spend the night in there Bruce. The truth is out, you believe in these things just as we do." One woman said. Another asked if I would be taking my teddy bear with me if I went. I was shocked when my wife said,

"It's time to put up or shut up, Bruce. Either do it or apologize to our friends."

My big alcohol fueled mouth slipped back into gear.

"Apologize! Never! Sure I will go tomorrow night. It is a little inconvenient for me, but for the sake of putting this idiotic matter to rest in your minds, I will spend the night in the house. It will be well worth it just to see you all humbled to your knees."

I had a notion, despite the fact that I was feeling no pain, that my last sentence was a little over the top and that it might come back to haunt me. Why did I use that phrase? I ask myself. Well, it seemed that my big mouth was the catalyst for breaking up the party, at least that was what Beryl my wife suggested as she drove me home.

"You were boorish rude and insulting to our hosts and the other guests Bruce. It is all well and good to have your own opinions, but to suggest to others that their opinions are invalid is inexcusable. You are ignorant and loud Bruce and I am angry with you, as I am sure are the other ladies at the party you have most assuredly broken up."

I only understood part of what Beryl had said, my seventh rum and coke had turned my brain into a blacksmith's anvil and someone was pounding out horseshoes on it. I have only a vague recollection of getting into bed, but a vivid recollection of waking up feeling awful. Beryl, in her anger and her inability to sleep with my violent snoring, had spent the night on the sofa. Instinctively, I knew this was not going to be a good day. Beryl would react in one of two ways. It might be the silent treatment and the, don't you dare touch me routine. Or it might be the yelling and the forcing of a guilt trip on me. Either one was a daunting prospect. I needed sympathy and an understanding of the severe hangover that throbbed throughout my head, but I knew I would be denied it.

Beryl put on the coffee. Can you imagine how I felt when I found out she had only made one cup. Hers. So it was to be the silent treatment after all. I tried to remember what had happened at the party that had made Beryl so upset. I made my own coffee and then I asked,

"I think I had too much to drink at the party last night Beryl, did I make a fool of myself?'

The silence was deafening but I did get a look of utter disgust. I pride myself in the ability to read faces and I read in Beryl's that I had indeed made a fool of myself at the party. Unfortunately, I could not remember what I had done to induce such wrath in her. I knew if the impasse between us were to end, I would have to find out.

My tongue felt as though it was covered in cat fur despite trying to scald it off with my coffee. It felt as if someone had attached lead weights to my eyelids as I slept, and I could hear the sound of my blood pumping through my head like it was being pushed in rhythmic thumps by a sausage-making machine.

"What did I do or say Beryl, darling?" Her eyes slowly rose above the

Sunday paper and fixed upon me as though I had slithered out from under a rock. For a moment I thought she was going to tell me, but then her lips, now also visible above the newspaper, pursed tightly.

"You know what you said and did. You disgust me at times, Bruce." Beryl had always had a special look about her when she was angry.

"You look really pretty this morning, Beryl," I said. As soon as I said it I knew I had chosen the wrong moment.

"Do you really think you can get round me by a bit of sweet-talk. How many more insults are you going to send my way on top of the ones you gave everyone at the party?"

Ah! I am getting somewhere I thought, she is beginning to explain.

"I have insulted you? Darling, you know I would never do that on purpose. I love you, surely you know that? If I did insult you it must have been the drink talking.

"Talking! Talking! Last night you were shouting insults not talking them. I really don't know if I want to go to Ruth and Emmett's house again, I was so embarrassed at your outbursts."

"Can you refresh my memory, darling, I really can't remember much about last night."

"Don't darling me Bruce; I am still hurting from your boorish remarks. Among other things you called all the women dizzy broads and you suggested we were all idiots."

"Why did I do that Beryl?"

"Because we differ in point of view from you regarding the haunted house and by the way I hope you enjoy sleeping in the damn place tonight."

"What are you talking about Beryl? Why on earth would I be sleeping there?"

"Because you said you would, to show us idiotic women there was nothing to fear and that there were no such things as ghosts. Mike and Dianne will be at the front of the house at dusk and Hank and Melanie will be at the back, sitting in their cars to make sure you keep your promise."

"I can't do it tonight Beryl. I have to be at work early tomorrow. I will need my rest especially after feeling like I do."

"How you feel today is entirely your own fault Bruce, you won't get any sympathy from me. As for tonight, you promised and if you try to renege on your promise I will make damn sure you don't sleep here either. Your big mouth got you into this situation but it will not get you out of it, only your actions will. Oh, and by the way, just before we left last night, you invited them all to a party at our house next Saturday without even asking me if it was alright, just so that you could gloat over proving us all wrong."

"Oh God what have I done! No wonder you are angry with me. I will phone everybody and cancel the plans. I will tell them I had way too much to drink and said things I didn't mean."

"You will not! I will rip the phone out by the roots if you even try. You were so cocksure last night that you were right and we were wrong. You will go through with it or you can sleep in the car. The choice is yours."

I know Beryl. We have been married for ten years and when she is this angry I cannot win, simply because she will not lose. I find the aspirins, make some toast and then I lie down for a while. The aspirins do not work and at lunchtime my head was still pounding. Beryl prepared lunch for one and it wasn't mine. By dinnertime I had begun to feel marginally better, but the thought of sleeping on the floor of an abandoned house did nothing to improve my state of mind. Beryl prepared a chicken breast with Chinese vegetables for her dinner and when she was done, I warmed up a can of beans for mine. I collected my sleeping bag a spare pillow and threw them into the car. Just before dusk Beryl said,

"It's time for you to go big boy. I will have a good breakfast ready for you at seven o clock if you live through the night."

I sniggered at her then I drove to the haunted house and circled around the block. Mike and Dianne were sitting in their car at the front and Hank and Melanie were in theirs at the back. I parked right behind them and grabbed my gear. I gave them a cheery wave as I entered the big old house. I had to decide which room I would sleep in before it got completely dark. It was terribly messy. Children had been playing here during the holidays. Loose wallpaper hung from the walls and boards were missing in places from the floor. It was an eerie place and it was easy to see why people were suspicious of the house. I placed my sleeping bag in a corner of a downstairs room, climbed in and put my head on the pillow. I was so tired after the ordeal of the last twenty-four hours; I felt I would drop off to sleep right away. A light wind through the unglazed windows made an odd noise as it passed through the house. Occasionally a piece of the loose wallpaper would flap with a mild slapping sound. Instead of sleeping I found myself listening and as the night wind increased so did the strange sounds within the house. At somewhere near midnight I was wide-awake wondering what the next sound might be. It was then that I heard the unmistakable sound of footsteps on the stairs. I sat bolt upright. Were they coming down, or going up?

"Who's there?" I shouted. But no one answered. I heard a rustling sound from upstairs. Could it be the hem of a long dress trailing along the floor? There was no doubt what the next sounds were. They were sighs, long human sighs. Had I been wrong all along? I decided I didn't want to find out. I grabbed my sleeping bag and ran out of the house to my car. Hank and Melanie's car was gone. I drove home like a wild man and let myself in. Beryl was in bed so I undressed and got in with her.

"So we were right I take it," she said.

I didn't answer. I didn't think I needed to. The following Saturday, I helped Beryl prepare for the party I had offered to give. Thankfully no one mentioned the haunted house until after the third drink. Without warning the group began laughing and pointing at me. I began to squirm.

"So you ran out of the haunted house at one o clock Bruce? Did you see the ghost? Was it the sound of footsteps that did it, or the sound of the crinoline?"

"How did you know about that Mike? I haven't told anybody what happened."

"Everybody who has ever slept in the house has heard the very same things, Bruce." Then everybody began laughing again. I couldn't understand it. I knew they were laughing at my expense but why? It wasn't until the fifth drink that they told me it was they who had made the noises to teach me a lesson. I always knew there were no such things as ghosts.

"It's all Hogwash," I said. "There are no such thing as ghosts"

THE WATER MAIN.

"YOU WILL have to replace the line to your house from the water main," the man from the water board announced. "The cost is the homeowners responsibility, either we can do the work at municipal labour cost, or you can do the job yourself which you would find to be much more economical."

"I will do the replacing myself," I answered him. It was no big deal for me to do the work; after all I was doing almost a complete restoration of the house anyway.

I had come to live here in Ashton looking for a respite from the rat race of the city. Allison and I were living in our motor home while we tackled the restoration project on the big Victorian house which we had bought, for very little money, on the outskirts of Ashton. We had instantly fallen in love with the rambling but sadly neglected house. It had sat empty for at least twenty years, according to the realtor who sold the place to us. The family of the previous owner lived clear across the country in Arizona, and had no interest in living in the house of their long deceased uncle, apparently a medical man. They had set too high a price on the place and consequently it remained unsold until we came along and offered a low bid which they accepted, we presume to be rid of paying the annual taxes on the house. It had been a beautiful home in its heyday with fine Victorian fretwork all around the eaves and porch. But now the faded and peeling paint, made the place look neglected and decrepit. The front steps had a few boards missing adding to the sad appearance of the house.

I recognized immediately upon seeing the house that making the exterior beautiful again was, for the most part, cosmetic, not requiring a lot of structural work. Allison and I made the decision to begin our project by restoring the outside of our new home first. Rather than spend weeks scraping and wire brushing the peeling paint, we brought in a sandblasting company who finished the job in two days, doing it better than we could have done by hand. The same company spray painted the fretwork, eaves and trim with two coats of bone white. And the main part of the building forest green.

We were now ready to begin the longer task of working on the interior. The kitchen plumbing had to go. The old iron pipes were rotten and the sink looked like it was out of the dark ages. The bathroom fixtures were utterly outdated and since I had to replace the entire amount of iron pipe in the house with copper, we chose to install a modern bathroom suite while we had the room torn apart. With the plumbing work completed it was time to turn on the water.

I called the water board to open the valve at the water main on the street. Out of our faucets the most disgusting rusty liquid dribbled into our new plumbing fixtures. We had virtually no pressure and eventually we had none. That was when I had the conversation with the water board man, telling me I had to replace the line from the main to my water shut off valve in the basement of the house. As we spoke, water was bubbling up through the unkempt lawn and making its way to the road. I measured inside the basement where the house shut off valve was located and marked the location on the outside with a stake. I now had to dig a trench between the stake and the underground brass connection on the road to lay in new pipe.

I decided to begin digging in the basement, where the pipe coming into the house was encased in concrete. The concrete around the pipe had been poured long after the original floor; it appeared to me that the pipe had been replaced at an earlier date. First I had to smash the concrete to get at the soft soil beneath it. Then I started digging piling the soil up alongside the excavation. I found the elbow connecting to the line coming in from the street. Every thing was covered in rust and I needed to make the excavation deeper and wide in order to use my tools to disconnect the two pieces.

My spade touched something solid below the pipe making a hollow sound as though it were an underground tank of some kind. Surely this would not be a septic tank? Not only would it be irregular, but in all likelihood, illegal. My curiosity was piqued so I began to enlarge the excavation only to discover the roof of the tank, or whatever it was, spread further under the basement floor. When I tapped on it, there was definitely a hollow sound. I continued breaking concrete and digging across the floor. Then I felt that I should get on with the job at hand and re-pipe in from the water main in order to get clean water flowing into the house. Then I would get back to this mystery when I had more time.

I finished the job late in the day and let the water run into the sinks and toilet until it came out of the faucets clean. The following day my curiosity made me go back to continue digging in an attempt to find the end of the tank or whatever it was. Since I had to bring in a concrete pump to redo the front path, as well as replace the concrete in the hole in the basement floor, it didn't matter that I would need a little extra mix.

I dug along the tank until I came to a big cabinet holding ancient paint cans and garden chemicals. There the tank ceased being level and rose vertically to the base of the cabinet. It made no sense. I examined the cabinet carefully. On the floor in front of it were scuffmarks suggesting that it had, at some time, swung open like a door. I noticed a casing on both sides. Using my claw hammer I tore them off the wall. On the left side I discovered hinges that were dry, and had been hidden for many years; on the right a door lock with the knob and shaft removed. Using a large screwdriver I turned the lock. The cabinet swung to the left side, revealing steps that descended into darkness.

Stale air rose, had it been a septic tank it would have smelled foul. I went upstairs to the kitchen where Allison was removing layers of old wallpaper.

"Allison I have found an entrance to that tank thing I was telling you about. The old paint cabinet swings back and there are steps going down. Do we have a flashlight?"

"Yes Brian there is one of those big ones in the motor home under the bench seat. Get it and I will come with you." With the lamp in my hand, Allison and I went to the basement. Shining the light down the steps to the tank revealed the spider webs of many years.

"You had better get a broom before we go down to investigate, Brian." With Allison holding the lamp behind me I furiously swept the cobwebs aside then descended into the blackness. Allison followed me down the steep steps until we were standing together on the dry floor of the tank.

"Well since it's dry Allison. I would assume it is not a septic tank as I suspected it might be. Hand me the lamp and let's see exactly what this thing is." I took the lamp and flashed it round the walls. I reeled back in horror. Allison screamed. Just inches in front of us a skeleton, with the remains of men's clothing hanging from it, lay on a bench. Further along in the corner three more skeletons sat on the floor in grotesque positions.

Along the end wall, another skeleton hung with wrist shackles still holding it off the floor. I shone the lamp on the wall behind us. It contained an array of torture equipment under which two more skeletons that had fallen apart, their bones lay in profusion on the floor.

"Get me out of here!" Allison screamed. I shone the light onto the steps, and she ran up them. I followed her. In the basement we stopped and stared at each other.

"My God Brian, what have we got ourselves into here?"

"I really don't know Allison. But I think we had better call the police and tell them what we have just found." I dialed the non-emergency number of the Aston police department.

"I have discovered a group of human skeletons in a room under my basement floor." I told the officer answering my call.

"Have you been drinking sir?" He asked condescendingly.

"Certainly not." I retorted. "I recently bought the big Victorian house out on Lambeth road and when I was replacing the water pipe to the mains, I discovered this room under my basement floor in which there are a number of human skeletons."

"Sir. It is the first of April. Do you take me for an April fool?" I became frustrated; this small town cop would not believe my story and finally hung up on me.

Now that I was over the initial shock, I decided to go back down and have a better look at the tank and its contents. There was obviously nothing to fear, the human remains had lain undisturbed in the tank for more than twenty years. I took the lamp and found an electric light switch just above the entry door. To my surprise a light came on in the tank. A single light bulb illuminated the tank so that I could examine its interior more carefully. The eye sockets in the skulls seemed to be looking at me as I reached the bottom step.

I wondered what kind of monster would shackle and leave the bodies that had encased the skeletons so many years ago. Under the steps to the tank I found a filing cabinet. Maybe the answer was inside, so I opened the top drawer. Inside I found a ledger marked, Pain Threshold Studies, by Doctor Wilhelm Schroder. The first entry was dated March 11th 1939. It told of a patient Frank Morris, brought here from the state mental hospital in the care of Dr. Schroder. The entry listed the torture that Patient Morris had endured before expiring on March 27th The entry ended with the notation that Morris had a low pain tolerance, a surprising result considering his mental condition. I had assumed that because of his extreme mental disorder, pain would not bother him too much.

Entry after entry, listed terrible suffering by patients removed from the mental hospital into Schroder's custody. According to the ledger more than forty patients had met a grisly experimental end in this underground tank. I wondered where their remains had been removed to, since there were only five skeletons here in the tank. It seemed highly unlikely that the State health authorities would have sanctioned these experiments, nor not allowing for proper funerals for the doctor's victims.

I went back up into the kitchen and told Allison my findings.

"We have to go to the police, Brian if they don't believe us, we will call the State Patrol."

"O.K. Allison. I will go into town and talk to the police again. If I go in person they have to take me seriously."

"I'm coming with you. I'm not staying in this creepy place alone, Brian." We drove the motor home to town and reported the matter to the police who grudgingly agreed to send an officer out to the house. When he saw the tank and the human remains in it, immediately he declared our house a crime scene. We were ordered out of the house and so took our motor home to an R.V. park. Over the next two weeks our yard was dug up and many human remains were located where the long unused vegetable garden had been. The police investigation team found even more mummified remains under the basement concrete floor.

When we were allowed to go back to continue our restoration of the house, we parked the motor home alongside the house and connected the electricity and water. The first night, Allison sat bolt upright in bed and shook me into wakefulness.

"Brian! I can hear screams coming from the house!" she said frantically. I too sat up. Then I could hear the most blood curdling screams coming from inside the house. In seconds goose pimples covered my body.

"You had better go and see what is going on in there Brian." I quickly dressed and went outside the motor home. The appalling screams burst from every door and window in the house. Not knowing what to expect I grabbed a shovel to use as defense against whatever it might be. I hurled open the front door and went inside. I determined that the agonized screams came from the basement, so I nervously made my way down the steps to the dug up floor. The sounds were coming from the open door to the tank.

My blood ran cold at the sound of the appalling screams of agony.

I turned on the light and went down. The police had taken all the human remains away, and the screams came forth out of thin air. My first thought was that the remains had gone, but their spirits lingered on in agony. I tried making a noise, but the screams continued unabated. There was nothing I could do, so I went back to the motor home and told Allison what had transpired. We could not sleep, the screams were much too disturbing so I disconnected the services from the vehicle, and we drove away parking on the road so we could get some rest. All was quiet when we returned in the morning. Had we not spent the night parked on the roadside, I might have thought we had shared the same nightmare.

At midnight the blood curdling screams started again. Thank goodness we were not sleeping in the house or I think we should have gone mad. We knew that if this was to be a nightly occurrence we could not live here, despite all the work we had put into the place. We sought the help of the priest of the local church who he referred us to an exorcist. He spent the night in the house and heard the screams.

"They are real enough," he said. "But they are not the screams of the damned, they are the cries of spirits unable to leave the place of their torture and demise. They are the screams of innocents and I know of no way to help them. The methods used to cast out the Devil are of no value, for the Devil is not present here. I do not know how I can help the tortured souls or you. The only suggestion I have is that by opening the tank you have given the spirits a voice. By closing it and burying it deep underground, you just might bring them peace and silence. But it is my feeling that they will reside there for all time."

"I cannot live here knowing what lies under my house, Brian. We should do as the exorcist suggests. Seal off the tank, finish restoring the house then resell it, for I will never sleep one night under this roof."

The nightly wails continued until we had completely sealed off the tank and poured a ten-inch thick concrete floor in the basement. When prospective buyers asked why we had put in a new basement floor, we told them it was because I had replaced the pipe to the water mains.

BEACHCOMBER.

I ALMOST DIDN'T pick it up. Half buried in the sand and covered with algae, the bottle didn't seem like much of a find. It laid semi concealed by a pile of wind and tide borne logs. I have no idea what possessed me to bend down and look at the bottle. On the surface it was no different than a million others just like it. But the moment I removed from the sand it was immediately apparent that this bottle was different.

The top had been corked and sealed with red wax. Through the algae coated exterior I could see a roll of paper inside. I figured some romantic teenager had put it in just for a prank. I have been beachcombing every weekend for at least ten years now. I suppose you could describe me as a loner; I am not a very good looking man; fairly short, and my hair has a huge cowlick in front which tends to accentuate my plain features needless to say, I am very much aware of it. So I tended to spend my weekends alone at the Pacific shore beaches. I had my own apartment on the outskirts of town and a job in the crab packing plant.

The big prize in beachcombing in this area is the large glass ball fishing floats that drift in from Japanese waters. Over the years I have found over twenty of them, plus numerous smaller ones. I find many other odd things of course and I enjoyed the mind games of where the objects originated. I slipped the bottle into my backpack to be dealt with later. I combed about four miles of beach to the north returning to my pickup to eat my lunch sandwich washed down by can of diet coke. I listened to the noon news on my truck radio and emptied the backpack before I headed south to work the other stretch of sandy beach.

Pickings were lean on the south beach; there was nothing really worth taking, so I wandered back to my truck. It was one of those days, about ten miles of walking and nothing much to show for it. But on the up side, it had been a good walking day, with not too much wind and it hadn't rained. I slipped the bottle behind the seat in my cab preventing it from rolling around, making a noise or breaking.

When I got back to my apartment, I forgot all about the bottle. It was about a month later when I remembered it. I removed the wax seal and used a regular corkscrew to open the bottle. The paper inside was bone-dry and I could not twist it small enough to remove it through the neck. So I wrapped the bottle in newspaper and smashed it. Retrieving the note, it read,

Finder. Please write and tell me
Where the bottle was found and
Something about yourself.

Box 1184 Fairbanks Alaska.

Wow! This bottle was a long distance traveler I told myself. I noted that there was no indication if the sender was male or female. I wrote a return letter right away.

> *Dear sender, I located the bottle high on the beach at Marsden, on the south Oregon coast. It would have been close to noon on the 10th of April. My name is Walter Marshall. I am 35 years of age, and I have been a beachcomber for about ten years. Your note did not indicate if the launching of your bottle was part of an official tidal flow study. Yours truly Walter Marshal.*

I dropped the letter in a mailbox later in the day when I went for my Saturday visit with my parents. As usual my mother asked,

"Have you got a girlfriend yet?" I get tired of her asking. It wasn't as if I were still living at home and under her feet all the time. Sure! I would like to have a lady in my life. But I am not a handsome young buck. I do not feel I am attractive to women and I accept that, let's face it I am thirty-five now and no woman has ever shown any interest in me so far. Any dreams of romance I had as a teen and young adult have long faded, I have accepted that I will remain a singe man. For the most part I enjoy my job at the plant and beachcombing seems to fill my emotional needs.

Ten days after I had mailed the letter to Alaska I received a reply.

Dear Walter, Thank you for responding to my note in a bottle. It has been traveling for just over two years. I too am thirty-five. I am unmarried and live a somewhat lonely life in the bush about sixty miles outside Fairbanks. I go in to town twice a month for my supplies and the mail. Your letter did not indicate if you were an unattached man. If this is the case then I should like to hear from you again. If not then thank you for responding to my note. Regards, Francis Wade.

I knew immediately that I would respond. My dealings with the opposite sex have been severely limited and here was an opportunity to develop a non-threatening relationship with this person named Francis. She need never know that I considered myself as being ugly, or that I was terribly shy as a result of it. I could send a letter and feel as though I were Robert Redford or Gregory peck. We would never meet so where was the harm in it. So I began to write, but I quickly discovered that I could not be untruthful and deceitful in my letter, so I tore up the first one and penned the second.

Dear Francis. Thank you for your response to my initial letter. The fact that I am writing to you indicates that I am indeed single. I too have a somewhat lonely life, I am not the tallest or most handsome tree in the forest, and as a result I have always been shy with females. I suppose the fear of rejection has caused me to live my life so far almost reclusively. My greatest joy is beachcombing and I spend every weekend doing it. I go to the movies by myself on Saturday nights, and I read a lot. I thank you for the opportunity to correspond with you. Yours. Walter Marshal.

I mailed the letter, but I figured that by being honest it would be the last communication between us. After two weeks had gone by with no reply, I felt that my suspicions had been confirmed. After four weeks I was sure of it. Then I found a letter in my mailbox after coming home from work. It was from Francis.

Dear Walter. I must have missed your letter by a day and didn't get it for another two weeks. Remember I only go into town twice

> *each month. I did enjoy your letter, your life sounds very much like mine. I prefer my own company for the most part, for I too was not born the prettiest flower in the garden. I too have fears of rejection and tend to avoid it by keeping very much to myself. I have taught myself to paint, and a gallery in Fairbanks distributes my work to other galleries in the lower 48. I manage to eke out a living at it, but at times the loneliness here at my cabin becomes intense and I crave the company of a man who will accept me for who I am. Believe me no one understands better than I how you feel. Please forgive me for prattling on. Yours truly. Francis Wade.*

The letter was better than a spring tonic. I felt elated for I had found a kindred soul. At last in my lonely life someone understands how I felt. Her letter brings me hope that somewhere there is a woman who might love me as I am and not as society would have me look. I made a journey the following Saturday all the way up to Portland to check out the art galleries for Francis's work. I found a smaller gallery who had several of her paintings on display. They were similar in that they were landscapes of Alaska. They were painted in a style with heavy brush strokes, but the strokes conveyed admirably the ruggedness of the wilderness scenes. I drove home pleased to have seen her work and I would tell her what I had done when I wrote my reply. There was a message on my answering machine from mother, wanting to know why I hadn't called by at the house today. I sat down to write a return letter.

> *Dear Francis, Thank you for your letter. It would seem we have a great deal in common. Today I drove to Portland three hundred miles there and back to see some of your work at the waterfront gallery. I was very impressed; you obviously have a great talent for painting. I am afraid I have no such talents; mine are limited to finding strange and wonderful things on the beaches.*
> *I know this is very forward of me, and I have never done anything like this before That is to say, well I have two weeks off in August, and I wonder if I were to fly to Fairbanks if we could meet. It seems to me we have much we could talk about. If I am being too bold and you don't wish it to happen, I will understand.*
> *Yours truly. Walter Marshal.*

I mailed the letter to Francis and hoped for an early reply, It would be great it she would agree to meet me. Who knows where such a meeting might lead us. Her reply came to my mailbox three weeks later.

Dear Walter, How pleased I was to receive your latest letter. Of course, I would like to meet you. I too believe we must be kindred spirits and brought together in the oddest way. Let me know what dates you would expect to arrive, and I will pick you up at the Fairbanks airport. Failing that I could have my closest neighbour pick you up, he drives in daily to work. There is no need to book accommodation, I have room to put you up. Please forgive my boldness now, but I cannot help but wonder if fate has longer term plans for us. I suppose only time will tell. Looking forward immensely to your visit.
Yours truly, Francis.

Suddenly after reading her letter, I was on cloud nine. Perhaps there can be love in my life after all. My mind began to draw a picture of us, together by the fire in her cabin, hand in hand and then going to her bed. I begin to imagine the softness of her skin, the fragrance of her hair as our bodies meet. I have never been with a woman before and my mind runs riot at what I might expect. I felt that though neither of us may seem beautiful to the outside world, we will be beautiful to each other. I find myself not sleeping properly, I toss and turn. I see Francis with her arms outstretched beckoning me, wanting me. I cannot wait until morning. I have to rise from my bed and answer her letter.

Dear Francis, How good to get your latest letter. I am thrilled that you were not offended, and want me to come and stay with you. I shall count the hours until we meet. I will check on airline times from Oregon to Fairbanks, after the second of August. I will let you know as soon as I have tickets and flight confirmation. Is there any thing I can bring with me that you cannot get in Fairbanks? Even though we have not met as yet, I have a feeling things will go well between us. I will be frank with you Francis, I have never had a serious relationship with anyone before and I am just a little nervous that you may not like me as well as I hope. I will write as soon as I have travel dates. Yours, Walter.

I mailed the letter that morning, and on Monday I would go to the travel agency. The agent booked me on a flight from Eugene direct to Fairbanks on August the fifth with an arrival time of three p.m. I sent Francis another letter giving her the details. Her next letter comes to my mailbox.

Dear Walter. Thank you for your two letters. I will be waiting for you in the airport arrivals lounge. No there is nothing I can't buy in Fairbanks but thanks for the offer. Walter dear, do not worry yourself that I will not like you when you get here. From your letters I read honesty, and a willingness to accept me, just as I am willing to accept you. I have a good feeling about us, and look forward to sharing an intimacy between us that possibly neither of us has had before. Bring the letters I have written to you and we can make a scrapbook of them together. Until August the fifth. Love Francis.

I was in seventh heaven. Francis had finished her letter with the word love. She obviously felt as I do. The weeks and days dragged at the packing plant, I could hardly wait until the flight time. My mother was curious as to why I was going to Alaska, but I had no wish to let her know until I am sure that Francis is willing to marry me. I did not like lying to mother, but I told her I am going on a fishing trip for King Salmon. She was a little suspicious, but she accepted my explanation. Finally it is the fifth! I drove to Eugene and boarded my flight. I had a window seat and I marveled at the scenery below. The plane began its bank into Fairbanks airport. Then we were on the ground. Clutching the huge bunch of Oregon flowers and my flight bag I entered the arrivals lounge. It was full of people greeting each other. I looked around for Francis but I did not see a woman alone. The crowd thinned out and she was not here. Finally I am alone so I sat down to wait for her. The door swung open and a shabbily dressed woman wearing a toque and large boots stepped inside

"Are you Walter?" She asked in a rough gravelly voice. "Welcome I am Francis Wade."

This was not what I had visualized. Francis looked more like a lumberjack than the soft pretty woman I had expected.

"Yes, I'm Walter," I said. I knew I had made a terrible mistake by coming here, but since I had, I would try to make the best of it. Francis led me out to the parking lot and a ramshackle old pickup truck that looked as though it had never been cleaned out since new. Our conversations on the way back to her cabin were strained to say the least, but in just over an hour we reached it and I was in for another shock. The place looked more like a junkyard than the varnished log cabin with smoke curling from the chimney, I had expected to find.

The interior was even worse. An easel, with a painting on it, sat in the middle of the floor an unmade bed and a disgustingly dirty sofa sat against one wall, a stove and table cluttered with paints and unwashed dishes sat along the opposite one. My heart sank at what I saw. I knew I could not live for long under these conditions, and I had absolutely no desire to get naked with Francis; all thoughts of a wonderful first love-making had fled. In view of what happened to me in the night, that too, was a mistake. I had rejected her invitation to sleep with her and I woke up on the sofa with a shackle fastened round my ankle.

It had become painfully obvious that Francis was quite mad, utterly deranged. She got out of her bed fully clothed, put on her boots and went outside. She returned with a logging chain and padlocked it to my shackle. She led me outside and chained me to a sturdy tree along with several husky dogs.

"You will never lead another woman down the garden path, Walter. Men like you deserve what they get." For the next few weeks I survived by stealing some of the food Francis gave the dogs. But I began to weaken, and the intense cold at night took its toll on me. I lived in hope that someone would come to the cabin and find me, but it didn't happen and one freezing night I just fell asleep.

There is nothing the Oregon State Patrol can do, Mrs. Marshal. There could be a hundred reasons why your son has not returned from his Alaskan fishing trip. You have no information on his destination, so there is nothing for us to go on. He may even have drowned while fishing and his body swept to the ocean. Or he may just have decided to abandon his old one and make a new life for himself.

THE ACCIDENT.

IT HAD been a great party. Friends they hadn't seen in ages were there. Some of them, not since he and Sheila moved to Bowville six years ago. Fran and George Brown were excellent party hosts. Fran had a knack for producing good food and keeping an eye out for any guest who had imbibed too much of the free flowing beverages. Also she and George had a way of wheedling the car keys from any they thought were too tipsy to drive home afterwards.

The permanently grinning and portly George was just the guy to keep the party hopping. He was the personnel manager for his company and had an instinct for reading people. The same applied at his parties; if he saw a guest becoming a little morose he could cajole them back into high spirits. Sitting here, I remember him asking me,

"Are you planning to drive back to Bowville tonight Frank?" I can recall my answer,

"Yes George. I have a business appointment at nine in the morning. Why do you ask?"

"Well you know Frank, that I don't like my party guests to drive after having a few and I notice that Sheila looks like she is feeling no pain."

"Thanks for the concern George. But we had already agreed that I would drink lightly, Sheila has been going through a bit of a rough emotional patch lately and I think it is good that she is letting her hair down." Sheila a thirty something pretty blonde sat staring blankly ahead, her normally smiling face looking dark and serious.

"That's O.K. then Frank. I was just a little concerned. You have to drive over the pass to Bowville on winding mountain roads and the weather, as we both know, can change so rapidly up there."

"Don't worry George, I am quite sober and intend to stay that way,"

I answered.

Then I remember him turning away to see to another guest.

They were playing a waltz on the record player so I stepped up to Marjorie Telford and took her hand. She stepped into the circle and we began to dance. I had worked with her husband Jack before I moved to Bowville and I always liked dancing with her even back then. Marjorie liked to be held close when she danced. The feel of her body against mine, as always, felt exciting. It had never gone anywhere; it was just one of those momentary things we both silently enjoyed. Besides Jack was a good friend, but given the opportunity I think I could forget that for a while.

As we danced, I caught a glimpse of Sheila staring at me, her eyes seemed glazed and angry, George was right, she looked like she had had one too many. I pulled Marjorie closer to me and she responded I could feel her breasts pressing into me through our clothes. As we turned, her leg slipped between mine and I had a feeling she wanted to know me much better than just friends. Who knows what has transpired in her life in the last year or so, maybe her marriage was not all that it seemed and needed a little spice. Then I quickly realize that I must behave myself; I am married and Sheila is watching my every move.

I have a recollection of returning to Sheila and asking her if she wanted to go home yet. Her terse reply surprised me,

"Yes. Take me home right now."

We thanked our hosts at the door we saw it had begun to snow lightly.

"Drive carefully Frank. Better still, if you want to wait until daylight, we can find a place for you to catch some sleep," George suggested.

"I'll be alright George, I'm perfectly sober and I have good tires on the car"

It is a three-hour drive to Bowville in good weather; it would take me a little longer in the snow. The clock in the dash read eleven thirty. I wish I didn't have an early appointment and could have stayed. I could have had another dance or two with Marjorie.

I glanced at Sheila; she sat erect in her seat with her eyes closed.

"Did you enjoy the party?" I asked. Her eyes slowly opened as she turned to face me.

"Bastard!" It was the only word she uttered.

"Wow! You really did have too much to drink." I answered. She said it again,

"Bastard!"

"What the Hell has gotten into you Sheila? Are you annoyed because I danced a few times with Marjorie? I have danced with her at parties before and it has never bothered you!"

"Bastard!"

"You are starting to sound like a broken record, Sheila. Spit it out. Say what is on your mind and get it out in the open so we can deal with it. Are you jealous because I danced with Marjorie and not you? You had been drinking heavily, Sheila, you couldn't have danced even if you had wanted to." She did not answer so I decided to drop it and concentrate on my driving. It was snowing much heavier now. The film of compacted snow on the road made it quite slick.

We were climbing steadily and with the higher elevation the snow fell thicker. I slowed for a series of tight curves and I could feel the wheels slip in each one. I passed a line of truckers installing tire chains in a lay by. I figure with my new snow tires I will be O.K. and besides I don't feel like being out in the stuff in my good clothes to put my tire chains on. On top of that Sheila is sulking and will not speak her mind. The thought of it angers me and I press a little harder on the gas pedal.

We have been married ten tears now and we have no kids. Maybe that is what is bugging her; women are so damned hard to understand in these matters. She has been suggesting for a while that we go to a doctor together, but I don't believe for a moment the problem is with me. If she is the one brooding about it, she should be the one to go. But why bring up the issue at a goddamn party if that is what is bugging her. I glance at her. I see tears on her cheeks from the reflected headlights in the snow.

"Are you going to tell me what is bothering you Sheila? Or are you going to suffer in silence. For what it's worth, I'm sorry I danced with Marjorie so many times without asking you."

"You lousy stinking bastard Frank!"

"For what? You surely can't be this angry over a dance with a woman who has been friends with both of us for ages?"

"I can't? Why can't I? I have lots of reasons to be angry about. Marjorie is only one of them. The fact that you were slithering round her like a snake in heat is just another one."

"So bloody well tell me and then we can discuss them."

"You know what the issues are Frank, there is nothing to discuss. Words mean nothing to you. I want a divorce Frank?"

"A bloody divorce! What the Hell brought this on?" In my anger I momentarily took my eyes from the snow-covered road, and before I knew what was happening the car had left the road and was airborne. We were in mid air and the nose of the car started to dip. The headlight beams shone on treetops far below. Helplessly I saw the light beams quickly drop to the tree trunks at ground level. The car was almost vertical in flight, and then suddenly there was a loud bang and darkness. My face stung like it had been burned and just as quickly as it had inflated, the airbag deflated.

"Are you all right?" I screamed at Sheila. But there was no response. Then I remembered when I bought the car the auto dealer saying to me,

"Do you want the car equipped with dual airbags?" I had figured for the extra cost it was not worth it and I had refused.

"Are you all right Sheila?" I yelled again. But the only sound was the wind outside the car. I began to panic. I felt in the darkness to see if she had stayed with the car or had been hurled out in the impact. I felt for her. But she was still inside. There was a space where the seat should have been. I moved my hands up her back, but my seatbelt kept me from reaching her head. I undid the buckle but when I tried to get close to her I realized that my feet and legs were trapped with metal, crushed around them in the impact. I could only move my upper body and I could not reach Sheila's head, nor could I see it in the dark. I felt for her arm and lifted it toward me. I tried to feel a pulse, but never having done it before I still could not tell if she was alive. The temperature in the car began to plummet without the engine running. I tried the switch attempting to restart it, but the switch just clicked and the engine would not turn over. I glanced at the outside mirror and I could see moving light as a vehicle went by, high above us on the highway. Surely someone would see by the tracks that a vehicle had just left the road? I tried again to extricate my feet but they were held vise like, by twisted metal. It occurred to me that if our car became buried in snow we might not be discovered for weeks.

Even though we had been in this predicament for a few minutes I had a feeling we were going to die here. Maybe Sheila had already met her end, I would not know until daylight. I wondered how I would die, frostbite or starvation? Our only hope was that someone would report us missing and the authorities might begin a search. There was no sign of movement or sound of breathing from Sheila. I could not do anything to help her and I began to feel guilt about it. She had always been a strong woman and had asked for my help only on rare occasions. Knowing she was strong, I gave it begrudgingly. Now, as a result of my actions, she desperately needed my help and I could offer her none.

I began to wonder why she had said she wanted a divorce. I don't ever remember her being so angry before. Surely she couldn't have found out about Pamela Martin and I. We had always been so careful to keep our relationship a clandestine and secret one. It was in fact the secrecy of our meetings that added such spice to our lovemaking. When we did get together, on my out of town trips, we were like randy teenagers and we made love with wild abandon. How could Sheila have found out? We were so careful; we never wrote anything down or telephoned each other at home. Any arrangements had been made in the privacy of my office, as my secretary, Pamela made damned sure things were kept just between the two of us.

She told me that her husband suspected nothing when she explained that she went on retreats with the church group. In fact, he had told her he didn't mind her being away because he could play golf on both Saturday and Sunday.

I began to think it was not possible that Sheila had found out; she must have been incensed at something else. Maybe it was the fertility thing after all? Possibly she had a point. I never took precautions with Pamela, or with the broad I met at the health club. Marsha, I think her name was. Maybe I do have a problem? Maybe it was my fault that Sheila never got pregnant. I have to admit to myself that I really didn't want kids anyway; they would have put a major cramp in my lifestyle.

I am starting to get really cold now, and though it didn't seem so bad at first, my trapped feet are becoming quite painful. Sheila never questioned the monthly Friday night card game with the guys. John Willard used to bring in some wild broads, and for fifty bucks the sky was the limit. But it couldn't have been that she was angry at, we haven't had card night for over a year now and we had all swore to secrecy.

Sheila has shown no signs of life. I wonder if she is dead. If I could get her coat, I could keep myself warmer. I will not know until daylight if she died in the crash or she is just unconscious. Since I am unable to do anything else, I try to sleep. It is a useless exercise; the pain in my feet and the cold will not allow it. Imperceptibly the light of the dawn begins to filter into the car and I see that Sheila's head is outside the car through a hole in the broken windshield. She is still trapped in her broken seat. I cannot see her face; it looks forward toward the trees. Lying on the top of her head is a blob of fresh snow and a touch of her frozen hand tells me she is dead. I try to take her coat from her, but I cannot get it, due to the seated position I am trapped in. Outside the snow is almost to the top of the windows now and it is still coming down heavily. If it does not stop, I estimate the car will be completely covered within the hour and to boot, my car is a white one. The chances of it being spotted so far below the highway are close to nil, until the spring warmth melts the snow. I now know I will die here alongside Sheila.

In the morning light I see her purse on the floor. With an effort I reach it and bring it to my knee. Sometimes she carries candies in here. I open the purse and begin to rummage through it. There are no edibles, but I find an envelope tucked behind the lining and I begin to read the letter inside.

> *My darling Sheila, Thank god you have decided to tell Frank it is over between you this weekend. I cannot live another day without you in my arms. I know you are fully aware of Frank's dalliances and have known for quite some time. I suppose your disgust and disappointment at him have helped to drive you into my arms. Come to me my love, I will soothe your soul and help to heal your emotional wounds. I have arranged for a small apartment for you so Frank will not be able to find you until the divorce is finalized. When that day comes, I will fire Frank effective immediately. And we will both be free of him permanently. I love you, Gerald.*

I fold the letter and prepare to die, with Sheila's body grotesquely frozen at my side. So she did know about my infidelity, terrible feelings of guilt rush like wild horses into my brain. I am responsible for her unhappiness through my own lack of character. I am responsible for her death in this white wilderness. I realize now, just how much I really loved her and how much I have hurt her. Sheila was never a vengeful person, but unknowingly she will taunt me until I take my last breath in this frozen Hell we share.

I scream out my regrets, but the sound is muffled by the snow covering us and is heard only by me. Another night approaches and with it sub-zero temperatures. I shall not see another dawn.

THE BEACH.

THE SMALLEST arc of the setting sun remained above the horizon. The brilliant red orb cast its glow onto the wave tops and the surf breaking on the beach. The surf took on the colour of a foamy strawberry milkshake as it rushed up the beach spreading itself thinner and thinner, until it melded with the dark wet sand losing its grandeur. The moist sand pushed up between my toes forced upward by the weight of my body was a delicate grainy and damp feeling, highly pleasurable. It was a feeling of communing with nature in the simplest way.

We walked together wordlessly. She took smaller steps than I and yet, she did not lag behind but stayed at my side as we traversed the shore. Sometimes our feet were in several inches of water. At others, as the initial rush of tidewater returned to the sea caressing my ankles, I found my feet sinking deeper into the sand aided by the moving water. Then, suddenly the water had gone and we again walked on hard wet sand.

To the south, the moon in a lightly clouded sky began to appear much brighter now, as the sun had almost gone taking with it the strawberry hued light. Almost miraculously, several stars joined the moon in their nocturnal visitations. Minute by minute more of them appeared as the sun finally sank below the horizon leaving just the light in the western sky a pale muted glow.

The full power of the new summer moon illuminated the shoreline, aided largely by its brilliant reflection on the surface of the boundless waves. We walked silently to where we rested for a short while, before coming back. The moonlight picked out white quartz stones amid the sand, polished and cleaned by a thousand tides, their whiteness a stark contrast against the now dark beach. By now the surf's hue was a pale primrose yellow and the wave tops resembled an endless string of little white Christmas tree lights dancing and moving to the rhythm of the inbound waves.

We left the water's edge to sit at the base of a large rock high on the beach above the summer tide line. Here we would sit and contemplate the beauty of the muted scene before us and listen to the sound of the waves breaking, far out where the land meets the sea in timeless conflict. I sat in the sand and leaned my back against the moonlit rock. She sat down quietly at my side. I did not speak, for the wonder of a summer's eve at the beach said it all.

For a moment I closed my eyes. The visions ended, but the sounds continued on unabated. Straining to hear, I heard the bark of a distant seal from far out where the surf broke. From the land behind me, I heard the sounds of trees sighing in the ever-present summer breeze.

I opened my eyes. The surf retained its primrose hue. The surf still roared in the distance and the trees continued to sigh. I extended my arm and gently stroked her head; she turned and looked at me with soft eyes lit by the moon high above us. I did not speak, there was no need. My hand stroked her head. Her eyes looked at me. Words were not needed, or even wanted. Truth be told, words might even destroy the magic of the moment for both of us. We tarried a little longer soaking up the surrounding ambiance. Together we rose and ambled back down to where the incoming tide softened the freshly washed sand.

The sky had darkened and the stars, now more prominent in the subdued light, sparkled like diamonds hurled onto a table of black velvet. . With the moon now behind us, two shadows preceded us across the sand, one tall and one shorter. I felt an incredible oneness with nature, a primal satisfaction. It was a sense of deep peace knowing that what I was experiencing at this very moment had been experienced by countless others over millions of years, and it would likely be experienced by many more far into the future.

Sea meeting shore was timeless. It had always been this way; the only thing to change was the seasons. The tranquility I felt in my heart at this moment would in the storms of winter, be less calm. Rather it would be one of awe at natures fury unleashed, as the sea meets the land in unbridled violence. I glanced at her as she walked in silence beside me and I wondered if she shared my thoughts. Our eyes met when she looked up, but hers gave no indication that she did.

Far off, high above the shoreline, the pale yellow glow of our cabin window beckoned us. Barefoot still, I walked in a straight line across the beach toward it. The shadows we were making, now were off to the one side with the slight change in our direction. The moving shadows cast to the sand were now stunted and twisted. Quite unlike the bodies making them in the moonlight.

It was harder to walk now as we passed through the jumble of weeds, sticks and miscellaneous flotsam left by the last high tide The water packed sand now gave way to sand that was loose and dry. The dry sand clings tenaciously to wet skin. It is smooth as glass and soft underfoot, but toes sink in displacing it, leaving stunted and unrecognizable tracks.

I find the place where I had left my shoes, brush off my feet and put them on. Together we climb up the steep track to the treed plateau above the beach. The cabin is close now. I think of the fresh clam chowder simmering on the stove, made from the clams I had dug at daybreak from the same wet sand.

She leaves me now and runs ahead, but waits for me on the cabin steps. In the light spilling from the cabin window, I can see her waiting for me. The soft light shining upon her hair causes it to look golden now instead of black. Patiently she waits for me to come closer. Even in the low light I see love for me in her eyes. It is a love that has not waned since we first cast eyes upon each other. But then nor has mine for her. I reach the steps. Her eyes look deeply into mine begging, searching, and I know instinctively that she desires my touch and the sound of my voice. So I extend my hand stroking her head, I see that she too perceives the aroma of the simmering chowder somehow escaping the confines of the cabin. It is tantalizing, it teases the senses and it beckons us.

"Good dog." I say, "Are you hungry too?" And then we go inside together.

THE HOMECOMING.

My fellow prisoners and I stared in disbelief as our captors climbed into the back of a military truck. The truck moved to the camp gate and stopped. The two guards from the gate towers ran down the steps and swung the camp gates wide open. They passed their rifles inside and climbed into the canvas-covered vehicle with the others. With a puff of blue smoke the truck lurched forward. With a roar and a cloud of rising dust it drove through the gates leaving them wide open.

We had been told nothing. We had been held prisoners of war, in this God forsaken camp for longer than most of us cared to remember. None of us knew how the war was going, or even if it had ended. I had a dreadful urge to run to the gate and escape this terrible cage. I could tell that our senior officer sensed that many of the others felt the same way.

"Wait!" He shouted. "It may be a trick to mow us down as escapees."

His words quickly quashed the urge to run, there may, indeed, be concealed machine gunners waiting to close the books on the camp. We stood in line after our final roll call. We were all, I believe, trying to make sense of this most unusual camp occurrence. Had the war actually ended? Were our captors running to save their own skins from advancing liberators? If so who were the liberators? I stood with the others in the tattered remains of my uniform, wearing oversize boots without laces, boots I had salvaged from the body of one of my deceased campmates.

The longer I stood there, my thoughts of freedom grew. I thought of Andrea. Where was she now? It had been almost five years since our lips touched. At our parting, we knew not what the future held for us, but I had a premonition that catastrophe teetered above us, ready to fall.

More than a thousand nights have passed since that night of farewell and each of those thousand nights, I have dreamed of Andrea. Her memory and my determination to again lie with her in my arms had been the catalyst that has sustained me through this dreadful ordeal. It forced me to live, when I wanted to die and have it all end.

The senior officer's voice brought me back from my thoughts of Andrea.

"Is there a volunteer to test the waters and be the first out of the gate?"

I did not hesitate for a second. I stepped one pace forward. My actions were not based on bravery, or even concern for my fellow prisoners. They were based on my determination to go and find Andrea and not waste a second doing so. If it were a trap waiting for us outside the compound and I were the first to die then, I should meet my end in the knowledge that I had reached out for her in my final moment.

The officer nodded and I began to walk toward the gate. My mind's eye saw Andrea's face beckoning me from beyond the wire. My walk turned into a run. My boots were loose upon my feet but I didn't care. My nutrition-starved body hurt in every weakened muscle, but I kept running. I did not look back. It was Hell behind me and somewhere ahead far down the road Heaven laid waiting for me. I ran like a man deranged, I did not care if bullets crashed into my body. Dead or alive I was going to Andrea. I thought nothing of the men in the compound waiting to see if I died on the road, the victim of a cruel hoax. As far as I was concerned there was no military force back at the camp to control me any longer. I was done with the military. I had but one thought in my mind, getting to Andrea. Nothing else mattered. My loose boots were beginning to hurt my feet, so I paused running for a moment and took them off. I would run in the soft grass at the roadside carrying the boots in my hand. For the first time I glanced back toward the compound. Beyond the wire I could see the prisoners still in line, watching and listening to see if I would go down.

"Run you bloody fools," I shouted. I supposed they hadn't heard me, for the ranks stood fast. "I'm coming to find you Andrea," I shouted in elation. And then I began running again. I ran for several miles, until I fell to the ground exhausted. When I had recovered somewhat, I began to think logically. I had no idea where I was, not even which country I was in. I knew that at last I was free, and that I intended to find Andrea, but common sense demanded that I had to have a plan. I could not walk aimlessly, and I had to find sustenance or I should never find her. In which direction had the guards fled? Whichever it was, I had to be sure to go in the opposite one or I could end up being captured again.

Off in the distance I spotted a stream winding through the countryside. I began to run to it, my throat was parched as I had partaken of no liquid yet today. Reaching it, I thrust my head into the cold clear water and sucked it into my mouth. I drank until I filled my shrunken stomach. Standing up I saw the reflection of myself in the pool and I was appalled at the sight. As I gazed at the rippling reflection it seemed that Andrea stood next to me. I felt ashamed at my appearance. She might not welcome me looking so filthy and decrepit so I peeled off my ragged clothes and lay down in the crushingly cold stream. I could see the body lice, which had fed from my emaciated body float free and sail off to their doom downstream. Returning to my clothes I took them into the water with me, I washed them as best I could. I would have to wear them until they dried, but at least they and I would be clean.

I lay naked on the grass with the muted sunlight slowly warming my body. I closed my eyes and began to dream of Andrea. She would cry when she first saw me but she would take me in her arms and comfort me. I would feel her hands on my body stroking my skin and I would place my head between her breasts. My fingers would stroke her flaxen hair and I would know that I am home.

The raucous sound of a crow in a nearby tree broke my thoughts. Is someone coming? Could it be soldiers? But from whose army? I grabbed my clothes and struggled to put them on, but the wet cloth stuck to my skin. I listened intently for the sound of human voices but I heard none. Instinct told me to avoid using the road from now on. Even though I do not know where I was, I had a gut feeling I should be heading southeast towards the sea. I decided to go across country as secretly as possible.

As nightfall approached I found myself at a deserted farm, the house had suffered some war damage but the roof was still on. I checked inside to see if I could find any food but the place had been ransacked. I discover only a can of lard so I go to check out the barn. I found a sack with some crushed oats, obviously the feed for the decomposing horse lying on the stable floor. I would mix the oats in lard; it would be a strange meal but a nutritious one.

I collected straw from the stable floor and made myself a bed. I would have my first sleep as a free man in many a year and sleep I did. I dreamed I had found Andrea and we lay naked and warm under clean sheets, our bodies touching and giving comfort to each other. When I awoke at first light, the dream spurred me to hurry on my way to find her. I walked for several weeks across country keeping clear of other humans and eating whatever I could forage.

One morning, I stumbled upon a military camp; the soldiers were wearing the same uniforms that mine had once been. I walked into their midst and declared who I was, and why I looked so terrible. I must admit to shedding a tear of relief to find myself among friends again. They took fed me and found me some better clothes. They treated my sores and blisters and told me of the progress of the war. It was all over (but for the shouting) they told me. I convalesced with them for a week and then they gave me a military travel pass and put me in a truck headed for the coast. I was going home.

Thoughts of Andrea filled my mind; survival was no longer a priority. Not only did she share my dreams at night, but also she filled my mind in my waking hours. Every moment we were closing the gap of miles and minutes between us. I was given new papers and boarded a homebound ship. Goose pimples coated my arms and legs as I thought of her; and the welcome she would give me. I wanted to scream at the ship's captain; surely this old tub could sail faster than this. Andrea was somewhere waiting for me and I was desperate to be with her. After an eternity, the ship docked and I ran down the gangplank. I inquired of the train station and I ran like the wind to it. No longer was our separation remaining days, but only hours. I arrived at my destination and ran to the street where she would be waiting, but not expecting me.

I stopped dead in my tracks. The entire row of houses, we had lived and loved in lay demolished, a pile of rubble and broken bricks. I sucked in a breath of despair. Had I fought the will to die in order to come home to Andrea, only to find that she had died first and was waiting for me somewhere else out of this mortal world? I sat down on the rubble, tears came to my eyes but they seemed pointless. I stared at the dirt at my feet. I did not know what to do. But I do know that I do not want to live without Andrea.

A hand comes to rest on my shoulder. I looked up and saw an elderly woman looking down at me.

"Have you just got home, soldier?" She asked. I nodded. For words do not want to come forth from my aching soul.

"The people who lived here have all been moved away, soldier. If you go to the council they can tell you where the people are now."

"Where is this council?" I asked.

"At the City Hall, soldier. They can tell you the whereabouts of your family."

My hopes of finding Andrea are buoyed. I run all the way to the City Hall. Yes. They tell me Andrea is re-housed not far away. I get the address and run to find it. My heart is bursting, she is so near. I find the house. My blood pounds furiously through my veins. In seconds we will meet. She will see me. She will hold me. We will cry. We will share our stories. We will make love and all the hurt will melt away like ice in the spring sun. I approached her door trembling.

It is then that I heard a strangely familiar sound from inside. I tried my best to remember what it was, but the memory of it would not come to the fore of my mind.

The darkness of the passage to Andrea's door causes me to open my eyes wide. It will only be seconds now before she is in my arms. My wide-open eyes see the straw in the bunk above mine. Then a loud voice shouts,

"Everybody out! Roll call."

The dream door to my Andrea is gone. I climb out of my flea-infested bunk to face still another day in this Godforsaken camp. I stand in line with my fellow captives. I cannot cry real tears and dent our collective moral so I stand to attention with the remnants of my sustaining dreams of Andrea. With my head reaching for Heaven, and my feet stuck firmly in Hell.

ESSENCE OF A LIFE.

It is as if no one cares.

I have lain here without moving for a long time now. Before I relate to you my tale of triumph and tragedy, there is much you need to know. I begin with a broad overview of life as it is and not as I would have it.

Since the earliest of times, man has had a creative side. It is much more evident and stronger in some individuals than others. Those with a profound sense of creativity have been able to generate the *essence* of life in their works. Dedicated Greek artists chiseled statues from rock and marble and somehow achieved this *essence* within the work. Roman sculptors too, produced works of art containing this illusive *essence* embedded within their creations. Over the centuries, great painters have captured this into their masterpieces. To the casual observer, the work may appear to be just a picture created by daubing paint upon a canvas, however those gifted individuals, able to discern the essence within an inanimate object, are able to enjoy the creation on a much higher level.

How do I know? I know for I am one of those inanimate objects, with this entity wrought into me at the hands of man. I cannot speak or write of my thoughts or wishes, they must lie silent until they can be captured and revealed within the mind of those elite who can interpret and understand that my ilk and I have this *essence* within us. We have an ethereal life, unlike any other life. We are a being without form in the conventional sense. I have deep knowledge that you are among the few able to receive and understand the vibrations emanating from my core created by human hand.

Now I believe we have an understanding so I shall begin my story.

My creation came about in late 1927. I am a product of many hands and the dreams of a few. I am neither sculpture nor painting and yet I contain the elements of both. In many minds I am art, but I am the art of an industrial world. Even though I am an inanimate object, I am aware beauty is in the eyes of the beholder. Many will love me with an enduring love while others will summarily reject me.

I accept that.

My conception came about as a blueprint and design on paper. Economic dictates spearheaded my conception; I had to come into being to prevent a financial disaster of great magnitude. Many thousands of jobs were at stake my introduction to the world at the end of 1927 was vital. My arrival was awaited by an entire nation clamoring for the first glimpse of the newcomer. My predecessor was quickly dying. I became the replacement several nations of the world demanded. I had big shoes to fill. I had to be strong. I was expected to be good looking and at the risk of sounding conceited, I believe I am. It was incumbent upon me to be reliable above all else and I was expected to be fast for the day. I was to be different from the run of the mill and at my introduction, the public assured my manufacturer that I was.

There would be no lingering at the place of my creation, the world outside demanded, with a loud voice; I go out to them forthwith. I did go and I went proudly with my ilk to the far corners of the continent. Everywhere we were greeted with acclamation. We were wanted, needed and yes even loved, all these years later some of us are still loved and cherished. But, the intervening years have not been good years for all of us. Some of us have been abused and badly treated, many of us were simply abandoned and others wantonly destroyed. The larger of our numbers simply vanished back into the industrial world that spawned us.

As for myself, I have been spared. That is not to say I haven't had my share of the bad times. I have, but I also enjoyed the care and love of one man an understanding man such as you are. He knew instinctively I had the *essence* of which I have spoken. I am an inanimate object to be sure, but he understood there was more to me.

We were together for only five years and as so many men do, he abandoned me for one younger and I suppose, in his opinion prettier than I. Life seemed to go downhill for me after that. I had several more men in my life, each successively caring less for me; none of the latter men recognized the spirit and *essence* of life dwelling in me.

The Second World War changed everything. It seemed I no longer had any value and found myself abandoned under a stand of trees. I lay leaf-covered for a good many seasons mostly unseen and definitely unwanted. I had the strongest feeling I would die there and the earth would reclaim me. I became badly deteriorated and terribly despondent. I knew it should not be like this, but the spirit and *essence* within me had not expired.

Things changed suddenly and without warning for me in the spring of 1972. Two men came to my side and I knew instantly that one of them understood I had the illusive *essence* of life. He walked around me and I felt a gentle hand touch me. I was embarrassed to be in such a decrepit state, but I also could tell the man overlooked my shortcomings. His eyes saw me as other eyes had seen me back in late 1927. There was a connection between us, my spirit was revitalized and I knew he felt it, for he was just like you, able to receive the vibrations from an inanimate object.

"I'll take her," he said to the other man and my spirit soared.

Thus began a new and different phase in my life. There was now another man who loved me for what I am and not what I used to be. We went home together. He showered me with affection, tended to my bruises and helped with my cosmetics. It took a little time, but before too long I looked young and beautiful again. He was proud of me, he could not hide it, and my own pride of earlier years returned. The first time we went out together was utter joy for both of us. My man would take me out often just to show me off to any who would look.

I knew I was lucky, I had another chance at life that many of my sisters did not. But dark clouds were ahead, clouds I did not foresee. The trips out became less frequent, my man had brought home another. She was much younger than I, and by my own admission prettier. I saw my man look at her with desire and anticipation. He would take her out and I would stay behind, my spirit crumbling bit by bit.

It has been a long time now since he and I went out together and I am becoming despondent again. Thank you for coming to see me while he is out with her again and thank you especially, for being a person who can read and understand my vibrations. I feel better for communicating with you and for you caring about the life of a Model A Ford.

SHAVING.

I OPENED THE medicine cabinet to bring out my shaving things and stood before the mirror. The face in the glass stared back at me. I looked deeply into the grey-green eyes that appeared to be fixed upon my own. The eyes in the mirror stared at the real eyes in my face. There was a kind of impasse between them. The eyes in the mirror looked critically at me it was if they saw something that my real eyes hadn't.

With the turning of the mirrored cabinet door, the watching eyes broke their gaze and as I closed the cabinet door again, the eyes in the glass resumed their piercing look into my own. I stared back. But I saw nothing there that had not been there before.

I moved my eyeballs to the right and the ones in the mirror followed suit. They seemed to be trying to tell me something. Something that I should know but didn't. I refused to play this game anymore and took my gaze from the mirror and ran hot water into the basin. I washed my face to soften my beard, and then I placed my razor and shaving cream on the counter. I wondered how on earth they managed to put so much shaving cream into such a small container. I imagined a short little man stuffing foam into the metal can then trying to seal it before all the foam popped back out again. I then raised my head and found the eyes still engaging me with their intense stare. I looked again and tried to understand the message they were clearly trying to deliver to me. But I couldn't read it. I took the cap off the shaving cream and placed a daub of it onto my fingers. I began to spread the cream onto my beard, but the eyes in the mirror kept on calling me to look into them and my aim with the shaving cream faltered. I think to myself, I hope the razor doesn't go where the foam has gone. I wondered too, who puts those little blades in the disposable razors. It must be a very tedious job. I wrench my gaze from the eyes in the mirror, moisten the razor and begin to shave. I always begin near my right ear and work downwards. I look at what I am doing, but the eyes in the mirror take away my concentration, and draw me back to them.

What is it that I do not understand? I have shaved almost daily over a whole pile of years and I have never had this problem before. The eyes in the mirror had no ready answer; they just stared back at me, still and cold, yet strangely they beckoned. I continued shaving and the eyes in the mirror followed the razor's every move transfixed. I did my best to ignore them and completed my shave although I had nicked the skin under my nose a little. I ran fresh hot water and washed my face clean of the remaining foam. After toweling my face dry, I happened to look up and the eyes in the mirror were insistently calling to me again.

They stared pleadingly into mine. I lean forward to be closer to the mirror and stare back at them. I am not vain, nor do I have a narcissic personality and I am not in the habit of admiring my image in mirrors. Yet here I am doing these same things. But why? I lean forward so that my face is within an inch of the mirror and stare into the eyes that are staring into mine. I look deep into the iris. It seems clear, tunnel like. As I gaze deep into the tunnel, it widens and seems to beckon me to a place beyond. This is foolish, I think, so I back away from the basin and turn to leave my bathroom. I turn the light off and as I start to close the door behind me, I again see those pleading eyes in the mirror, further away from me now, but just as compelling. I hesitate. I am torn between leaving or going back to the mirror. The forceful orbs there win the conflict. I put the light back on and return to the mirror. I do not know why I am doing this, it makes no sense, am I going mad? Yet I am drawn, compelled even, to gaze into the eyes that all common sense and reason tells me are my own eyes in reflection. I notice I have neglected to put my shaving things away, so I pick them up and open the cabinet door. As I do so, I have the strangest feeling accompanied by goosebumps that I will find myself inside the cabinet staring back at myself. My feeling is groundless, I am not in there. I close the cabinet door and the eyes are waiting for me, staring, piercing, begging, as the door clicks into place.

Once again I draw close to the mirror and see the tunnel in the iris. In an odd way I am nervous about what I might discover if I should follow the tunnel, to the Lord only knows where. But then I think logically, it's really my own reflected eyes that are so insistently calling me, what could there possibly be to be afraid of in a mirror image. Having reassured myself, I allow my own eyes to travel into the ones in the mirror. The tunnel is short and in semi-darkness, and I am emerging into light at the end. Adjusting to the brightness I see myself standing there. But how could this be? I am now a young man of twenty years again. I am quite handsome in a rough kind of way and looking at the younger me I could well remember how I felt back then. I was strong; I had dreams, I had ambitions; I had plans for all manner of things and I thought that life for me would go on forever. I was invincible. But as I looked upon my younger self, I realized that I had, of course, been wrong. The man who is me outside the mirror, had grown much older, and now knows that the length of my life is limited and knows also that I am not invincible.

"We have done many things together you and I," the younger me said. The words surprised me. His voice was my voice. I answered him,

"I am terribly confused. I just came to have a shave, when this strange happening occurred. I know you are me, and I know you summoned me here. But why and how."

"My other self, it is time for you to look at your life in a different way. Your time is limited. By how much I am not prepared to say. Think older self. How many of your dreams and ambitions have not yet reached fruition. How many of your plans lie unfinished. I your younger self, languish amid the ruins of a life not lived to the full. I bid you go now, older self, redeem us both. You have still time to reach those ambitions that once lived so strong in you. Time to make the dreams you had come true and time to finish the unfinished plans. You said you were confused and only came to shave, but it is no accident that we meet. I planned it this way. For there comes a time of realization for every man, that he could have lived his life better, had he mustered the courage to do so and carried through with his plans and dreams. When you shave from now on, you will remember your younger self. You will see me and the young face will become the old and the old will become the young. Go now, older self and do what you still have time to do."

I blink my eyes, and the younger me is gone. The reflection in the mirror reveals only the older me, with thicker brows, and lines where once there were none. There is sadness in the droop of my jaw and graying at my temples. I reflect on the words spoken by the younger me.

His words have scraped a raw nerve somewhere deep inside my brain. I could have lived life better, but somehow it was easier to let ambition slide. I could have fought to make my dreams come true, but instead I abandoned them. I could have worked for the fruition of my plans, but it was easier to let them slip away.

But he did say I had time still. So I shall discard my mantle of slothful behaviour and face life renewed. Younger me, has given me the courage to change how I do everything and each morning when I put a razor to my face in front of the mirror, the younger me will spur me on to better things and end his languishing among the wreckage of my life. I shall begin today.

DINNER PARTIES.

I met Carlotta in Brazil in 1997. I was in South America on a culinary exchange programme. I was there to learn Brazilian cooking methods and the different foods produced in the southern hemisphere. I found the lifestyle different and exciting. The city of Rio de Janeiro glittered at night and the beaches in the daytime were crowded with the wealthy and beautiful people of the western world.

I was taking my training at the prestigious Hotel Brazillia. Preparations for lunch kept me busy in the late mornings and there never seemed to be a real break before we began preparations for the dinner crowd. I tended to go to the beach between nine and eleven in the mornings; the sun was still not too hot, ideal for tanning and girl watching. Many but not all, went topless. Girls who knew they had great bodies shared the view of them with great pride; Carlotta was such a girl.

A mutual friend introduced us and we seemed to hit it off right away. Carlotta was a native Brazilian and she expressed a great desire to hear about my hometown of Chicago. She told me she had always wanted to move to the United States. In retrospect I realize now that Carlotta was a temptress. She certainly had me wrapped around her finger in no time flat and as a result I asked her to marry me as soon as we could get the documentation dealt with. We married at a small church in the neighbourhood Carlotta's family lived. After a blissful honeymoon, I went to the U.S. Consul's office to arrange for her immigration papers so that she could accompany me when I returned to Chicago.

Carlotta moved into my apartment for the next two months when we were due to fly home. I brought back to the States a new bride to show off to my parents and a line of South American cuisine to entice my employer's hotel dining room customers. Carlotta loved living in Chicago although she said she missed the Rio beaches. We were as happy as two clams. At least I thought so. With my job keeping me at the hotel until late at night, Carlotta took to going out alone in the evenings. I didn't mind her going to the occasional movie but she began to go to bars and parties she had been invited to and frankly I was jealous.

One night she didn't come home at all and I was furious with her and we had a major quarrel. When it happened a second time I cracked. Carlotta walked into the house at nine a.m. with her hair messed up, and her lip-gloss smeared all around her mouth. I knew instantly that she had spent the night with another man. It was obvious to me that we had a one sided relationship and I could not deal with it. My jealousy completely took over my sense of reality. Carlotta had hurt me immeasurably with her actions and I suppose I went berserk but in a calm and calculated way. I went to the basement and laid a plastic sheet that I had bought for house painting and spread it over the laundry room floor, then made a few other preparations.

I called Carlotta down saying I needed help with the laundry and when she entered the laundry room and saw the plastic sheet, she asked,

"What's this for Aubrey?" I didn't answer her. Instead I plunged my carving knife into her chest. I had aimed correctly; for the blood pumped out in spurts that I caught in a bowl I had ready and waiting. It didn't take long for her to die with me holding her immobile. I poured the still hot blood into the toilet as I flushed it. So far there was virtually no mess. I tied a rope round her ankles and hung her from the beam like a slaughtered hog.

I had received some butchery experience as part of my chef's training so I knew what had to be done. I disemboweled her, catching the entrails in a laundry tub, the lungs, heart, liver and kidneys I put in a large cooking pot and placed it on the stove to cook. Boiled and cut up it would feed many of the local dogs running loose in the area around the park.

I put an edge on my paring knife and began removing her skin, it was a laborious job but I did get it done. I put it in a separate pot and set it to boil, it would mix well with the dog food. Next I cut off her long black hair and put it in a plastic shopping bag in the garbage. I hadn't decided what to do with the head, so I put it aside to deal with later. Next, I cut all the meat from the bones and put it in freezer bags and placed them in the deep freezer. With the bones separated, I placed them in the plastic sheet from the floor. I would wrap the whole thing in brown paper and take it to the local landfill concealed in a garbage bag. My murder scene was spotlessly clean. There was no evidence that could lead investigators into believing there had been a murder here.

I put Carlotta's head in a plastic bag and put it in my refrigerator. I had already decided what I would do with it but at a later date. When the liver and kidneys etc were fully cooked and cooled, I cut them into small pieces. I mixed a pound of Quaker oats with the meats and took it after dark, to the local park and spread it around under the shrubbery. By the time I had finished, several dogs were gorging themselves on the delicacies and more had caught the scent and were racing to the feast.

Carlotta's disappearance had to be explained to my family and friends; it had to be believable and convincing. I told everyone that Carlotta and I had quarreled and that she had left me and returned to Brazil. I wrote to her parents and told them the same story with the exception that she had gone out to Hollywood in California to try to get into show business and to be closer to other Latinos.

I got in touch with one of those people who advertise in magazines that for twenty-five dollars you can get a certificate for almost anything. I paid for and received a Brazilian certificate of divorce. I organized a dinner party to celebrate my divorce from Carlotta and to advertise that I was a free bachelor again. I decided there would be drinks and canapés before sitting down to dine.

I ground up some pork along with an equal amount of Carlotta's flesh and added spices to make sausage meat. I made mini sausage rolls with a light and delicate puff pastry and sausage meat stuffed mushroom caps which I thought would go well with a chilled chardonnay. For the main course I marinated strips of Carlotta's meat with red wine and soy sauce then I sautéed it with shallots in fresh cream. I gave it the name, Brazilian Venison. For afterwards I made a head cheese out of Carlotta's head just the same way as it is made from the heads of hogs. Laced with gelatin it made a hearty head cheese to be served with specialty crackers and cheddar. The dried out skull I broke into pieces with a hammer and wrapped them in a plastic shopping bag to go in the garbage.

My dinner party was a resounding success. I had the divorce certificate as a table centre display. Everyone adored my food and some asked for the recipe but of course I kept that to myself, chef's privilege. I had three dinner parties before Carlotta had been totally consumed. As host, I didn't partake in the meals but served them with flourish and kept the wine flowing. I was much too close to Carlotta to have taken part in eating her.

It was two years after the parties that the police called round. Carlotta's parents had asked for an investigation when she did not contact them. They asked if I would mind them looking round the house simply to eliminate me as a suspect. I said,

"Please look wherever you will." I knew I had nothing to fear, for I remember the words I heard and heeded when I first went for chef's training. Cleanliness is the paramount thing you need to observe if you are to become a top rated chef. There are still occasions when my friends complement me on my Brazilian Venison and make subtle suggestions that I prepare it again. I smile wryly and say,

"Maybe."

RED SKY.

I LEFT THE hotel lobby and glanced at the early morning sky as I made my way to my station wagon in the parking lot. My cursory glance at the sky and what my eyes beheld caused me to stop and take a longer look. I ceased walking and with my briefcases in my hands, I stood and drank in the vision of various shades of brilliant reds splattered across the entire eastern sky. I had seen red morning skies before of course but this one was spectacular in its vividness. It immediately brought to mind the old saying. *Red sky at night sailor's delight. Red sky at morning, sailor take warning.* I had often heard my father say those words growing up on our prairie farm, but never did we heed the warning part for nothing ever happened, although the evening sky often meant a clear day for tomorrow's harvesting. I stood stock still, surveying the splendour of the sky. Never had I seen such a display of colour and the depth and variance of it held me captivated.

As a hardware sales rep I had a lot of territory to cover today. My station wagon was filled with samples and catalogues, paint colour chips and order forms. My two briefcases were filled with completed orders, from clients I had already visited so far along this leg of my monthly tour of the state. The wagon's gas tank was filled ready for an early start with no delays and my first stop would be Greenville, about a hundred miles upstate. I took a final look at the sky and started the engine of the wagon. As I waited for the engine to warm up and begin to run smoothly, I once again affixed my gaze on the sky.

My father's words came into my mind again. *"Sailor take warning."* Take warning for what? I asked myself. Surely the words were just so much mumbo jumbo from that silly farmer's almanac. After all they had been printing the same rubbish for almost a hundred years. But

I reasoned that is the way of the sales game, some of the stuff I sold was hopelessly outdated, but the public still paid hard cash for it. I eased the station wagon out of the hotel parking lot and headed for the Interstate.

I would exit just a few miles south of Greenville, and follow Side road Fifty Seven into the town, to my next two calls; the Greenville Farmers Supply Depot and the Johnston Brothers hardware store in the downtown core.

About an hour's drive up the interstate, the brilliant sky began to fade to pink. The peacock-like display had passed its splendour and greyness with a darker centre began to replace it. Concentrating on my driving I did not notice how the sky had taken on an ominous black and stormy appearance. When I happened to look up I could see that I was heading right into a storm. Such things were not unusual in this area of the country; thunderstorms came and went with regularity. The resulting rain filled the water holes and nourished the wheat and corn crops. It didn't take long before the first drops of rain spattered my windshield, softening the remains of bugs that had met their fate upon it. Turning on the wipers, at first spread the goo from the bugs across the glass, but then with the rain increasing, eventually the glass was wiped clean.

The sky darkened even more. I figured that if this kept up I would have to use my headlights. Without warning the rain began to fall in sheets, making visibility difficult. I turned on the headlights and reduced my speed down to about thirty miles per hour. I suspected that the speed change would delay me by only a few minutes for I felt I would pass through the storm's centre quickly. I found it not to be the case; the water just fell from the sky harder than I had ever seen it before, forcing me to slow down even more. All the freeway traffic was following suit except for the big trucks that passed sending plumes of water over my station wagon temporarily reducing my visibility to nil.

For some inexplicable reason the words *"Sailor take warning"* passed though my mind. I thought that this time at least, the saying had a ring of truth to it. The rain was falling so hard that it could not run off the road fast enough. I was driving through about two inches of water so I reduced my speed down to ten miles per hour. I felt that this situation could not last much longer; surely the sky could not hold much more water? But it proved me wrong. It began to come down with increasing intensity. Visibility was completely obliterated, causing me to pull over to where I felt the freeway shoulder should be, to wait out the downpour.

I realized instantly that I had made an error in judgment when the nose of the station wagon dipped forward. I felt a sensation of being afloat. I rapidly wound down the side window and saw an ocean of fresh water. The freeway was not visible, only the tops of a few shrubs showed above the flat-water surface completely surrounding my vehicle. The rain poured in wetting my lap so I wound the window back up again.

With a loud hiss of steam from my hot engine, it stopped. The only sound now was the rain thundering down onto the metal roof. Suddenly my feet were wet. I looked down and the water was gushing into the wagon through the pedal holes on the floor. Again I had the sensation of being afloat and with it a forward motion. I wound down the window again, and the shrubs that had been there seconds ago were gone. It was then that I realized I was being swept away in a fast current to God only knows where. I had a choice. Climb out the window and abandon the vehicle to whatever fate might await me, or stay with the wagon and hope that it might get hung up on a hillock or fence.

In a millisecond I chose the latter. Unfortunately, the more the water gushed in through the holes in the floor, the deeper the water inside became. I realized that very soon I would have to leave the wagon and start swimming. Suddenly the station wagon made a violent turn to the left and the speed in which I was traveling through the water increased dramatically. I saw a dark shape hurtling at me through the downpour I realized I was being swept under a freeway bridge. There was barely three feet of room for the station wagon to pass under so I ducked as I went beneath the first beam. With the weight of the engine, the car traveled nose down in the torrent; the rear of the car was sticking higher out of the water. The roof racks hit the underside of the bridge forcing it down deeper into the rampaging water. The impact with the beam smashed the rear window and water rushed in under pressure. I was sitting up to my chest in freezing cold water. I knew I had to get out if I wanted to survive, for the car would be submerged in seconds. With one hand I released my seat belt, with the other I wound down the driver's side window again and then attempted to get out. I made a lunge for the last wide steel beam before the vehicle shot out from under the bridge. My hands gripped one of the flanges and the station wagon pulled away from under me into the light and the downpour. I couldn't have made my move at a better time, for the vehicle vanished under the raging torrent.

The force of the moving water ripped at my legs like an angry beast trying to tear me from the safety of a tree. With a Herculean effort I extracted my legs from the water hooking them onto the beam. I hung from the beam like a gigantic bat with the water rushing just inches below my back. I could feel it tugging on my coattails hanging loosely behind me. I knew I could not hold on in this position for long; I had to find a way to climb just below the road deck where I might be able to hang on until the flood subsided. I reached up with one leg hoping to hook it over the beam. I struggled and stretched failing several times. My cold wet hands were beginning to slip from the flange but I knew if I let go, it would all be over for me.

I had just enough strength for one last try to save myself. I flung my leg for the beam, and at the same time my left hand slipped from the flange and trailed in the water rushing under me. Somehow my foot hooked over the beam, allowing me to reposition myself and climb up and hold on in a much safer and comfortable position. For the moment I was safe. I found it difficult to believe that within the space of a very few moments I had been whisked from my warm and dry vehicle to this cold and terribly dangerous place. I closed my eyes and began to think of my wife June. By now she would be sending the kids off to school and going about her housewifely duties. I realized that my salesman's job gave me lots of freedom while June was bound to the house and our family. As I clung to my uncertain perch, I suddenly knew how much of our married life we had spent apart and for the first time it didn't seem fair. I had missed seeing my kids grow older and I guess they saw me as the father who dropped by the house every second weekend, the father who always missed the school concerts and such. Mind you, June never complained. It appeared to me that she just accepted that this was the way things were.

But then I began to think that maybe she didn't feel that way at all and suffered in silence so as to not send me out on the road feeling guilty After all I did bring in a good income. We did have a nice house. But I wondered if it was just a house and not a home. I pondered what she would do if I did not get out of this thing alive. There was every possibility that my body might never be found. Would she think I had abandoned her for another woman and been diligent in covering my tracks?

I opened my eyes and looked down. To my horror I saw that the water had risen to the bottom of the beam and was still rising. If the water kept on rising as rapidly as this, I would only have a few more minutes before I would be swept away or make the decision to let go and take my chances swimming hopefully finding a tree to cling onto further downstream. I did not want to die, there was so much I wanted to do in my life but had always told myself I was too busy. At this moment in time clinging to the underside of a bridge like a gigantic insect, the things I had been busy with meant nothing and I suppose in reality, just excuses.

I looked at the floodwaters careening under the bridge and noted that it had now risen over the flange I had clung onto mere minutes ago. I had only about 14 inches of space now between the flood and the underside of the bridge. Which meant that at the rate of rising, I had maybe only two to four minutes before the flood took me, or I let go in a possible futile attempt to save myself. I looked out into the light from the darkness of the underside of the bridge. The downpour continued unabated. It was obvious that the floodwaters would continue to rise, sealing my fate one-way or the other. There was now the moral question for me to grapple with. If I were to wait until the floodwaters took me, would it be cowardice on my part? Or if I plunged in of my own accord and failed to live would it be suicide? My religion views suicide as a mortal sin, could I be condemning my soul to the pit by attempting to save myself?

The water had now risen another four inches; I was trapped in a ten-inch space with death staring me in the face. I now knew without a doubt that I owed it to my family to try to escape. I hurled myself from the ledge into the maelstrom. Water grabbed me like a giant hand and pitched me out into the light. Instantly I dwelled in a world of water. It surrounded me; it pushed me and pulled me. It fell from above in sheets. I struggled with all my strength to fight the powers all about me. I found water entering my lungs no matter how I tried to avoid it. My eyes were blinded by water and I knew I was close to my end. I thought I had reached the surface and drew a deep breath, but only water entered my lungs. I fought with all my limbs thrashing, despite all that was happening I let out a scream of agony and despair that expelled water. My world went black as I gave a final shriek.

"Wake up Jim. You are having a nightmare. You kicked me out of bed. It's time you were up anyway, it's seven thirty. There is a lovely red sky this morning."

THIRTY SECONDS.

ALICIA GLANCED at the handsome man sitting askew on a stool at the bar, with a dark coloured drink held loosely in his right hand and his left elbow set firmly on the bar. In the second it took to notice him, she saw that he wore a pair of well pressed grey slacks, a dark blue blazer with some kind of badge on the top pocket, a crisp white shirt open at the neck, but with a striped blue tie hanging loose at the front with the part around his neck still neatly tucked under his collar. He appeared to be about the same age as she, twenty-four years. He moved positions on the stool into a position that placed him in full profile. Not wishing to appear to be staring at him, Alicia quickly turned her gaze to the half consumed rum and coke held with the long shapely fingers of both hands. As she made the move, Alicia saw in the corner of her eye that the man had turned his head to look at her.

Alicia hadn't really wanted to come to Mary's party. She felt that working alongside a person eight hours a day was quite enough without spending the Saturday evening with them also. But this particular Saturday she had been at a loose end and Mary had been so insistent that she come along, she had accepted the invitation. It had been only six weeks since she had moved to the city to work in the Bandross Corporation offices and Mary had kindly taken her under her wing. From her very first day at Bandross, Mary had helped her to understand the office routine and had tried to make her move to Welford an easy transition both domestically and socially. Alicia was grateful being fully aware that without Mary's help the move would have been much harder to handle.

She wondered if the young man seated at the bar might come and ask her to dance. Maybe he was shy and might not dare. It was possible too that he was married, and his wife might even be in the room chatting with someone else. Alicia allowed her gaze to return to the man, she might even be able to see if he wore a wedding ring. His ring finger was behind the glass of dark liquid he held. She raised her gaze to his face he really was quite handsome and the shape of his body through his clothes suggested that he was fit and athletic. But the very moment she looked at his face, she realized that he was looking at her. Instantly they both turned away, she a little embarrassed at being discovered looking at him.

Alicia swirled her rum and coke around in her glass hearing the tinkle of the ice cubes. It was just a regular house party with about fifteen of Mary's friends. There had been the usual round of introductions, but Alicia knew she had not been introduced to the man in the blazer, she would not have forgotten that. Nor did she remember seeing him come in alone, but she reasoned that she might have been chatting with some one.

Unable to really help herself, Alicia turned to look at his face again. He was a handsome creature and she was drawn to him. She was not expecting it, but their gazes met head on and nervously she glanced away again, but as she did, she saw his lips flicker into the hint of a smile. A couple dancing broke the line of vision between the two of them and the fleeting moment was broken and she looked down.

Alicia wondered again, if now that there had been a minor breaking of the ice he might ask her to dance. It had been months since she and her ex boyfriend had been out together and the thought of dancing closely with the man in the blue blazer, appealed to her. When the dancing couple passed by, Alicia looked up but he was not there. The stool he had been sitting on was empty.

Alicia firmly stirred the drink in her glass by turning it in sharp circular motions. Had he left because he did not think her pretty enough to ask to dance? Surely not. She glanced at her long lithe fingers grasping the glass. They were exquisite hands; she had been told so several times. Earlier she had taken great care doing her nails coating them with a smart silver grey polish. Alicia recalled how she had carefully pressed her dress with the white lace collar and cuffs and found a pair of white high heels and white purse to accent the dress. She had checked herself front and rear in the mirror and was satisfied that she did indeed look pretty.

The feeling came suddenly; that all her preparations had been pointless now that the one person she would have liked to dance with had gone. Alicia wondered if she could quietly leave the party without offending Mary. She felt out of place, a bump on a log, a single in a room full of pairs. Mary Manson had been kind and thoughtful to invite her to the party knowing that for entertainment she only had the Saturday night T.V. lineup at home. Alicia swirled her drink around for the final time then swallowed it. Having made the decision to leave and go home, she would explain to Mary on Monday why she had left early.

Before she could take the first step to place her glass on the bar, she had a strong feeling that he was here, close by. She hesitated. The thought raced across her mind, if he was still here I will be missing the opportunity to meet and possibly dance with him. Her slender fingers gripped the empty glass and Alicia made another instant decision to stay at least for a little while longer. Despite having just drained her glass, her throat felt dry.

It was not so much thirst that caused her to take the first step, but an excuse to step up to the bar where she could have a better view of the room to see if he was still here.

Alicia poured ice water from a jug into her glass. Without consciously thinking about it she placed her free hand onto the stool. It was still warm from him sitting there. It gave her the oddest feeling, a connection, but a connection like no other she had ever experienced. In one sense it felt like she had actually touched him, but her common sense told her it was just the lingering heat from his body. She ran her fingertips lazily over the surface of the stool absorbing the dissipating warmth. As she raised her glass to sip the cold water through the collection of floating ice cubes, a strong sensation ran through her body like a frosty morning shiver. It was a sensation of presence. Completely unexplainable but real.

A light but musky hint of perfume came to her nostrils. It could have come from any of the fifteen or so guests milling around in noisy laughter and loud music, but her feminine instincts told her that it was unmistakably he. Somewhere he was close by and her heart quickened.

Alicia took her hand from the stool and prepared to go back to where she had been standing when this odd chain of events had begun. The hint of aftershave touched her senses again. He was very near and she knew it. With the speed of light her brain received a message telling her, this is silly; you do not know him or even his name. At equal speed another part of her brain responded, but I want to know him, I want to touch him; I want to know the feeling of his hand holding mine; I want to look into the eyes that I have not yet seen properly; I want to feel the roughness of his chin against my cheek as we dance; I want to feel the strength of his arm around my waist as we turn on the dance floor.

Alicia turned from the bar to discover he was standing next to her. Suddenly they were face-to-face mere inches apart. Now she could look into his eyes. They were dark, deep mysterious eyes, friendly eyes, eyes that spoke of understanding and tenderness. The brows over them were not overly thick but smooth, complementing them. His lips parted into a warm smile revealing even clean white teeth and his chin was not rugged but firm suggesting tolerance. The clean-shaven chin had a darker look the hint of a beard that would match the well-groomed dark hair parted on the right side of his head. With his loosened tie, he had a relaxed, but smart look about his person.

Alicia returned his smile. She felt wonderful about receiving his. She was instantly glad she had decided to stay at the party. But at the same time they had not been introduced, nor had they spoken. Clutching her glass, Alicia moved to step aside and go to where she had been before. In a millisecond she felt annoyance at her host Mary, for the lack of an introduction. It would have made this moment in time so much easier. She wanted so much to speak and dance with this man whose name she did not know.

Etiquette dictated that she not be brash and introduce herself to him. The ball was in his court but would he play? Alicia saw his hand leave his glass and felt it touch her arm. It was cold from the icy drink, but warm in that it was what she had really wanted to happen. He had noticed her. He probably thought she was attractive or he wouldn't have done it. A warm feeling ran through every vein in her body, it was like a shiver, but it was not a shiver of coldness or shock it was more a feeling of well being, of warmth and of wondrous things that might happen now that she had felt his first touch.

But would he speak? Alicia looked directly into his eyes and he looked back. It was a magical search of each other's hearts and souls. She felt his gaze pierce the wall of propriety separating them and it released the most beautiful smile from deep within her. She waited for him to respond in words. His broad lips began to move and she knew that he would. His fingers found Alicia's and gently pried the glass from them placing both his and hers on the bar.

"Please, will you dance with me, Alicia?" He said in a soft tone.

Alicia's heart soared. He knows my name; Mary must have told him all about me. He must think me pretty or he wouldn't have approached me. She fought her instinct to beam at him and say yes, she did not want to appear to be forward or over eager. For eagerness on her part might be construed as unladylike. Instead she smiled sweetly and answered a simple,

"Yes."

She felt his hand take hers and his arm slid gently but firmly around her waist and they began to dance. In the first turn their bodies touched and Alicia's senses savoured the moment and memory of it.

"Forgive me Alicia. I am Michael, Mary's cousin. She has told me much about you and asked me here to meet you. I told her I didn't want an introduction like in a blind date, I wanted to meet you on my own terms. And now having seen and met you I want to know even more about you from your own lips."

Alicia knew now, for sure, that he did find himself attracted to her, he liked her, his words indicated it. She did want to share the story of her life with Michael and she wanted to hear his. It had been a mere thirty seconds since the first glance connected them; it was to be the most important thirty seconds of her life.

A SEAMAN'S STORY.

"TORPEDO! TORPEDO off the starboard bow, sir, it's coming right for us." Matt Dirkson yelled at the top of his lungs to his gunnery officer. He waited anxiously for instructions from the officer, but none came. His fear heightened as the torpedo rapidly closed in. Matt felt the torpedo would strike the destroyer Oliver just below where he stood. He dared not leave his battle station for fear of the consequences. He saw the line of foam vanish from his view below the ships outer rail. He heard an ear splitting explosion and felt himself hurled into the air. A searing white light blinded his eyes then all became dark and quiet.

In the darkness that enveloped me I found it easy to recall the events that had brought me to this point in my life and how I came to be aboard this ship. Dark clouds of an impending war had appeared on the European horizon affecting many thousands of lives. By nineteen thirty-nine the dark clouds of the European war had begun to affect the lives of Canadians. Advertisements had appeared in the Nation's papers and magazines calling on young men and women to serve the flag. At age twenty-one I was young and strong. I had experience being at sea as a fisherman, so filled with dreams of glory, I wrote to the Navy. The brochure they mailed me back had colour pictures of happy smiling sailors with tropical maidens on their arms and dollar bills sticking out of their pockets. The brochures convinced me to join the Royal Canadian Navy.

The gangplank groaned under the weight of the embarking crew each of us packing a heavy kitbag on our shoulders to the spotless decks of the H.M.C.S. Oliver. The newly commissioned destroyer had just been delivered to Halifax to take aboard her crew of officers and men for her first foray into the North Atlantic. I shuffled up the gangplank tired and weary from the long train ride from the West Coast to the East and the long march from the train to the dock.

The six day train ride had become almost unbearable toward the end of the journey. I had been unable to sleep properly as crew members from different cities across Canada boarded the train. In time the atmosphere became almost party-like. Booze flowed from clandestine bottles and there were never ending noisy card games. Some of the recruits bragged about wildly exaggerated tales of sexual conquests. The trip and the march had left me drained and exhausted.

When we were all aboard we were ordered to assemble in the crew mess compartment for instructions. Ten men, I among them were assigned guard duty on deck. I thought it was pretty silly that I had to guard the ship in its home port; I wondered whom I had to guard it against. I struggled to stay awake during my four-hour watch as I paced the deck with my unloaded rifle in hand. At the end of my four-hour stint I went below decks to discover all the narrow bunks had been taken and found myself assigned to a hammock hanging from the overhead pipes. I fell out twice before I got the hang of getting into it, but eventually I slept an exhausted sleep oblivious to the noise around me.

I was just one of an untried crew aboard an untried ship. This meant day after day of intense training before the H.M.C.S. Oliver could take her place escorting the convoys of merchantmen crossing the Atlantic to England and Ireland carrying vital war supplies and foodstuffs. At basic training camp I had volunteered to be schooled as a gunner on four-inch guns. I also took training in the depth charge launching apparatus. We endured six more solid days of training aboard ship, from dawn until dark, as the destroyer, Oliver, remained tied to the dock. On the evening of the sixth day some of the crew received a four-hour pass ashore in Halifax. The following morning at 0800 hours the Oliver slipped easily away from the dock on her way to begin sea trials. Her crew in dress blues stood at attention at their battle stations to salute the assembly of officers on their shore side viewing stand. On the dock the Navy band played Hearts of Oak. The Oliver gleamed, not a single rust spot or paint chip could be seen.

On the bridge, Captain Willis felt intense pride. The Navy had chosen him to captain the H.M.C.S. Oliver, she was the newest destroyer in the fleet and according to her sea going tests, possibly the fastest. Willis had served the Canadian navy in a series of older vessels and he felt the Oliver was his reward. He was always impeccably dressed setting the standard for his officers and men. Willis was quite small in stature but made up for it with his commanding attitude. He was a fast sharp thinker; his bidding was carried out without question. When the ship reached mid harbour, Captain Willis, through his second officer, ordered the men assembled in the enlisted men's mess hall where he would address us. The men stood at attention when Willis entered. The second officer gave the order to stand at ease and Captain Willis began to speak,

"Men you are fortunate to be aboard the newest and fastest destroyer in the Canadian Navy. Let me make this quite clear, we have a big job to do. German U-boats are sinking vessels at an alarming rate, it is our job to protect the convoys and destroy the enemy U-boats. We have the advantage of speed but do not let it lull you into a false sense of security, for we too are targets. Most of you men are new recruits. I intend to mold you into a crack fighting unit. I expect the absolute best of every man serving under me. We will be cruising in some of the roughest water on the globe. Many of you will be seasick. No matter what you may think at the time, you will not die from it. Once the ship leaves the protection of the harbour, we are in danger of attack from under the sea at any time. When you receive an order from any of my officers you will carry the order out immediately without question. The lives of all of us depend upon it. You will find that your Captain runs a tight ship. Any seaman shirking his duty will be dealt with swiftly and harshly." Nodding his head to the second officer the Captain saluted, turned and left the mess. The men went about their individual duties according to the daily roster.

The Oliver cruised out of Halifax harbour. Upon reaching open water the captain ordered three quarter speed. The Oliver leapt forward valiantly into the waves beginning to take on the rhythmic motion of the Atlantic's heavy seas. Dipping and surging through the ever-increasing wave heights. Her bow ploughed through the mountains of greenish water setting the decks awash. Within a short space of time crew members unfamiliar with this daunting new environment began to spill their guts. Raw recruits from the prairies were filled with terror at the huge and mountainous expanse of water crashing over the Oliver's hull, the men clinging to almost anything that gave them some stability. Even with my seagoing experience aboard the fishing vessel, M.V. Lillian on the West Coast, I felt in awe of this new experience. I had encountered storms at sea but never with waves as powerful and deep as these. I didn't get seasick as I had plenty of seagoing experience, but I did have a genuine sense of fear. For I knew the mass of surging water could sweep a man to his death, unnoticed, should he not take all precautions.

On the bridge, Captain Willis, eager to get the feel of the Oliver, ordered full speed ahead. The ship crashed through the waves sending spray up and over the bridge windows. Below decks men heaved their breakfasts, groaning as they clung to solid steel pieces of the ship trying not to fall down into their own mess. Captain Willis, impatient to try out the green untried crew, ordered the battle stations klaxon sounded. Vomiting, nauseous seamen ran, walked and crawled to their respective battle stations. Frightening thoughts rushed through my brain. Are we really under attack. I don't think I can make it to my station, why the hell did I join the bloody Navy? I want to die at home in bed not here in this hellish ocean. Clinging on like grim death to anything I could, I made it to my battle station, promptly beginning to prepare the weapons for firing following my training to the letter. I looked out into the raging cauldron that was the ocean expecting to see the enemy. I saw nothing but mountains of green water hurtling past the Oliver's hull. The gunnery officer issued orders to charge the guns for firing. The seamen loading the shells were both seasick and experiencing great difficulty staying on their feet. The gunnery officer bellowed threats and profanities at the unfortunate men who somehow summoned up the strength and will to complete the task. From the bridge Captain Willis watched the proceedings with a keen eye noting that far too much time had elapsed to make the Oliver battle ready. He gave the signal to stand down the battle stations. The men unloaded and covered the weapons then went below. The deck officer followed them and looked around.

"These decks are a bloody pig sty." He thundered at the men. "This is a Royal Canadian Navy ship not a bloody farmyard! Clean the bloody deck now. I want everything shipshape fast." The swabbys went to work on the run, cleaning up the barf and spilled food in the mess hall and companionways, under the eye of the scornful deck officer. Fighting the leaping motions of the ship the unhappy men did their best. They had not fully completed the task when again the battle stations klaxon blared throughout the ship. The seamen scrambled to their stations pulling on their outer clothing as they ran. From the bridge Captain Willis noted the men had reduced their readiness time by two minutes.

"That's better number one, but it's far from good enough. Fire several rounds from the four inch guns to acquaint the men with the noise."

I set the controls to the numbers given me. The officer fired four rounds. The noise deafened me, the recoil scared me. The disengage battle stations klaxon sounded. The men went below wondering what the Oliver had fired on. Someone started the rumour we had sunk a German submarine. The ship and her crew spent four more harrowing days at sea practicing for the real thing. Back in port, in Halifax, half the crew received a twenty-four hour leave before the Oliver sailed to join other ships in the R. C. N. fleet, to escort a convoy of merchant ships assembled in Bedford Basin destined for Northern Ireland. I had shipboard duties so I didn't get to sample the nightlife in Halifax.

At 0600 hours a light snow had begun to fall, dusting the decks of the Oliver just before she cast off. Around the Navy yards, other ships prepared to sail. They would meet at sea and take up their positions on the flanks of the assembled merchantmen. The heavily laden merchant ships traveled three abreast. They were much slower than their Navy protectors making them a much easier target for the marauding U- boats.

Three Destroyers, two Battleships and four Corvettes had the job of keeping harm from the merchant ships by patrolling the flanks of the convoy of some thirty ships. I stood at attention at my battle station as the Oliver sailed toward the harbour entrance. The snow, driven by an east wind, made worse by the speed of the ship, stuck to my face and clothing. The biting cold found its way through my uniform chilling my legs and hands. Not until the Oliver reached the harbour entrance did the order to dismiss, filter down the chain of command.

Once the ship reached the open ocean I could see the merchantmen ploughing through the turbulent ocean three abreast and about a half mile apart. Beyond the convoy, two corvettes and a destroyer patrolled in zigzag formation. Breaking spray caused ice to form on our clothing and gloves, the cold from the wind was excruciating.

I thought grimly of the brochures the Navy had sent me containing pictures of smiling sailors with tropical maidens on their arms. The brochures had failed to mention the bone numbing cold and the mountainous freezing ocean. I was suddenly torn from my thoughts as the battle stations klaxon sounded its raucous warning throughout the ship. Men scattered to their stations slipping and sliding on the icy decks. With difficulty I prepared my weapons for use. Between the Oliver and the closest merchantman, the conning tower of a U-boat broke the surface. The gunnery officer yelled out the range and trajectory numbers, the Oliver opened fire. Within seconds the submarine began to dive with shells bursting all around it. The Oliver veered toward the spot where the U-boat had dived then the depth charge crews were put on full alert.

Having ceased firing I looked out at the convoy. My eyes perceived a massive explosion several seconds before the tremendous sound reached my ears. A munitions ship had been hit amidships by a torpedo. The vessel rose from the sea, hurling debris, exploding munitions and seamen high into the freezing air. The ship broke in half; the front section plunged back to the surface and dived bow first beneath the waves. The stern section clung desperately to the surface before the towering waves took her down. At full speed ahead, the Oliver began to drop her depth charges into the area the Captain felt the submarine might be lurking. I saw debris and merchant seamen dying quickly in the frigid water. To my horror and amazement, no attempt was made to aid them. The Oliver cruised right past their pleading faces leaving them to die. My sense of decency and compassion caused me to become angry instantly. Under my breath I cursed Captain Willis. I felt he was a cruel hard-hearted bastard who had no concern for human life. I felt that no decent human being would leave his fellow man to die such a terrible death without offering aid.

The U-boat outsmarted the Navy ships, surviving to wreak more havoc and death another day. When the convoy had outrun the enemy submarine battle alert was lifted allowing the men to go below to warm up. Captain Willis spoke to them on the ship's intercom.

"Men, on this day you have had your first taste of battle. You will see many more. Today a number of you saw men left in the ocean to die. I know it is a terrible thing to see, but for the safety of the fleet and the general safety of the convoy the orders are, there is to be no stopping for any reason. A moving target is a hard to hit target. I hope men, that you can understand. War is not pretty. We have a hell of a job to do. Carry on."

For me, and my crewmates, it was a stretch to see the bigger picture of war. We saw only the terror filled faces in the water pleading, ignored.

The fact did not escape us that should the Oliver be hit, we would share the same fate as the merchant seamen, freezing, lonely, abandoned to die. Life below the Oliver's decks became subdued among the lower ranks, our baptism of fire led to a greater appreciation for our own lives. The convoy reached the coast of Ireland without any further enemy action, arriving at dockside minus only the one merchant ship.

The Naval vessels had five days in port awaiting an outbound convoy destined for Halifax. All ranks were allotted shore leave. Along with my shipmates I eagerly got acquainted with the local pubs, dancehalls and bars. Some of the men drank too much, some got into brawls with the locals and a few found willing girls whose reputations were quickly shattered by the braggart's back aboard ship. For myself, I found solace in the local beer and stout as I tried to erase the memory of the faces on the men dying in the merciless waves.

The leave ended all too quickly. The crew and officers of the Oliver prepared to sail with the assembled convoy. On this voyage the men knew what lay ahead, shipboard moral was on a lower plane. The Oliver took up her position on the outer flank of the convoy now free of the ice that had coated her on her entry into port. She steamed confidently northwest with the convoy towards Halifax. Less than fifty miles away from the Irish coast the Klaxon shrieked its urgent and frightening message. The ships sonar had detected two submarines lurking in the area. A frantic search failed to locate them, but the enemy managed to disable two of the merchantmen, however not sufficiently enough to sink them. The convoy left them to fend for themselves as they returned to port for repairs, while we sailed on to Halifax. Mid Atlantic the convoy encountered a lone U- boat. The naval ships hunted the depths for it without success. When the hunt ended, the submarine surfaced on the horizon as if to taunt the navy ships.

On the next escort duty the convoy continued on unhindered, but three days outside of Halifax the ships began icing up, keeping the entire crew busy chipping it from the decks and superstructure.

One morning at sea, all hell broke loose aboard the naval ships. A pack of five German U-boats had penetrated the convoy by lying in wait until it was directly overhead. All five recorded a hit. Five merchantmen were damaged, two sinking almost immediately. A third vessel, an oil tanker, exploded into a giant inferno setting the sea ablaze with its volatile liquid cargo. The two other disabled ships sat helpless in a sea of burning oil slowly sinking forcing the unfortunate crew to decide how they should die. The choice, drown, freeze, burn, or both. Men from the merchant ships swam through the flames, their bodies and legs freezing their hands and heads on fire. As the stricken men swept past the Oliver's hull I knew that as long as I was fortunate enough to live I would never forget the appalling scene now etched onto my brain.

The naval ships frantically searched for the subs, finally we got a kill. At the surface the German sailors begged to be taken prisoner, but they too were left to perish amid the havoc they had caused. As the convoy sailed on, the sea behind them still burned, hundreds of men dotted its surface, dead men, burned men. The lucky dead were those trapped in the hulls of their sunken ships in a mile deep watery grave.

The Navy ships herded the merchantmen into the mouth of the river Mersey in Liverpool and into their individual docks like cattle into a stockyard. The ships were still not really safe for here they were subject to nightly bombing from the air along with the city itself. The men discovered that leave in Liverpool was a different kettle of fish; the city was in blackout after dark. They stayed in the port only twenty four hours just sufficient to refuel and supply. The brass felt the ships were safer moving at sea, than as sitting ducks in the Mersey. The return trip to Halifax passed relatively uneventfully. The convoy encountered only one U-boat and its torpedo swept by, wide of its target. The Oliver chased after the sub but it had dived below the point where the sonar could detect it.

The Oliver sailed on her next convoy duty with a fleet of forty- five merchantmen. The voyage went smoothly until we reached mid Atlantic. Two U-boats fired torpedoes without success. Three Naval vessels commenced attack using depth charges while the Oliver maintained her position on the outer flank. At my gunnery post I watched the battle off in the distance. I took my gaze from the horizon then glanced at the waves close by, to my horror I saw the white wake of a torpedo heading straight for the Oliver's hull.

A lone body flew high into the air away from the ship. With arms and legs askew the body landed on the crest of a wave as the Oliver's hull sped past.

Mr. and Mrs. Dirkson the admiralty regrets to inform you.------

THE CRATE.

IT FELL from the back of a truck I was following. The crate bounced haphazardly down the road. I had seen it vibrating toward the rear of the vehicle as I trailed it down a bumpy road surface driving my pickup truck. Of course I have no way of knowing if the driver had been negligent in leaving the roll up door open, or if it had rolled up accidentally as a result of the bumpy road.

The crate had obviously been well put together, or it would have broken apart on impact. I braked, not wishing to bump into it. A thought shot quickly through my mind. 'I have scored myself some free goods if the truck driver hadn't noticed the crate fall off, or see it in his mirrors.' Obviously he wasn't aware, for the truck rounded the next corner without slowing down. I drove around the crate, parking in front of it in order to load it into my pickup.

The sturdy crate was about six feet long by two feet wide and deep. It was very heavy. I figured a crate this size and weight, must contain a small woodworking lathe. It would make a great addition to my workshop. I checked for any labels. There were none, they must have been rubbed off on the road surface. This was an excellent opportunity to exercise finder's keepers, in the absence of the names of either shipper or the intended recipient. I struggled to get on end onto my truck tailboard. Then with a Herculean effort I lifted the heavy end and slid it onto my pickup box. I assumed the heavy end is where the electric drive motor would be.

I looked around to see if I had been observed, but saw no one. This baby was all mine. At home I backed up to my workshop door and struggled to get the crate onto two sawhorses. I closed the door with the intention of letting things cool down just in case there was a hue and cry over the loss. I itched to open the crate and inspect my new lathe, but I contained myself and waited for two weeks checking the newspaper's lost and found section every day. I could wait no longer. I cut the steel-straps, then using my electric screwdriver I took the lid off the crate, eager for the first glimpse of my new lathe.

My heart leapt to my throat. I gasped for breath. Inside the crate lay a highly polished coffin with bright silver handles. "My God! What do I do now?" I yelled. I lifted the lid. Inside, someone's Uncle Randolph lay wide eyed and terribly dead. I slammed down the lid in a mild panic. Closing the workshop door, I went to the house and poured myself a large Scotch. I had to think about what I was going to do. I could not put an ad in the paper saying "Found body on road please claim by identifying." I certainly could not go to the police after sitting on my find for two weeks, such an admission screamed of theft. Had I become a body snatcher, a grave robber?

Finally I reached the decision I would take the coffin and crate back to where I had found it, but try to hide it in the long grass and shrubs at the road edge. I dared not make my move in daylight in case I was spotted. Tonight was out of the question, Martha my wife, went to her quilting bee on Tuesdays while I minded the kids. So I would do it Wednesday night after dark.

Martha arrived home about nine thirty.

"It was the strangest thing Harold. Just as I was leaving I could swear I saw a man coming out of your workshop, but the door was still closed. I figured my eyes were playing tricks on me so I ignored it, continuing on my way to the quilting bee."

Goose bumps rose all over my skin. Sweat began pouring from my brow. I ran out to the workshop and opened the door. I switched on the light. The coffin was empty. What the Hell have I done? I have released one of the undead to go about his nefarious night-time forays. I had of course read the Dracula stories. I knew the undead returned to their coffins at dawn.

I spent a terrible night listening intently while watching for moving shadows. Finally the sun came up and I went out to the shed. The coffin's inhabitant lay still with eyes wide open. I slammed down the lid and installed the crate top. I put in extra screws then loaded it into my truck. At the place where I had found it I backed off the road. I was in the process of hiding the crate in the shrubs when a police patrol car stopped.

I am serving sixty days for theft by conversion and six additional months for the crime of an indignity to a human body.

TICKET TO RIDE. A True Story.

MY TICKET to ride came to me as a result of a conversation with my friend, Mike and his wife Dianne. At the time, Mike was a gillnet fisherman. When at sea fishing, Dianne acted as cook and crew for her husband aboard the Esperanza, a thirty-foot, sea-going Gill-netter. The conversation revealed that Dianne had no love for life on the ocean wave. She dreaded the final voyage of the season down the inside passage on the British Columbia coast, to bring the Esperanza to the lower mainland for the winter. My ears picked up. I felt opportunity knocking at my door.

"I should love to go to be cook and crew." I said. "I love the sea, I love boats also I can cook like Chef Boy-Ar-De. My baked beans are the talk of the town; they have a unique ability to produce methane gas in copious amounts."

"Would you really like to go?" Dianne asked, ignoring my last remark.

"Yes I am serious." I replied. "I have always fancied knowing what life is like aboard a fishing vessel. I know that I can keep Captain Mike happy with my meals and crewmanship.

So the die was cast, I was hired on as unpaid crew. It was arranged that I would be picked up alongside the highway leading to the Tsawassen Ferry Terminal. When my ride arrived, it was related to me that two vessels were to come home to the Lower Mainland, one on a trailer by road, the Esperanza by sea. Thus began the journey to the north end of Vancouver Island. Three burly men surrounded by supplies for the voyage, sat hip to hip in a rusty pickup truck, excepting for time spent out of the cab on the ferry ride to Nanaimo.

I was silently thankful that we had not partaken of a meal of my beans, for I fear my fellow travelers, maỳ have abandoned me on a lonely stretch of the Island Highway. In Campbell River we stopped for dinner. After our hips had become unglued from each other we left the truck and trailer. Between us we devoured a gigantic pizza; I prayed that the onions smothering it would not have the same effect upon our persons as my beans may have.

We are northbound again; darkness falls on the highway save for a glimmer of light filtering through the trees overhead, from an almost full moon. We drive through beginning wisps of fog, which seems to thicken as we venture further north. Eventually the fog attains the clarity and texture of white cheddar.

"We are here. This is port Hardy." The driver announces after traveling through blinding whiteness. How he knows this I am not sure, for the white cheddar looks the same here, as it did miles ago. We begin unloading plastic hampers of? Since I have no idea what is in them I shall refer to it as stuff. Carrying one of the hampers, I follow the sound of footsteps ahead of me and find that I am on a wooden boardwalk. Suddenly it ends. A ramp as steep as a house roof, leads down to a floating dock.

"Stack them here." A voice says through the cheddar. I follow him back up the waterslide, previously referred to as a ramp. Three trips later, a voice says,

"See you in the morning Mike." Another voice from somewhere amid the cheddar replies

"We will have breakfast at the hotel before we load your boat on the trailer." It is Mike's voice. I have a nagging feeling that Mike is trying to delay sampling my cooking skills.

"Grab your gear." Mike says. I pick up my packsack then follow him into the fog. I do not understand. We are at sea level, yet we are hiking up a steep hill. Suddenly we are going down a hill so steep I almost lose my footing. We come to another ramp with wheels on the bottom. We are on another floating dock. An overhead light casts its paleness through the fog, through it; I perceive the Esperanza tied to the dock like an errant dog.

"Put your gear below decks." Captain Mike ordered, as he busied himself opening hatches. It was pitch black, foggy, and the middle of the night. Esperanza's diesel engine roared to life shattering the coastal silence.

"We are going to the other dock to load our stuff." Mike yelled over the din. At times like this it is important to have complete faith in your captain. "Let go the aft lines." He shouted. The Esperanza eased away from the dock. My last connection with terra firma had been severed. With either incredible skill, or outhouse luck, the Esperanza kissed the other dock right by the stack of our stuff.

"Let's get this stuff into the main cabin. Then we can get some sleep." Captain Mike ordered. The Esperanza had been tied up for weeks in the damp air; consequently the bedding was clammy to the point of almost being moist.

"Your bunk." Captain Mike said, pointing at a tray fastened to the inside bend of the bow. It measured two feet wide where my shoulders were, three inches wide at my feet. Sleeping this way I thought, is like being a ballet dancer without the tutu, but wrapped in wet burlap. Three feet away across the companionway, my captain slept the deep and innocent sleep of a child.

Next morning after loading the other boat on the trailer, we bade farewell to our traveling companion, then sailed out to the fuel barge, with full tanks we went to sea. The fog had lifted, the September sun blazed down, the sea glassy calm. I busied myself bringing seawater from over the side, swabbing and swilling the deck and hatch covers of the accumulated dust and grime. Captain Mike didn't tell me to do it, but I figured why try to test him on my crewmanship since I don't swim very well. When I went below to make my galley shipshape, I discovered that the stuff in the plastic hampers was actually food, packed by Dianne.

The frig had been left un-emptied in haste weeks ago, it had things in there that I could no longer recognize due to the sprouting, hair like, growth of bacteria. While the Captain was engaged in the wheelhouse I jettisoned the offending food hoping that a series of fish in the food chain did not perish on my account. Then I cleaned out the frig restocking it. After wards, I prepared my first meal. Dianne had packed fresh meat for us, so I thought I should use it up first. We docked late that night in Kelsey bay. I managed to sleep cross-legged, ballerina style, for a short while. I thought that this morning I would cook a special Louisiana type breakfast for Mike, so I invented fiery Cajun scrambled eggs. After eating my masterpiece, beads of sweat burst from his forehead. His eyes were open so wide, I thought he was trying to read the tide chart from across the cabin. It was obvious to me that he absolutely loved my creation. All day long he would put the Esperanza on autopilot and go below to the head. He must have had a damn good novel down there, for I could hear moans and groans floating up as I stood out on deck. Later, Mike developed a migraine headache; I think it must have been caused by travel stress. So we put in early at the Campbell River Government dock. After tying up, Mike took to his bunk.

By now, after so long without my daily shower, my body had taken on the odour of a Mexican army boot and sock locker. I found a washroom on the dock with hot running water. I went back to the Esperanza to bring a towel and soap, leaving Mike a note, in case he awoke and made the decision to sail off leaving me there. I plugged the washbasin with a paper towel, filled it and stripped. While in the middle of my stand up bath with one leg on the counter, Mike pounded on the door.

"There are showers in the other side of the building." He informed me.

"Thanks." I answered. I made another meal, after which we went to bed early in order to have an early start on the last leg of the voyage to Victoria. Somehow, maybe it was revenge on Mike's part who is totally deaf without his hearing aids; the alarm clock shocked me into wakefulness. I rose and put on a pot of coffee. I went to nudge Mike. It was then noticed it was only one in the morning. Now wide awake, I spent the night walking the streets, followed and watched carefully by a security guard who seemed convinced that I was probably a wanted man up to no good. We left the dock at five A.M. and sailed all day. That night Mike went somewhere to pick up some vintage car parts for his model T Ford leaving me aboard, sleeping an exhausted sleep. I awoke to a terrible noise. I rushed on deck to investigate. Mike with a big grin was dragging a model T axle across the deck to the fish hold. I was so shook up I could not get back to sleep after that. I made Mike his last on board breakfast of utterly blackened toast, as we sailed to Swartz Bay. I swear I heard a fish coughing up the toast Mike had heaved out of the wheelhouse window. We tied up, gathered our gear, boarded a bus and went to catch the ferry. This time,

I bought a Ticket to Ride.

IMPOSSIPAKS.

IMPOSSIPAKS! DON'T look in your dictionary for the word. It's not there. I just invented it. I shall of course expect to be rewarded by Webster's and the Encyclopedia Britannica for this creation to add to the glorious array of words in the English language.

While you may not recognize the word Impossipaks, you will most certainly be familiar with the product. We have all of us, without exception, made a purchase of a particular item locked firmly and tightly in a plastic sarcophagus. Even the nimble fingers of Middle Eastern carpet makers could not break into this clear hard as concrete bubble to extract the item you have just bought and taken home. All manner of things are packaged this way from pencils to flashlight batteries. Even some food items resist the most determined fingers to get inside, as the product taunts you from within the security of the rock hard bubble.

For example, you have purchased a pair of scissors, but you cannot get them out. They are entombed in an Impossipak. The fact is you need a pair of scissors, or a bevy of road building equipment to extract them. At first incorrectly believing you can open the bubble by hands alone, you make the attempt. Five broken and disfigured finger nails later you go in search of a tool to puncture the bubble. As you search the cutlery drawer you think perhaps a steak knife will do the trick, it is pointed and sharp. Common sense indicates there should be no trouble piercing the bubble in order to get a finger-hold and tear the granite hard plastic away from your purchase. Carefully, you position the blade point atop the bubble with one hand, while holding the serrated knife edge in position with two fingers.

You press sharply down on the handle. All things being equal one would expect the point to puncture the Impossipak. The bubble is so incredibly hard the knife slips off to the side of the bubble pack causing a deep gash in two fingers. Bleeding profusely, it is obvious you need several band aids or a long gauze bandage. You know you have some band aids you recall that you just bought them last Wednesday. Dripping blood all over the kitchen floor, you make your way to the bathroom medicine cabinet having left a trail reminiscent of a heinous crime scene. You open the cabinet door only to find that the band aids you purchased are still encased in the Impossipak you brought them home in. No doubt assuming you would be able to open the Impossipak at your leisure at some later date. You wrap your bleeding fingers in a wad of toilet paper while searching for something to break into the band aid, Impossipak. Perhaps the nail clippers with the sharp points can break the seal between the two parts of the bubble. With your blood soaked paper encased fingers, you attempt to stick the pointy end of the clippers through the seal.

It slips from the diamond hard bubble. Two points sink deep into the base of your thumb. Now both hands are injured and bleeding but you are determined to get those band aids and scissors out the accursed Impossipaks no matter what it takes.

You wrap your other hand in toilet paper. Cursing audibly you make your way out to the workshop where you know you store the utility knife. Now you remember that recently you lost the old one, replacing it when you were in the hardware store. You brought it home then hung it on the workshop wall. You stare in disbelief. The new utility knife is sealed like an Egyptian mummy in a clear Impossipak. Your loud screams attract the next door neighbour. She comes running into your house and follows the blood trail. Finding you in hysterics she sees your blood-covered hands. Assuming the worst case scenario, she runs from your house to call 911. Within minutes, the fire trucks and ambulances, plus the swat team in full riot gear, surrounds the house of the reported axe murderer.

"Come out of the house with your hands over your head! Lie face down on the lawn with your hands behind you." With automatic rifles aimed at your chest, you do not argue, but comply.

"Whom did you murder in the house?' A voice demands of you.

"No-one. I was just attempting to get something out of an Impossipak. In doing so, I injured myself."

"O.K. You can get up now. The ambulance men will patch you up. Madam, you are the fourth call this week we have had to attend to with Impossipak opening problems. You should get yourself a pair of scissors. Believe me; life will be much simpler for you."

BIOGRAPHY

Alan's interest in writing began at age seven when his teacher praised a five page composition on his summer adventures.

During his working years he gained insight into many different levels of society ranging from Vancouver's sleazy east side to corporate boardrooms. He continued to write on a small scale. He became West Coast correspondent for his national company's quarterly magazine. He won three awards for his contributions and an award for adult fiction.

Upon his early retirement, Alan began to write seriously, encouraged by the Penticton Writers and Publishers group. He writes several genres of poetry and has been published in three countries.

He performs his cowboy poetry at cowboy poetry festivals. Alan has recently published a book of humour, *Out Behind The Barn* along with four other novels as yet unpublished and a published booklet of twelve short stories about the history and people of Okanagan Falls. His novel, *(I Never Saw My Father Smile*) a story of an abusive childhood, military life, a love affair, murder and madness, is published by Trafford Press.

This book of short stories, *24 Hours In Hell* follows on the heels of a co authored work by Alan and Shanna Ahmad. *(Lost In The Sand)* is an amazing story of life under Saddam Hussein, a story of love of country and espionage, brought by Shanna, from war torn Iraq. Translated from the handwritten and readied for print by Alan.

ISBN 142515971-0

9 781425 159719